SWITCHEROO

OTHER TITLES BY AARON ELKINS

Gideon Oliver Mysteries

Fellowship of Fear

The Dark Place

Murder in the Queen's Armes

Old Bones

Curses!

Icy Clutches

Make No Bones

Dead Men's Hearts

Twenty Blue Devils

Skeleton Dance

Good Blood

Where There's a Will

Unnatural Selection

Little Tiny Teeth

Uneasy Relations

Skull Duggery

Dying on the Vine

Chris Norgren Mysteries

A Deceptive Clarity

A Glancing Light

Old Scores

Stand-Alone Thrillers

Loot

Turncoat

The Worst Thing

Lee Ofsted Mysteries (with Charlotte Elkins)

A Wicked Slice

Rotten Lies

Nasty Breaks

Where Have All the Birdies Gone?

On the Fringe

Alix London Mysteries (with Charlotte Elkins)

A Dangerous Talent

A Cruise to Die For

The Art Whisperer

SWITCHEROO

Edgar Award-Winning Author

AARON ELKINS

THOMAS & MERCER

This is a work of fiction. Names, characters, organizations, places, events, and incidents are either products of the author's imagination or are used fictitiously.

Published by Thomas & Mercer, Seattle
www.apub.com

Amazon, the Amazon logo, and Thomas & Mercer are trademarks of Amazon.com, Inc., or its affiliates.

ISBN-13: 9781477827680
ISBN-10: 1477827684

Cover design by David Drummond

Printed in the United States of America

CHAPTER 1

Jersey, the Channel Islands, Great Britain, June 1940

The Nazis were coming.

It was all anybody could talk about. The capitulation of the French, making official what everyone knew to be a fact anyway, was now a week old, and the coast of Occupied France was only twelve miles away, visible even on a cloudy day. On a clear one you could pick out the cars on the roads. With binoculars, you could see that they were tanks and personnel carriers, not cars. Already the Germans were entrenched in the fortified coastal city of Saint-Malo, fifteen minutes by *Luftwaffe* bomber from Jersey.

Meanwhile, what the islanders called "the Homeland"—England—was ten times more distant, across virtually the entire width of the English Channel, and the Homeland had thrown them to the wolves. Once the threat of a German invasion of the Channel Islands had become both certain and imminent, London had shocked the islanders by withdrawing all means of defense. The British soldiers stationed on the two main islands, Guernsey and Jersey, had been hurriedly—some said furtively—evacuated. And there was no air cover, no Royal Navy vessel within call. The British government had declared the islands a demilitarized zone, in effect an invitation to the Germans to march right on in. And the inhabitants had been left to cope on their own.

All this only weeks after their beloved (no longer quite so beloved) Winnie had made his stirring call to arms:

We shall fight on the beaches, we shall fight on the landing grounds, we shall fight in the fields and in the streets, we shall fight in the hills . . .

"He forgot the part about 'We shall fight everywhere but in the Channel Islands,'" went the sour joke making the rounds in Saint Helier and Saint Peter Port.

The outrage and shock of the abandoned islanders prompted London to provide ships for those who wanted to evacuate to the Homeland before the occupiers came. Many whose roots were too deep in the soil elected to remain, but there were thousands desperate to get out with their families before it was too late; even in 1940 they'd heard about the Gestapo and the concentration camps. But there weren't enough ships and there wasn't nearly enough time (the evacuation was to run for only three days) to accommodate them all.

The entire hastily put-together process was a mess. Evacuations were not announced until June 19, at which time islanders who hoped to leave were told to register and get their tickets at the Saint Helier Town Hall by ten the next morning (and pay for them if they could afford it) and be ready to board that same day if necessary. Altogether, it meant less than twenty-four hours to decide if you wanted to leave the Channel Islands at all (many for the first time), perhaps never to return; to figure out what you would do (and how much *could* you do?) about the property you would leave behind—your livestock, your debts, your possessions, your business, your bank account; and to be packed (with a limit of twenty-eight pounds per person) and ready to travel.

The exodus started smoothly enough, with polite queues (they were still British, after all), but within hours the famously tranquil social fabric of the islands tore apart. There were fistfights, hair pulling, screaming accusations of cheating, and, inevitably, appeals from those who didn't make it onto the register.

The final decisions on these appeals were in the hands of senior government officials, soon overworked and harried to a man, one of whom, Senator Roland Makepeace, the seventy-three-year-old chief deputy to the bailiff of Jersey, had been given the particularly touchy task of dealing with appeals from "important" citizens, which, alas, meant pretty much the same thing as it did with the unimportant ones, viz., turning virtually all of them down.

By midafternoon of the second day, he had seen thirty-eight such petitioners, only one of whose appeals he'd been able to approve. It was a heart-wrenching job, and Senator Makepeace, good soul that he was, wasn't holding up very well. He was physically and emotionally drained. So many fearful, frenzied people, so much misery, such a limited ability to help.

"I'm very sorry, Mr. Wright, there's nothing I can do," he was saying to number thirty-nine. "I'm sure you understand that we cannot make exceptions to the rules by which so many people have already abided."

"Of course I do, Senator, and I appreciate it. I'm not asking for myself. I'll stick it out. But my father is eighty-nine now, and my mother is only a year younger, and neither one is in good health. Frankly, I don't see how they can survive the hardships that are sure to come when the Germans get here."

Makepeace repressed a sigh. How many variations of this had he heard in the last forty-eight hours? His heart went out to Scott Wright, and to his aged parents, as it had to everyone he'd already seen. But there was nothing he could do, nothing that wouldn't be unfair to so many others.

"I'm sorry," he said again, and this time Wright could see that that was the end of it.

He nodded and rose. "Thank you for taking the time to see me, Senator Makepeace," he said woodenly.

Makepeace got up to shake his hand. "Good luck, Scott. It's a terrible time we're living in. And good luck to your parents."

"Good luck to us all, Senator. We'll need it."

The senator sat alone for a few minutes, smoking a cigarette and pulling himself together for the next interview. He felt every bit as old as Scott Wright's mother and father. Still, this was part of his sworn duty, and he flicked on the intercom to speak with his clerk.

"I'm ready, Dickinson, let's get on with it. Send the next one in."

"It's Howard Carlisle, sir," Dickinson whispered, and Makepeace's heart sank even lower.

Carlisle was indeed one of those "important" people. The Carlisles had been important since 1872, when Howard's grandfather was surprised to learn that the unsightly black sludge that had been seeping forever from the base of a rock outcropping on his dairy farm was some newfangled stuff called "asphaltum." He had been even more astonished at the annual fee that a Newcastle construction company had been willing to pay him for access to the sticky, smelly stuff. The money had been enough for Carlisle to buy up two thousand acres of prime farmland in bits and pieces over the next few years and stock them with cattle from France and England, making Carlisle & Son Dairies the island's biggest dairy farmer. It still was, with its herd now standing at four thousand—all the land could support—and Howard Carlisle, the son of the "Son," was one of the island's richest men, if not the richest. And if that wasn't enough, in 1933, Carlisle had ended the Newcastle firm's lease on his asphalt and turned the deposit to his own ends, opening his own road-construction company, Carlisle Paving, which had quickly become the Channel Islands' major road builder.

Like Makepeace, Carlisle was one of Jersey's ten legislative senators, a formidable man, not only of wealth but of influence, and used to having his way. He was, by most measures, an admirable man, if sometimes perhaps a little too self-assured. Makepeace shrank from having to see him do something that in all this time he'd never seen him once do: beg.

But when Dickinson ushered him in, Carlisle didn't look as if he had supplication in mind. Wherever he was, Howard Carlisle looked as if he owned the place, and this was no less true in Makepeace's own office, which annoyed Makepeace, and not for the first time.

"Good afternoon, Roland. I appreciate your seeing me. I know how busy you must be. I'll be brief." The words were civil enough and politely delivered, but the tone indicated that Carlisle had the impression he was the one who would be running this meeting.

Makepeace's spine stiffened further. Unconsciously, he helped it along, aware at some level that his irritation with Howard would make it easier to do what had to be done. He grunted acknowledgement and gestured to the carved chair beside the grand desk. "Sit down, will you, Howard?"

"Let me get directly to the matter at hand," Carlisle said as he took his seat.

But Makepeace wouldn't let him get started. "I know what brings you here, Howard." Best to get this over with as quickly as possible.

Carlisle smiled and lifted his chin. "Do you, now?"

"Yes, the same thing that everyone else who's been here today has wanted. You've decided you'd best get your family to England—and to safety—after all. And believe me, I would help you if I could, but I'm afraid it's out of the question. It's simply not possible."

"That's a bit peremptory, wouldn't you say, Roland?" But his smile seemed a little forced now, his posture rigid rather than erect. "I know you've been dealing with people's problems all day—"

"And all day yesterday."

"—but surely you'll agree that my circumstances—my son's circumstances—are of a different order than most. My situation genuinely *is* extraordinary—and desperate."

"Not really, Howard." Makepeace cleared his throat, or tried to. His voice was ragged from too much talking, too much tension, and too much impotence. "Your situation, as you put it, in simplest terms, is this: When the directive to register for evacuations was published the day before yesterday, you decided to remain, to stay at your post, and therefore didn't act on it, a reaction I commend. But now, after the registration deadline has passed and there is no more room on the available ships, you have changed your mind—you and many dozens of others. I don't criticize you for this, but I have told them all, and I will tell you, that it is too late."

"Now, Roland, you know me. You know it's not for myself that I'm concerned, and not for Grace either. We could get by, just as I know that you and Penny will. But Roddy . . ." When he said his son's name, he sagged visibly in his chair. "I simply . . . I . . . there has to be some way . . ." His fingers went to his temples, and then he leaned his head heavily on both hands. The starch had gone out of him as suddenly as if it had been doused with a pail of water.

Oh, dear, Makepeace thought with horror, *is the man about to cry? I am far too old for this.* He lowered his eyes to his own fingers, drumming softly on the desk.

Carlisle quickly recovered himself. "What you say is true," he said in a tight monotone. "When I refused to register, I was reacting on instinct, on patriotic instinct, if you will permit me to call it that. Patriotic fervor, I should say. Like you, as a senator, I felt that I had a duty to see this thing through—"

"Yes, yes, I understand all that."

"—to serve our people in whatever way I could in the difficult time ahead. But then . . . then . . ."

The tears were there behind his eyes again, and Makepeace most assuredly did not want to see them. "But then, when you came down from your patriotic cloud, when it was too late, you thought about Roderick. Or more likely, Grace made you think about him. And—"

"And when I did, I realized that I was signing his death warrant. Roddy was born prematurely, as you know, a tiny, delicate thing, and even now, at almost three years, he weighs less than two stone. We both know that there are hard times to come, Roland, and I don't think he could survive a German occupation. Grace is quite right. It's essential that I get him out of here and to England. Although after Dunkirk, with the way the war's going, who knows if even England, or any place at all—" He stopped himself, aware that he was babbling.

"And how would you suggest this be accomplished?" Makepeace asked stonily. "*You* decided not to register. Now you've changed your mind and you expect me to remove from the manifest three people who have followed the rules in good faith, so that you, Grace, and Roderick can leave in their stead?"

The change in tone took Carlisle aback. "I . . . I . . ."

"Tell me, Howard, do you have a suggestion as to which particular family I should cancel to make room for the Carlisles? Would you care to be the one to inform them of the change?"

It had been meant as irony, but Carlisle, a very different man from what he'd been when he walked in five minutes earlier, grasped at it. "Yes, absolutely, whatever's required! I can make it up to them. They can set their own price. I'd pay whatever I had to."

With no response from Makepeace, Carlisle stopped again but then spoke in a wretched whisper, not looking at Makepeace but staring down at the tabletop. "Roland, if there's anything you *personally* can do for me—as a friend, I mean—I'm, I'm sure I could, I could show my appreci—"

Makepeace ended it before Carlisle could demean himself any further. "I'm sorry, Howard," he said abruptly and with authority. "Dickinson!" he called out.

Almost instantly, the door opened and Dickinson's head popped through. "Sir?"

"Will you escort the senator out, please, and bring in the next person."

"Sir."

Carlisle rose, gathering around him what was left of his dignity. "Thank you, Senator. I understand completely. Please don't bother, Dickinson. I can see myself out."

CHAPTER 2

Around the corner and across the street from Town Hall, on Seale Street, was an old pub, the Merrie Monarch, named for Charles II, who was given sanctuary in Mont Orgueil Castle by Jersey's Loyalist government (neighboring Guernsey was on the other side) when he was on the run from Oliver Cromwell and not yet so merrie. Later, after he had claimed the crown and Cromwell had suffered the singular fate of being posthumously beheaded, the grateful king presented Jersey's faithful bailiff with a tract of land in America, between the Hudson and Delaware rivers. In 1776, this tract became one of the Thirteen Colonies—New Jersey.

Possibly because of this history, but mostly because of its proximity to Town Hall, the Merrie Monarch had become a haven to the government workers, the pub of choice for an after-work pint. It was here that Carlisle went after leaving Makepeace's office, almost without thinking about it.

At this hour, five o'clock, the bar of the Merrie Monarch would typically be buried three deep in chatting, laughing mid- and upper-level civil servants: gentlemen in dark suits and ties, with a mug of beer in one hand and a cigarette in the other, their tightly furled brollies stowed in the umbrella stands. A few women would be among them, drinking sherry or ginger beer. Behind the bar, two men and a woman (Sadie, the proprietor) would be working at the beer taps as fast as they could, barely managing to keep up.

Not tonight. With the island on the brink of subjugation by a hostile army, it would be a long time before those jolly scenes would be seen again. Only Sadie was behind the bar, and only Sadie was needed. At most, there were a dozen long-faced customers. Mostly, they sat in booths, talking quietly to the accompaniment of many sober shakes of the head. Nobody was doing any laughing. The place even smelled different. Without the usual fug of tobacco smoke to mask it, the odor of a century's worth of spilled beer predominated. Not that Carlisle noticed it. He had gotten a pint of almost-black West Country stout from an uncommunicative Sadie, sat himself at the booth farthest from the bar, and, without being aware of it, opened a pack of Player's.

Beside the table was a glassed-in display case of rosy-cheeked Toby jugs, and Carlisle imagined his cheeks were almost as red. He'd come within a millimeter of offering Makepeace a bribe . . . a *bribe* to Jersey's living monument to moral integrity. He would have done it too, if Makepeace, out of the decency of his heart, hadn't cut him off before he was able to get the words out. Good Lord, what was he coming to? But he was sick with worry, ready to do anything, risk anything for the boy, only what was there to do?

And it was all entirely his fault; that was the worst of it. Out of prideful self-importance—how could Jersey possibly make it through the Occupation without his presence?—he had signed his child's death warrant, and now, as he saw it, he had only one hope left. Outlandish as it was, he intended to press for it. If it didn't work, he'd—well, he didn't know what he'd do, but he'd do something. He swallowed some ale in hopes that it would stop the headache building at the back of his neck, then lit a cigarette, took a long, long drag, leaned back, and closed his eyes.

He was fifty years old—he'd been forty-eight when Roddy had been born—and Roddy was his first child. He had expected to be a good father when the time came, and he had looked forward with a certain pleasant anticipation to the prospect, but until the night Roddy was born, all of his concern had been for Grace, who had endured a difficult pregnancy, and at the hospital he was so filled with relief on hearing that things had gone well that he had to be reminded that he could go and look at the baby. When he did, the surge of emotion that squeezed his heart had overwhelmed him, and in the nearly three years since, his love, his need to protect this sweet-tempered, sickly, defenseless little thing had grown even fiercer as the child's frail constitution became more apparent. It seemed to Carlisle, although he never expressed it to Grace, that the boy's connection to life, to this earth, was frighteningly flimsy. Two or three times a night Carlisle would get up to make sure his son was still breathing. He smiled now at the memory of the happy, sighing smile he would get if Roddy happened to be awake when he came in. Sometimes, if the boy were asleep, Carlisle would "accidentally" jog his tiny foot or shoulder just to see that dawning smile of recognition. (He never told his wife about that either.)

His own smile faded as the current situation came back to the front of his mind. Slowly, he exhaled the smoke—thin streams from both nostrils—and opened his eyes. When he did, he was startled by the sight of a thin, sallow man dressed in a black, much-worn three-piece woolen suit, uncomfortably standing a bare two feet from him, waiting to be acknowledged. The rest of the acrid smoke exploded from Carlisle's lungs, scalding his nose on the way out and making him sneeze. "Willie! For God's sake, man, how long have you been standing there? I thought you said you'd be half an hour."

"You said it was important. I thought I should hurry." William Skinner, Carlisle's brother-in-law, looked ill at ease. The Merrie

Monarch, all gleaming wood and polished brass and nineteenth-century hunting paintings, was not the kind of pub that he usually frequented.

"I appreciate that," Carlisle said, motioning him to sit down. "What would you like? Beer?"

"Half-and-half," Willie said.

Carlisle called out to Sadie: "Half-and-half, please, Sadie."

"Ale and bitter?" she called back.

"Ale and porter," Carlisle said, knowing Willie's preferences.

Sadie's disapproval showed as she pulled down the ceramic handle of a beer tap. Ale and porter was a rough-tasting Cockney concoction that could get you drunk in a hurry, and not often ordered at the Monarch. But then Willie was as true a Cockney as there ever was, London born and bred within the sound of Bow bells, in Watling Street, in fact, right around the corner from Saint Mary-le-Bow itself.

Carlisle waited for the beer to be delivered and for Willie to have his first nervous sip. "Willie, I have a very great favor to ask of you."

Willie blinked several times, his lips compressed, he sat up straighter. When favors had been asked and given between them in the past, it had been Willie who'd been the supplicant and Carlisle the grantor. And indeed, Carlisle had almost always granted them, usually in the form of small salary advances or modest string pulling on one minor governmental matter or another. Now, Willie appeared concerned that repayment day was at hand. As well he might be.

Willie Skinner had been married to Grace's angelic sister, Rose, who had since died in childbirth (the baby, George, had survived). Since then he had remarried, so technically the two men were no longer brothers-in-law, but the nature of their relationship, having been formed, remained.

It wasn't always an easy one. Willie, a few years younger than Carlisle, had emigrated to Jersey in 1932, when the Depression in England had been at its worst. Other than his luck in snaring the beautiful Rose a few years later, he had soon shown himself to be one of those people whom fate just seemed to have it in for. In the four years that Carlisle had known him, he'd broken his nose, his elbow (twice), and two of his fingers and had come down with appendicitis, gallstones, and (of all things) malaria. His luck with employment hadn't been any better. In the space of six months, he'd gotten himself let go from three different jobs (assistant floor manager at a chemist's, bookbinder's assistant, and deliveryman for a stationery store), his wages going down with each move.

It wasn't that he was an obnoxious or difficult employee, or that he embezzled, or that he was discourteous to customers; it was just that his attention would wander once too often, or he'd be too slow about things, or he'd make mistakes—and then make them again after being corrected. Or (this was Willie's own opinion) that he just wasn't cut out for that particular work.

Finally, at Grace's urging, Carlisle had hired him as an inventory-control clerk at one of his smaller dairy farms. There, under the knowing and sympathetic eye of the longtime plant manager, he was prevented from doing too much damage. The simple, old granite house that stood on the property had gone along with the job, rent-free. Willie had been, and still was, embarrassingly grateful, to the point of bordering on the obsequious, which made Carlisle uncomfortable to be around him.

Still, on his way from Town Hall, Carlisle had stopped at one of Her Majesty's red telephone boxes to ask Willie to meet him at the pub. Willie had said he'd hurry but it would take him half an hour to get there from the farm. And here he was, not fifteen minutes later. He'd driven fast. He was worried, all right; something was up, and he knew it. Like any true Cockney, he was distrustful of surprises, of pretty much anything new, really.

"What sort of favor?" he asked, fortifying himself for whatever was coming with another quick slug of his half-and-half.

"Willie, you're scheduled for evacuation to England tomorrow, is that still the case?"

Willie nodded. "Me, and the missus, and Georgie." The missus was Bess, Willie's second wife and young George's stepmother. She and Willie had gotten married only a few months after Rose's death, something for which Howard had eventually excused him (Willie was a weak-spined man; it was simply his nature) but had never quite forgiven him. To Howard, Grace's sister, Rose, had been the epitome of womanhood, generous, beautiful, intelligent, elegant . . . and far, far too wonderful for poor Willie Skinner.

"Good," Howard said. "I want you to take Roddy with you. That's the favor."

Whatever Willie had been expecting, that wasn't it. "You want me to . . . to . . ."

"To take Roddy with you to England, yes."

"But, Howard, he needs . . . well, he needs to be registered-like, to get on them boats. They won't let nobody on board without that, not even the babies."

"No, Willie, what he needs is an entry *in* the register. And there *is* an entry in the registry—currently in the name of George Skinner."

"My Georgie? But . . . you don't mean . . . no, wait . . . you want me to make as how your Roddy is my Georgie? And take him with me in his place?"

"I do."

"That's crazy, Howard. We couldn't never get away with it. They have a record of Georgie's weight, his height, even his picture. And he don't look nothing like Roddy. Blimey, Howard, Georgie's like five months older."

"Two, but what of it? I'm telling you, it's bedlam at the quay. They're not going to weigh the children on scales or compare pictures, I promise you. George is a two-year-old. Roddy is a two-year-old. Nobody is going to remark on the difference, or care about it for that matter. *One two-year-old boy . . . check. Next, please.*"

Perplexed, Willie shook his head. "So you want as Roddy should . . ."

"Should go with you to England," Carlisle said. "In George's place, yes." Carlisle's voice was beginning to tighten. Good Lord, the man was thick.

"So, Georgie wouldn't come with us." His eyebrows had drawn together with the effort to think things through.

Carlisle slowly nodded. "Correct."

"But, but . . . what would happen to him? To my Georgie?"

"George would remain here with Grace and me—in *Roddy's* place, do you see? And if we keep him to ourselves for a few weeks afterward, nobody is going to know the difference here either. At most it'll be 'My, my, hasn't Roddy grown!' And Willie"—he laid his hand on the back of Willie's wrist—"I hope it goes without saying that we would treat him as we would our own, with kindness and affection, and we know you would do the same for Roddy. Then afterward, of course, when—"

Willie finally got it, about one second before Carlisle's brain would have exploded with impatience. "You want us to . . . to *swap* one for t'other? Your Roddy would come away with me and the missus and live with us?"

"Exactly. To all extents and purposes, Roddy would *be* George. You and Bess would treat him as George, the authorities would believe he was your son, George, neighbors would believe it. *Roddy* would believe it. And the reverse would be the case on Jersey. For however long this bloody Occupation lasts, until you can come home again, George Skinner would be Roderick Carlisle."

This increased Willie's jumpiness. "Oh, no, I dunno. Lying to school officials and suchlike. Wouldn't that be breaking the law? Why couldn't they just keep their own names?"

"I'd prefer that too, but the German authorities—they'll be indexing everybody on the island, and the less we can do to arouse their curiosity—*This child, he is not yours, yes? Why does he then live with you?*—the better. For all we know, the same might be true of the English authorities. It's safer this way."

"But it might be years."

"So it might be," Carlisle agreed sagely, but through clenched teeth. He squeezed the bridge of his nose, shut his eyes tightly, but the actions gave no relief.

"But what happens when they find out they're somebody else? And what if we'ns can't *never* come back? What then?" The more agitated he became, the thicker the Cockney speech got.

"Willie, I don't have answers for you, damn it. How can I know these things?" *Shh, simmer down,* he told himself. "Look, what I do know is that here in Jersey there are sure to be hardships to come, and that Roddy is not a . . . a sturdy child who is likely to hold up under hardship. But George, why, George is robust, a tough little nipper who can take things as they come and deal with them. Remember the time that monstrous dog barked at him? How he just barked back and the dog was so surprised it simply stood there with its mouth open? I'm completely confident that he'll come through this perfectly well. And remember, I'll be staying on as a member of government. Even with the Nazis in overall charge, I'll have considerable influence. I'll be able to provide him with protection that other children won't have."

Not bloody likely, but he'd try.

"Howard, I'd like to help, you know that. God knows I owe you, but this is all, well, too bloody fantastic. How can you expect a father to leave his own baby boy behind to them dirty Nazis, so as he can take somebody *else's* kid to a safe place? It ain't normal."

"I know it's a lot to ask, Willie, but . . ." The cigarette he'd lit only a second ago was put in an ashtray and shoved to one side, along with his mug, so that he could lean more confidentially, more compassionately across the table. He lowered his voice. "Let's be honest with each other. It's all 'my Georgie this' and 'my Georgie that' right now, but we both know how you really feel about him. Don't you think it might be a good thing to be away from him for a while? For both of you? Don't you?"

This was a reference to conversations that he and Grace had had with Willie in the first weeks after Rose's death. Willie had been truly wretched, near despair, wondering how he could cope without her. (He certainly hadn't been coping well at the time; he was despondent and unfocused, he'd lost a lot of weight, and the shadows under his eyes spoke of sleepless nights.) Worse, he could barely stand to look at his little son. He hated to touch him, was repelled when he had to clean him up. "I know it's wrong," he'd told them. "I know he's innocent as they come and I'm a rotten dad, but I can't help it. Because of him, my sweetheart, the love of my life, is gone. He like as killed her! I'll never see her again, never hear her voice, ever. I don't know what I'm going to do."

The fact that two months later he married someone else raised in Carlisle a certain amount of skepticism as to the depth of Willie's devotion, but Grace had rightly pointed out that the new Mrs. Skinner was no love match for him. A plump, jolly chatterbox of a spinster who had lived with her niece at the time and was an indeterminate number of years older than Willie, she was there to impart motherly care to George, wifely care to Willie, and congenial company to both. In return, Willie would give her the home of her own that she longed for, support her as best he could, and treat her with husbandly consideration.

As far as Carlisle knew, both had come through on their ends of the bargain, and the marriage was happier than it might have been expected to be, perhaps because Bess had grown up in East London too. They were a couple of city-bred, streetwise Cockneys for whom London would always be home, but who now lived surrounded by rustics whose idea of a real city was Saint Helier. They needed each other just to have someone to talk to. As far as young George went, however, Willie's feelings about him remained unchanged. He rarely spoke of him anymore. The child was Bess's responsibility, not his; that was the deal.

"A good thing to be away from him for a while?" Willie mumbled after thinking things through. "Yes, I see what you're getting at." He sighed. "I suppose it might be." And then, with sudden intensity: "But Howard, don't you see—the responsibility of looking after a pale little tyke like Roddy . . . I don't know as I could—"

"Wouldn't Bess look after him, just as she does George now? Wouldn't she be a good mother to Roddy too?"

"Well, yes, I suppose so, but I meant the responsibility of looking after his needs—his special foods, his medical care, his—well, you know, better than anyone, I'm not a man of means." He shrugged and hung his head.

As the words drifted away to nothing, Carlisle worked to suppress a great sigh of relief, as if a terrible weight had been lifted from his shoulders. It was going to happen; the area of *yes* or *no* had been left behind. Whether Willie himself was aware of it or not, they had now entered the negotiations phase.

Carlisle had been holding an ace in the hole, two aces really, and this was the time to play them. "Willie, you've been earning what at the dairy, twenty pounds a month?"

"What? No, eighteen six."

"Well, let's make it an even twenty, simpler for record keeping. For as long as you have to be gone, I will send you twenty pounds on the first of every month. If it proves impossible to send anything to England, I will have it deposited here at Lloyds in your name, so that it's all waiting for you on your return. Does that sound reasonable?"

Willie brightened for an instant and then suddenly turned shifty. He too had grasped that they were now negotiating. "More than reasonable, Howard. Only—"

"I will also formally deed the farm to you, free and clear of any obligation on your part."

Willie stared at him, eyebrows drawn together.

Now I've overegged the pudding, Carlisle thought with dismay. *Made him think there's something dodgy about the entire thing.*

But Willie had merely been stunned into a momentary silence. "The farm?" he repeated. "Crikey, you mean the one I—"

"Yes, the one you live on, the one next to mine."

"D'you mean the whole thing?"

"Every bit of it. The house, the land, the cows—although I can't promise there'll be any animals left by the time this is all over. But what there are will be yours."

"That's all fine, Howard, it's wondrous, but there's another problem. Who knows what the situation's going to be in England now? They *say* as there's work waiting for me there, but . . ."

"I understand perfectly, Willie. Of course, you'll need money to get yourself going, and I want to help there too. The banks ran out of cash and closed their doors this morning, but I know I can get my hands on three or four hundred pounds by this evening, and you're more than welcome to it."

And that did it. Salary, property, that was all very nice, but they were off in the distant and uncertain future. Four hundred pounds—*today*—was another thing entirely. Willie's eyes glittered and danced like the numbers on a cash register. "*Thank* you, Howard, that would be a tremendous help. I swear to you, I'll pay you back as soon—"

Carlisle waved him down. "Nonsense, forget about that. I can't tell you how grateful to you I am for doing this. It'll take me a few hours to collect the money. Perhaps you and Bess could come by this evening? And I guess you'd best bring George."

It was all Willie could do to nod. Who would have thought that this bloody Nazi invasion was going to make him a rich man?

CHAPTER 3

Later that evening, at the Carlisles' town house in Royal Crescent, Willie and Bess Skinner and Howard and Grace Carlisle met to finalize the details. Because they agreed that a record of the arrangement was needed in case of future disagreements or confusion, Edmond Jouvet was also there. A young, newly minted solicitor, Jouvet had earned Carlisle's trust by performing several legal tasks for the dairies with discretion and integrity. And since they were the very first responsible jobs the young man had been offered, Carlisle had, in turn, earned Edmond's loyalty.

The two children, George and Roddy, were also there, both of them asleep in the next room, being watched over by Nuisance, the Carlisles' springer spaniel. It had been agreed that the children would be exchanged that night, mainly to give Roddy a chance to begin feeling comfortable with the Skinners before the next day's inevitable stresses and confusion.

It was after nine when they'd finished. The document was signed by everyone, and the money transferred (£455, more than two years of the average island salary). It was only at the very end, when Roddy was carried off by the Skinners and George left behind in his place, that

Grace showed signs of breaking down. She began to tremble. "Oh . . . Howard . . ."

Carlisle embraced her tenderly. "He'll be back, my darling, we'll get him back. This awful business can't go on forever."

Grace nodded, shuddering with the strain of holding back the tears but refusing to give in to them. "I know. I know."

"And at least he'll be safe."

Another nod, this time with a brave little smile. "And for that we should thank God."

"Amen."

An hour later, when they were trying to make friends with George and trying to make themselves call him "Roddy," Willie was back at their door. With him was a friendly little brown-and-white cocker spaniel puppy on a leash. Willie himself looked utterly used up, at the very end of his rope.

"Howard . . . Grace . . . I'm sorry . . . Bess, she don't know I'm here. She wouldn't let me ask you, but . . ." He gulped. "Could you take Bobbie too?"

"Take Bobbie?" Carlisle echoed.

Willie nodded hopefully. "They won't let us bring pets, you know. On them boats. People are just turning them loose to fend for theirselves. It's terrible."

No, Carlisle hadn't known, but he should have guessed. With the ships as jammed as they were, and few sanitary facilities, having pets aboard would have been awkward and unhealthy. He remembered now his surprise at seeing a pair of panicky-looking dogs wandering unattached in the street that afternoon and several more in the Parade Gardens. It hadn't really registered with him, though. His thoughts had been elsewhere.

"We can't bring ourselves to do that to him," Willie went on. "He's such a friendly little tyke, so used to being around people. And the boy loves him. And he's only three months; he'd be lost out there, wondering what he done wrong to be thrown out like that. Bess said we must bring him to the animal shelter to be put down. That's what they told us at the registration too, but—"

"We'll take him," Grace said.

"You *will*?"

"Of course we will," Howard said. "He'll be nice company for Nuisance too."

Grace bent down and lifted the little dog to her chest. Bobbie was in puppy paradise, his tail wagging—vibrating was more like it—and his tongue was trying to get at Grace's cheek.

Willie reached out to scratch behind the dog's ear one final time. "You little traitor. At least you could have made like you was a *little* sad." And to Grace and Howard: "God bless you both for what you done here." He squeezed their hands in both of his, something he'd never done before, and quickly left.

Before the door had closed behind him, Grace had buried her face in the puppy's soft fur, and only then did the tears she'd been holding back all night come pouring out.

"Oh, Howard, Howard, it's all so awful . . ."

By eleven the following morning, over two thousand people, more children than adults, were on the North Quay, about six hundred of them there to board the three old cargo ships waiting to take them across the channel to Weymouth, the rest there to see them off. The sky was a dull gray, the air sticky and oppressive, conditions that suited the grim mood. Occasionally, there were peals of childish laughter that briefly broke through the somber atmosphere. These came from youngsters too young to comprehend what was happening but old enough to know something funny when they saw it.

And their fellow evacuees did look funny, no doubt about it. Given the rigorous baggage limits, most were dressed in as many layers of clothing as they could stuff themselves into. "Cumberland sausages with arms and legs" was the way a reporter who'd watched the previous days' departures had described them. Many wore three hats, each one jammed onto the one underneath. Children flopped about in clown shoes five sizes too big for them because they were wearing a parent's over their own.

The Carlisles, leaving George with the nanny, had come down with the Skinners to wish them well and to bid farewell to Roddy. They had been standing on the quay for two and a half hours now, and the last two and a quarter of them—once Roddy had been hugged and kissed and doted over—had been painful in the extreme. Carlisle was depressed, Grace was teary, Willie tried visibly but unsuccessfully to find something to say, and Bess couldn't stop her nervous jabbering.

"Your attention, please," crackled over the loudspeakers, and two thousand heads came up. "The *Porthmorna* is now ready for boarding. Those with family names beginning from *A* to *L* are to report to the forward gangway, those from *M* to *Z* to the aft gangway. Please be prompt."

Carlisle rolled his eyes with relief. *At last, thank God!*

"Well, that's it, then," Bess chirped. She lifted the child from his baby carriage. "Want to say good-bye to little Roddy?"

We've already said a dozen good-byes, damn it, Carlisle thought. *If I have to do it one more time, my heart will break.* But Grace accepted the offer and hugged the cross, sleepy child to her. "Good-bye, my darling," she whispered through her tears. "Be well. I'll see you soon. Don't forget me."

Bess gently took the child back into her arms. "We'll take very good care of this little dear, don't you worry."

"And we'll take good care of George," Grace said.

"We'll wave to you from the deck. Oh, you can have the pram. They won't let us take it aboard."

"Thank you."

As if we needed another pram, Carlisle thought. *Go, go, go, I can't stand this misery any longer.* "You'd best get going," he said quietly.

Another loudspeaker announcement brought home his point. "A Royal Air Force group will arrive here from England in exactly one hour, at eleven forty-five, to escort the *Porthmorna* safely to Weymouth. The ship must be underway by that time. Those not aboard by eleven fifteen, one half hour from now, will be left behind."

That hurried things along. Carlisle was ready to go home right then, but Grace stayed him with a hand on his arm. She needed one last look at Roddy. It took almost the entire half hour for the Skinners to show up on deck and squeeze themselves in among the crowd at the railing, by which time the ship's horn had sounded three blasts and the water around the propellers had stepped up its churning. The Carlisles spotted them and waved, the Skinners waved back, and Bess waved Roddy's thin little arm for him. And the *Porthmorna*, looking like the tired, old coal carrier she was, slowly began to move.

It was then that the quavery but thrillingly pure soprano of an elderly woman floated down from the deck with the opening words of "Beautiful Jersey," that most unmartial of patriotic anthems. She sang in Norman French, until a hundred years ago the dominant language of the island, but now remembered by few people other than the old:

Man bieau p'tit Jèrri, la reine des îles . . .

The sweetly melancholic melody was known to all, however, and a few at a time, people began to sing or hum along with her. Before she reached the end of that first chorus, almost everyone, whether looking back from the too-quickly-receding *Porthmorna* or out from the quay, had joined in, but now it was in English:

Beautiful Jersey, gem of the sea,
Ever my heart turns in longing to thee.

Bright are the mem'ries you waken for me,
Beautiful Jersey, gem of the sea

By that time the crowd was swaying to the gentle meter of the song and unashamedly sobbing. Hundreds of handkerchiefs that had been in use all morning for dabbing away at eyes now waved in rhythmic unison.

Grace was crying and singing along with the others, but Howard looked as if he'd been turned to stone. She reached out and grasped his hand.

"Remember what you said last night: 'at least he'll be safe.'"

Howard nodded dumbly, then managed to get out a strangled, "Yes, that's right, he'll be safe now." And then, with a harsh, choked sob, he broke down and cried like everyone else.

CHAPTER 4

Five years later, May 8, 1945

Radio broadcast by Prime Minister Winston Churchill:

> *Hostilities will end officially at one minute after midnight tonight, but in the interests of saving lives, the "cease-fire" began yesterday to be sounded all along the front, and our dear Channel Islands are also to be freed today.*

So it was "our dear Channel Islands" now, was it—after half a decade of outright, explicit abandonment and neglect? But Winnie was Winnie, God bless him, and was quickly forgiven; he had done what he thought best for the United Kingdom as a whole, and who could blame him for that? And now at long, long last, the Second World War was officially over; the official decree had been read aloud in Saint Helier's Royal Square, and the Germans, as worn and nearly as starved as the islanders, had all been shipped off to camps in England. Already supplies had begun trickling in to bring Jersey back from the terrible deprivation of the Occupation's final two years. What was awaited now—awaited with all-consuming anticipation—was the return of those thousands of islanders, especially the beloved children, who had been evacuated at the war's beginning and lived it out overseas.

Like the evacuation itself, however, it didn't take long for the return to run into hitches. First, the ship that had originally been pledged to carry the returnees had shown up war damaged and would be unavailable for two months. When Jersey then requested planes to fly the returnees back, they were turned down in London. Finally, the War Transport Office agreed to divert a ship from the Dieppe–Newhaven run for returning servicemen, for as long as was needed, and it was then that the messages everyone had been waiting for began to arrive.

The Carlisles' came on June 24 in the form of a telegram, three white paper strips pasted on a yellow form:

Arriving St. Helier 27 Jun • All well • Roddy fine • Happy be home • Hope you fine too +++
Willie Skinner

It was the first time they'd heard from Willie in five years, the first word about Roddy's welfare in all this time, and it brought overwhelming relief and gratitude. All communication with England—with anywhere—had been cut off the day the newly arrived German military band first oompahed its way up Broad Street. (How plump and jolly the Germans were that day; if they'd been wearing lederhosen and forest-green fedoras with feathers in them, they would have looked like a band of merry innkeepers on vacation. And no wonder, they'd gotten a peach of an assignment, a quiet, beautiful island with only these pleasant, civilized limeys to worry about, while their brothers and cousins were fighting and dying among the unspeakable *Untermenschen* of Poland and Czechoslovakia.)

From that day on, there had been no letters from the outside world, no telegrams, no telephone calls. Residents were ordered to turn in their wireless sets; those found using them were sent off to the Nazis' notorious concentration camps in Germany or Eastern Europe. After the first few deportations, not many risked it. For the duration of the Occupation, islanders had to depend for their war news on the Nazi newsreels shown in the Forum Cinema in Saint Helier. Thus, it had come as a surprise when the Germans, so valiant and victorious in battle after battle on the silver screen, "suddenly" lost the war. Many of the rank-and-file Wehrmacht soldiers had been equally stunned.

But all of that, thank God, was over and done. They had their island back. The Germans were gone, never to return. And now, at last, their friends and relatives—their *children*—were coming home.

Three days later, June 27, Howard, Grace, and little Georgie were among the eager, impatient crowds on the North Quay who stood watching the battered, old hospital ship *Isle of Guernsey* glide into its berth, tie up, and let down its gangways. The mood couldn't have been more different from the one that had pervaded the crowd—many of them the same people—who had stood there five years ago to watch the *Porthmorna* depart. The good old *Porthmorna* itself was no longer in existence, having been destroyed by German fighter planes after being converted to a Navy raider.

Their joy was tempered only a little by reports from the day before—the first day of the transport—when there had been some fretting about the returnees, especially the young ones. They had become foreigners, many said. They spoke in the strange, flat accents of Lancashire, Cornwall, and Yorkshire. But as the returning children saw it, it was Jersey that was the foreign country. Any boys or girls under ten had spent the greater part of their lives in England. Their memories of Jersey were fragmented and confused at best, or more likely nonexistent altogether. To many of them, the rustic speech and manners of the islanders came as a shock that baffled or repelled them.

Howard was confident that that wouldn't be a problem with Roddy, who had been such an amiable, malleable baby and would be bound to pick up the ways of his homeland without any trouble. The Carlisles had brought Georgie along with them; they thought it was best for the boys to return to their parents right then and there. And, of course, they didn't want to wait even one more night to have Roddy back home with them. Over the past week, they had tried to prepare George for this moment, for his return to his own family, and they could only hope that the Skinners had done as much for Roddy.

"We love you very, very much," they'd told Georgie, and it was God's truth. To their surprise and happiness, Georgie had turned into a sweet, eminently lovable little boy, mild and generous. Their hearts had never stopped aching for their own Roddy, but that didn't mean it was going to be easy giving up Georgie.

"We're not really your mum and dad, you see," they'd explained. "We're really your Uncle Howard and Auntie Grace, and we've been taking care of you until your real mum and dad, who love you even more than we do, could come home. Only we weren't allowed to tell you that until the Germans went away. Well, now they have gone away, and your mum and dad will be back very soon, and they want you to come back and live with them, and who can blame them for that? And guess what, your name isn't really Roddy, it's George, isn't that a nice name? Isn't that lovely? You're named after a king, did you know that?"

And so on and so forth. The boy had seemed to take it in, but doubts were raised when, after mulling it over for a day, he asked: "But if I'm going to be George, who's going to be Roddy?" That had required some considerable explication, and they still weren't sure how much of it had taken.

Grace suddenly pinched Carlisle's wrist so hard that it hurt. "There! At the top of the gangplank! Isn't that Willie?"

Howard agreed that it was. A second later Bess appeared too, holding the hand of a tow-haired little boy.

"Roddy!" Grace exclaimed. Her hand went to her throat. "Oh, my God! Howard, look at how brave and straight he stands up there, look—" But she couldn't say any more before choking up with happiness and tears.

When they waved, the Skinners spotted them and waved jovially back as they came down the gangway.

"Are you sure that's him?" Howard asked when they got closer. "He looks so . . . so *sturdy*."

All of them did, for that matter. Compared to George and the rest of the skinny, hungry-looking kids waiting on the dock—with their faces mostly turned up and their mouths open, they looked like starving baby robins in the nest, straining for the worm that Mom had brought home—the ones coming down the gangway looked like fat Dutch burghers in an old Frans Hals painting. And the same went for the adults. It had been a hard five years for them here on Jersey, and the last two had brought them to the point of desperation; that was when the cats and dogs had started disappearing. On the other hand, for all the stress and dangers of nighttime bombings and V-2 rockets, the English had never starved, not really starved. The islanders had. Food was coming in now, thank heaven, but it would be a while before it showed on their scrawny frames.

"It's him, I'm almost sure," Grace said, "but we'll be able to see in a minute." She put three fingers to her neck, just under her right ear. After a moment, he understood. Their son, Roddy, had a group of three small, flat moles that formed a perfect little isosceles triangle there. When the Skinners got closer, they'd be able to tell for sure whether the child was their Roddy. They watched as the wonderfully well-knit little boy now made his way so assuredly down the gangway, holding Bess's hand in his own but confidently ignoring the railing on his other side.

And the moles were there.

Carlisle's heart quickened. "Hallo, Son!" he shouted, his excitement getting the better of him. "Welcome home, my boy!"

"'Ullo," Roddy called back, his voice barely audible.

Carlisle suddenly realized that George had been tugging on his hand for a while. He looked down. "Yes, Roddy"—*Damn!*—"yes, George?"

"That little boy?" George asked. "Is he me?"

So much for his having taken things in. "No, George, you're you, just as you always were. But we weren't allowed to tell you your real name."

"Oh." Now his hand slipped from Howard's and crept up to grasp Grace's.

"Now, Georgie," she said to him, "you go and greet your dear mother and father, just as we showed you."

George remained where he was, irresolute and uncertain, holding tightly to Grace's hand until she tenderly unlocked his fingers from hers and gave him a gentle shove.

He walked across the intervening few yards and gravely shook hands, first with Bess, and then, more reluctantly, with Willie. But his eyes kept pivoting back to Carlisle and Grace. They could see the whites; he looked like a panicked horse.

"Oh, Howard," Grace whispered, "this is all so awful. It has to be done, I know, but still . . ." She took in a little gasp and dabbed at her eyes with a handkerchief.

And now it was Roddy's turn. Willie knelt down beside him. "All right, then, lad, now you go and do the same. Go to your mum and give her a great hug."

Roddy walked confidently up to her and did as he was told. The hug was vigorous enough—rather overdone, in fact—but there was no warmth to it.

And why would there be? Carlisle thought. *Not yet. He doesn't know us; he doesn't understand what's going on. It's going to take time. Time for us too,* he realized. Grace sensed the boy's discomfort as well and forced herself not to let the embrace go on too long.

"And shake hands with your da, too," Willie prompted. "Go on, now."

Roddy then turned to Carlisle and held out his hand. "'Owdja do, sir?" he piped. "Very 'appy t'meetcher."

Carlisle burst out laughing. Good Lord, they'd made a proper little Cockney out of him! Well, that would be the first thing to be worked on, starting right now. "Very well, thank you," he replied in his clearest, crispest King's English. "And how do *you* do, young man?"

From the quay they went to the Carlisles' town house, where their maid had biscuits made with real sugar waiting for the children and cucumber sandwiches with synthetic honey and ersatz butter for the adults. On the way Willie told them that, unlike most of the evacuees, who had gone to the relatively safe countryside, they had stuck out the entire time in East London with his relatives. "We wasn't going to give them Jerries the satisfaction of running off, not us. And we all got through it too, with the bombings and them V-2s, and everything coming down all around. Right in the same street sometimes. The house right across from us got it one time. Right across!"

A look passed between Carlisle and Grace. They were glad they hadn't known that all along.

Once at the town house, the boys, who didn't appear to have taken to one another, were brought to the kitchen by the maid for tea and biscuits, which they unenthusiastically sipped and nibbled in uneasy silence. Meanwhile, the adults sat down to go over any remaining details with Edmond Jouvet, the young solicitor who had overseen the original exchange in 1940.

There was a moment's tension when Bess, who had clearly done her computing, pointed out that the bank statement that Carlisle had withdrawn for them from Lloyds the previous day showed Willie's account standing at £440, less than half of what the promised twenty pounds a month should have brought.

"Shush, Mother," Willie said, embarrassed. "Four hundred and forty pounds is a lot of money. They've had hard times here, a lot harder'n we've had."

"Well, I'm only asking what it says on that there paper. That's what we agreed." Carlisle's left eyebrow went up. Mrs. Skinner had grown more assertive during her years in London.

But it was Grace, usually so reserved, who responded, and with considerable heat. "Bess, you should know that it's only through Howard's generosity that you're getting that," she said hotly. "The Germans took over the plant the first month, for their military roads and whatnot. And the cows were all gone inside of a year. They paid us, yes, but the same way they paid everyone else—in Occupation marks. Oh, we still have plenty of those in a drawer somewhere, and if you want them, you're more than welcome to them. It'll save us the trouble of burning them."

"I wouldn't be in too much of a hurry to burn them," Edmond said. "I understand that London is going to accept them in exchange for pounds sterling."

"Yeah, sure," Bess said. "And what's the bloomin' rate of exchange to be? Ten thousand of them marks to one blinkin' pound?"

"It will be at face value, according to this morning's wireless," replied Edmond. "I'd say that's fair enough, wouldn't you?"

That surprising news cheered everyone and settled them down, and the meeting proceeded smoothly to its end. The Carlisles, the Skinners, and Jouvet re-signed the document that had been drawn up in 1940, attesting that the agreement had been fulfilled to the satisfaction of all.

They had their tea and sandwiches then, and soon, all too soon, it was time to make the switch a reality—the time for the Skinners to leave with their George and for Roddy to remain with his birth parents, but everyone was nervous, and they couldn't seem to bring themselves to close the circle for good. The conversation had grown desultory but still continued.

"Dad . . . ?" George was tugging at Carlisle's sleeve again.

"I'm not your dad," Carlisle snapped. "Your dad's sitting right there." And then, instantly regretting his tone, more gently: "But did you want to ask me something?"

George nodded. His eyes brimming with unshed tears, he leaned close to Carlisle's ear. "That other little boy—he's breaking my Spitfire."

And sure enough, in the far corner of the sitting room, which served as the play area, Roddy sprawled on the floor amid a jumble of metal Erector Set girders, wheels, and nuts and bolts, trying, with great determination, to twist the wings off a half-built toy airplane.

"Say there, son," Carlisle called, "if you want to take that apart, do it the right way. There are the tools right next to you."

Roddy looked sullenly at Carlisle, and then, for guidance, to Skinner.

"Now you listen to your da," Willie told him. "Don't act like you never seen a screwdriver before. You'll break it if you keep doing it like that."

Roddy received this sullenly. "I thought they was my toys now."

"Well, yeh, that's right, they are, but that don't mean—"

"Then I can break 'em if I want."

"Put that down this instant," said Grace, breaking her ten-minute silence.

Roddy made a face and threw the plane to the carpet, not quite hard enough to make it open rebellion, but hard enough to indicate he didn't give a damn. Then he just sat there with his arms crossed.

I should say something here, Carlisle thought, but he didn't know what it should be. And he was very suddenly tired, through and through. He simply gave the other adults an indulgent, mildly exasperated smile, which all but his grim-faced wife returned. *Boys will be boys.*

"Say, I was wondering," Willie said. "Did our Bobbie make it through? Do you still have him? I heard there at the end the Germans was stealing dogs and eating them."

"That they were," Carlisle said.

"Not only dogs, and not only Germans," Jouvet put in tartly.

"It's true, I'm afraid," said Carlisle, "but yes, Bobbie has remained uneaten. A fine animal, although a wee bit underfed, like the rest of us. Would you like to take him with you?"

Willie nodded. "We would. And I thank you for taking care of him all these years."

"He's an easy dog to get along with." Carlisle stood and went to the stairway. "He's upstairs with our Nuisance now. They tend to get overexcited when they hear guests, but I expect they've settled by now."

When he opened the door to the room the dogs were in, he saw that they had gone to sleep, pressed tight against one another, back-to-back. He bent to rub both of their smooth heads. "Bobbie, old boy, the war's over, you know. Time for you to go back home. Nuisance, you come down too and see him off. Your old friend Roddy's back too, although I doubt you'll know him."

At thirteen Nuisance was in his dotage and slow to awaken, but Bobbie, eight years his junior, jumped up with a start, ran past Carlisle, and dashed excitedly down the stairs, running from Willie to Bess and back again. Everyone else, even George, with whom he'd lived for the last five years, was ignored. Amazing, a dog's memory.

Roddy had gone to the bathroom, but now he came out, saw Bobbie, and went to pet him. At which point creaky, old Nuisance amazed Carlisle by shooting out from behind him and flying down the steps. Then, taking no notice of anyone else, he leaped straight up into Roddy's arms, bowling him over so that Roddy ended up on the seat of his pants, startled into blinking, open-mouthed silence, with Nuisance bounding in riotous circles around him, yawping and woofing like mad, and whimpering with joy.

The scene made them all laugh, most of all Carlisle. Good old Nuisance, loyal old Nuisance, he didn't have to check for neck moles to know his old pal.

CHAPTER 5

Nineteen years later, June 13, 1964

Jersey Evening Post
Missing Man Found Dead
Foul Play Indicated

The mystery that has gripped the island for the last two days was partly resolved yesterday morning when the body of George Skinner was found on the Saint Lawrence parish farm on which he resided. States Police have determined that his death was the result of a gunshot wound to the chest.

Skinner, until recently a high-level employee at both Carlisle Dairies and Carlisle Paving and Construction, had dropped out of sight on Wednesday last, along with Roderick Carlisle, the owner of both companies and the son of the late Senator Howard Carlisle. The two men had been the subjects of a police inquiry stemming from practices at Carlisle Paving and Construction, and it was initially believed that they had fled the islands to escape impending arrests.

"With the discovery of Mr. Skinner's body that theory is no longer tenable," said Detective Sergeant Mark Lavoisier. Making reference to the simultaneous disappearance of another Carlisle employee, assistant bookkeeper Bertrand Peltier, Sergeant Lavoisier said: "Now our main interest is in locating Mr. Carlisle and Mr. Peltier."

The investigation is ongoing, and anyone with information on the men's whereabouts is asked to contact the States Police Major Incident Bureau in Saint Helier.

Five years later, December 10, 1969

Jersey Evening Post
Shocking Findings
"Tar Pit Man" Identified; Not Prehistoric at All
New Questions Raised. Mystery Deepens

Human bones discovered last month in pitch deposits being extracted from the Carlisle Tar Pits, near L'Etacq in Saint Lawrence parish, have yielded appalling results. Thought at first to be the remains of prehistoric man, they are now believed to be the mingled remains of two men who have been sought by the States Police since 1964. One of the men has been identified as Roderick Carlisle, at that time the owner of Carlisle Paving and Road Construction (now Inter-Island Road Construction). The other remains are believed to be those of Bertrand Peltier, an employee of Carlisle's. Both men were the objects of police searches in connection with the five-year-old murder of business associate George Skinner.

"The likelihood of foul play is obviously extremely high," said Detective Sergeant Mark Lavoisier, "but reliable evidence of it has not been found on the remains. You must remember, however, that they are few and fragmentary."

The investigation is ongoing, and anyone with information of possible relevance is asked to contact the States Police Major Incident Bureau in Saint Helier.

CHAPTER 6

Málaga, Spain, April 15, 2015

Gideon Oliver was in one of his rare blue funks.

"It's not that I want to see any more people murdered," he mused. "It's just that, if people are going to get murdered anyhow, wouldn't you think a few more of them could be left out in the woods for a few months, or get buried in shallow graves that aren't discovered for a year or two, or tossed in the Sound, so that they don't wash up for a while? Is that asking so much?"

As an opening to a luncheon conversation between most married couples, this would be a nonstarter, but for Gideon and Julie Oliver, it was pretty ordinary stuff. Gideon was a professor of anthropology and the chairman of the Anthropology Department at the University of Washington's Port Angeles campus, at forty-two the youngest chairman on campus. He was also a consultant to law enforcement agencies in cases involving materials requiring the help of an expert in his peculiar and esoteric field of study—in a word, bones. His wife, Julie, a supervising park ranger at the Olympic National Park headquarters, also located in the quintessential, old Pacific Northwest timber town of Port Angeles, where the Olivers lived, had long ago gotten used to talk like this.

"Murdered so as to give honest employment to forensic anthropologists with time on their hands, you mean?" she said, without looking up from the ham and cheese sandwich from which she was using her fingers to remove a bit of ham rind.

"Exactly."

"In particular, forensic anthropologists who haven't had an interesting case to get their hands dirty on for going on, oh, say, six months?"

"Four, but it seems like six. Oh, and it would also be helpful if the remains were completely skeletonized so I don't have to deal with the icky stuff. Is that another half of a *bocadillo* that I see in there?"

"You're in luck," she said and handed the paper sack to him. "Half a can of orange Mirinda too."

Bocadillos were what the local Spaniards called their ham and cheese sandwiches—*bocadillos de jamón serrano y queso Manchego*—it was probably all those luscious syllables that made them so lip-smackingly good, that and the crusty Spanish loaves they came in. Orange Mirinda was a soft drink that tasted like every other carbonated, artificially flavored orange drink in the world—not even remotely like an orange but fizzy and refreshing, more than welcome on a warm spring day on the Costa del Sol.

At the moment, they were sitting on a wrought iron bench beside the Moorish-styled, multi-water-jetted pool in the botanical garden of the University of Málaga. Gideon was there to attend the biannual International Conference on Science and Detection, a three-day affair that was being held in the main auditorium of the Legal Medicine and Anatomy Building. For herself, Julie had arranged meetings with faculty members of the Department of Environmental Sciences to talk about issues of forest ecology. Happily, the spiffy but sterile-looking new buildings housing the two departments were only fifty yards apart, which made these pleasant lunches possible. With plenty of time to spare, Julie was also doing some local touring, and they were planning to stay a few additional days after the three-day conference ended today, so that she could show him the sights and they could perhaps range a little farther afield to Gibraltar or Tangier.

Once he'd eaten his fill, Gideon sat staring gloomily at the leftover crust in his hand. "Well," he said with a drawn-out sigh. "One more afternoon to get through. I probably should head on over to the lecture hall." But he didn't move.

"You sound thrilled," Julie said. "Not as much fun being one of the students instead of the professor, is it?"

"No, come on, Julie, that isn't it. You know I'm not like that."

She raised an eyebrow.

"Well, maybe a little," he allowed, and he supposed he was. He was, after all, very much used to, and very comfortable with, being a professor, and it was as a professor—a presenter—that he'd attended three previous Science and Detection conferences. This time, he was there as a learner, having begun to feel that he was drifting out of touch with the slew of recent developments in his field. Then, when he'd learned that the theme of this year's conference was "New Directions in the Forensic Sciences," he'd decided to sign up as a mere attendee.

"But more than that," he said, "I'm, well, not very interested, and that worries me. I should be interested in what's happening at the forefront, but I'm not. I'm just not. I think maybe I'd be happier just forgetting about it and letting myself turn into one of those carping, hoary old dinosaurs you see wandering around every campus. Or maybe it's too late and I already am one."

"Oh, come on," Julie said, smiling. "You're really not a very convincing whiner. And you're a bit young for dinosaur status. Besides, you've only got two more hours to go. It can't be that bad."

"You don't think so?" He opened his conference folder to the fourth page of the program. "Here, this is what I have to look forward to for the first hour. And the second hour's almost as bad. Care to join me?" He rotated the page so Julie could read it:

2:00 p.m. B8 "Multiplex PCR Development of Y-Chromosomal Biallelic Polymorphisms in Determining the Geographic Origin of Human Remains." S. J. Anjaneyulu, PhD, and Chandrashekhar Jeevarathinam, MA, Panjab University, Chandigarh, India.

She shook her head. "Cripes. Okay, I see what you mean. And this is in the anthropology section?"

"Yes, and that's my problem. I suppose it's useful, or would be if I understood what it means, but is it *anthropology*? I don't think so, not the way I see it. *Anthropos*—'man,' *logia*—'study of.' Well, you don't study *man* by studying biallelic polymorphisms. It's one more example of this increasingly reductionist direction that scientific research has been going in. Konrad Lorenz got it right a long time ago: 'Scientists are people who know more and more about less and less, until they know everything about nothing.'"

"That's not the whole quote. The other half of it is, 'Philosophers are people who know less and less about more and more, until they know nothing about everything.'"

"Yeah, he was probably right about that too. But look, I'm not saying that a holistic paradigm is necessarily the only one that should be utilized in the assessment of—"

Julie had tipped her chin downward and from under her eyebrows was giving him a certain look, which made him stop in the middle of his sentence and laugh, as it always did. "Earth to Gideon," was what it meant, "you've launched into lecture mode." It was a whispered commentary she'd started using a few years ago to let him know when his natural enthusiasms were overwhelming the people they were with. After a while, the single whispered word "launching" could do the job, and now the mere look that went along with it was enough.

"I'm sorry, Julie, you're right. Maybe what I really need *is* a captive audience—preferably one that depends on me for their grades."

"No, what you really need is a new case to remind you of what a dinosaur you're not. They don't call you the Skeleton Detective for nothing, pal. The FBI doesn't ask for your services on its trickiest cases because you're a dinosaur, you know."

"Thank you so much. Everyone needs a little patronizing once in a while."

"You're entirely welcome."

"So, people, how's it going?"

They turned at the cheerful greeting.

"Hi, John," they both called, and Gideon added: "How was the hamburger?"

"What makes you think I got a hamburger?"

"You mean other than the fact that that's what you always get when Marti's not around? Not much, really."

"Only for lunch," the aggrieved John pointed out, "and not *every* day."

Marti Lau, John's wife, was a nutritionist at Seattle's Virginia Mason Medical Center, where, on behalf of her helpless patients, she waged a personal war on fats, refined carbohydrates, salt, sugar, and just about anything else that tasted good. "The Dragon Lady of the Food Charts," they called her, and she loved it. She herself lived by dietary rules almost as stringent, but she knew better than to try to impose them on John. Still, he knew how she felt about it, and being a sensitive creature, despite his formidable presence—broad shouldered, hulking, and six foot two (only an inch taller than Gideon but seemingly taking up far more space)—he felt guilty indulging when she was around. But when she wasn't, then nothing stood between him and just about every hamburger, steak, and pizza he could get his hands on.

"You can get a hamburger in Málaga?" Julie asked.

"Julie, you can get a hamburger anyplace, if you know how to look," he said with pride. "You can trust me on that."

"You can trust him on that," said Gideon, who had been with him in quite a few different places. "So how was it? The hamburger?"

"Not too bad, Doc. Better when I scraped the hummus off it."

John Lau, a special agent with the FBI's regional office in Seattle, was a close friend of the Olivers', and especially of Gideon's; the two of them had known each other a long time and very literally owed their lives to each other. Despite this, John had been calling Gideon "Doc" from the first day they'd met. He just didn't like the name "Gideon," and as the only other choice Gideon had been offered was "Gid," Gideon opted for "Doc." John was here to present a session on ballistics, a subject he taught twice a year at the FBI Academy in Quantico, and to take in whatever lectures in the criminalistics section seemed potentially useful.

"Oh, by the way, Doc, you know Rafe Carlisle? Little guy, bald, natty dresser . . ."

"Right. DNA expert, isn't he?"

"Well, no, it turns out he's not. He's just fascinated by it and rich enough to do something about it. So he's gotten himself on the board of this DNA lab in England—in York, I think—and he's given them a big endowment, so he gets to mess around in their projects when he wants. Anyway, he's an interesting guy, and we got to talking, and he suggested why don't we all go downtown for dinner tonight—including you, Julie."

"That sounds fine, John," Julie said, "but there are two huge cruise ships in port. Something like six thousand day-trippers in town. It'll be elbow to elbow, and the restaurants and tapas bars will be wall to wall. Why don't you suggest we do it tomorrow?"

"Well, according to Rafe, the cruise-ship days are the best time to experience the town. And dinner won't be a problem, he promises. He seems to know Málaga pretty well; I'm game to take his word on it."

"If you will, then I will," Julie said. "Count me in."

With a nod, Gideon agreed. He checked his watch, arose, and let go another desolate sigh. “Okay, John, it’s almost two. Time to gird our loins.”

CHAPTER 7

They sat on rough-hewn blocks at the foot of a Roman amphitheater built in twentieth century BC or thereabouts, looking up beyond the rows of stone seating to the crenellated towers of the eighth-century Moorish Alcazaba that loomed atop the sheer cliff above, while listening to the plangent, twentieth-century *rasgueados* of a flamenco guitarist on a nearby street corner and munching on mini tapas from a sidewalk vendor dispensing his tiny morsels from a pushcart equipped with a state-of-the-art, twenty-first-century warming oven.

It was just the kind of chronological and cultural mishmash that Gideon, in most ways an annoyingly orderly sort of person, loved, and he was basking in this one. "This was a brilliant idea, Rafe. Perfect."

"Well, you know," Rafe said, "most Malagueňos stay away from the Old City on days when the cruise ships come in and those narrow little streets are clogged with gawking Brits or Germans or Americans, all of whom walk at a funereal pace that is just short of excruciating. But as for myself, I love it. With a flamenco guitarist playing on every corner and in every restaurant—which they don't do on other days of the week—it sounds like old *Espaňa*, you know, more than at any other time. The trick is to find a quiet spot a *little* removed from the hordes but still within hearing range of the guitars, such as"—he spread his arms—"you see."

Actually, the Roman Theater was right in the busy center of the city and one of Málaga's major attractions, with free entrance to it through the adjacent museum, so generally it was as full of tourists as the streets around it. But, today being Sunday, the museum had closed at two thirty. Rafe's lab was currently doing the DNA work on Roman bone fragments found at the site when it had been unearthed in the 1950s; in so doing, he had been spending time with the museum people over the last several weeks, and he had charmed the curator into breaking his own rules and letting the four of them in.

And a likable, altogether charming guy he was, upbeat, witty, and urbane, with enviable old-school—and distinctly old-fashioned—British manners and diction but without the meticulously civil but cool, condescending arrogance that too often went along with them. His few defects served to heighten his appeal by making him seem even more approachable: a slight tentativeness, almost but not quite a stammer, in his speech that suggested a beguiling uncertainty, as if he thought that anything he might say would be immediately (and justly) contradicted. His near-nonexistent eyebrows tilted slightly upward toward the middle, so that he looked as if he'd been caught off guard by—but also pleased with and interested in—the world he was in and the people he found himself in it with. Gideon guessed he was in his early fifties.

Not what anyone would call good-looking, he had squinchy eyes, thin lips, and a tiny snub nose, all scrunched together at the center of a moon of a face and lacking distinct eyebrows to set them off. A double set of dimples at each side of his mouth were cute additions, but his face could have used more help than that. As for the rest of him, three words summed him up: short, bald, and roly-poly. Still, he did the best he could with what he had. His shoes always gleamed, and the fluffy, graying fringe of hair above his ears was always combed. A careful dresser, he was one of the few at the conference who was never seen in anything but a conservative, impeccably tailored suit—never a mere sport coat—and an equally conservative tie. So far, they had been different every day, and their unfailingly high quality attested both to his taste and to the affluence that made them affordable.

"I like him," Julie had said after she'd first met him. "There's something about him that just makes me want to smile. He makes me think of the kind of guy you'd see in one of those old comedies—the puffy, stuffy old banker who gets his top hat knocked off by a snowball."

"Yep, that'd be Rafe all right. Except instead of getting mad and shaking his walking stick at them, he'd laugh and give the kids a nickel."

"Yes, or you could put the top hat back on, stick a walrus mustache on him, and you'd have the happy little guy in Monopoly, the one on the get-out-of-jail cards."

The four of them had been in the amphitheater for an hour this late afternoon, companionably chatting. The tapas had a mushy, prefrozen feel to them but had been quickly enough dealt with, and now they were relaxing, leaning back on the stone blocks of the row behind, sipping a flinty white Rioja from espresso-sized paper cups and feeling very privileged. This sense was heightened by Gideon's informing them that they were sitting in what would have been the orchestra back when people were snickering at the latest farce from Plautus; that is, the section strictly reserved for VIPs of the highest order. The ordinary citizens, the hoi polloi, would have been restricted to the cavea, the semicircular rows nearer the top of the theater.

"Your lab's DNA analysis," Gideon said when the small talk had run out. "Turning up anything interesting?"

Rafe poured himself a little more wine. "Haven't come up with the complete Roman genome yet, if that's what you mean. We've found a genetic connection to a third-century AD population from Tivoli, but that's hardly unexpected."

"Have they had an anthropologist look at the bones?"

"Gideon, these aren't what anybody would call *bones*. Or possibly you would. But they're only these little gray, flaky fragments, many of them burned. For most of them, it was only the DNA work itself that confirmed that they *were* human."

"Still, you never know. Even with only a little to work with, I might be able . . . well, never mind." He held out his cup, and John, closest to the bottle, refilled it for him.

Rafe was looking at him curiously. "Gideon," he said, with a bit more hesitation than usual, "is it possible that you're looking for work?"

"Funny you should say that," Julie murmured to no one.

"Because if you are," said Rafe, "I have something that might interest you. Have you ever been to the Channel Islands?"

A slight tilt of his head indicated that the question was addressed to Julie and John as well, and when all three said they hadn't, he told them that he had access to some far newer skeletal material—dating back only to 1969—from a murder case that had never been resolved, and he himself had some questions about them that he would love to have answered. It wasn't that the police had done a poor job, he explained, but that, as Gideon well knew, the forensic sciences were in a primitive state back then, and so he couldn't help wondering what a modern forensic examination might reveal.

"And so I was hoping, er, that you might be interested in, ah . . ."

"In looking at them to see if I can turn up anything that might shine a little light?" Gideon asked. He willed his brain waves straight at Rafe: *Say yes.*

"That's it exactly," Rafe said. "In coming on over to Jersey, having a look, and seeing what you might find, right. And?"

"I might be able to do that," Gideon said. "Tell me a little more about them." This was to convey the impression that he'd have to think about it, but nobody was fooled, except maybe Rafe. Gideon was going, and John and Julie knew it. When had he been known ever to turn down a hands-on chance at skeletal analysis? Of course he was going.

Rafe's immediate, bright smile—maybe just a tad overbright—suggested that he was pleased but no more fooled than the others. Nothing new there, Gideon thought with a sigh. He had learned a long time ago that hiding what he was thinking wasn't one of his long suits.

"Well, they were found in a pitch pond on our main farm. They were—what's the term for it? Amalgamated . . . conglomerated . . ."

"Commingled? Two or more people?"

"Yes, commingled. They were from two different people, both males, one twenty-six, I think it was, and the other, nineteen or twenty."

"Would you happen to know how that was determined?" Gideon asked. "The number of people? The sex?"

Forensic anthropology had indeed been in its infancy in 1969, he was thinking, and still the province of a very limited cadre of experts. Krogman's seminal textbook had come out only a few years earlier and was hardly likely to have been required reading in the Channel Islands. So what was the likelihood of a local Jersey doctor or police officer getting these things right, back then? Of course, if there were three tibias, say, or two mandibles, that would be a pretty good clue, even for a layman, that they were dealing with more than one person. But excepting something of that order, you had to wonder—

"*How* it was determined? No, I have no idea. But I do know that's what the postmortem reported: two men, one no *older* than twenty and the other no *younger* than twenty-six. Yes, that's right. I remember there was a six-year age difference between them."

So they aged them too, Gideon thought, right down to the individual year. Now there you were on really shaky ground. Sexing skeletons was a comparatively simple matter. All you had to do was toss a coin and you'd be right half the time. But coming up with how many years a person had lived? No, that was a different matter. Between immaturity and senescence (both of which had relatively obvious skeletal markers), you were left with a good fifty different choices of age. Not a job for the unanointed. And the possibility of having a trained forensic anthropologist available in Jersey in 1969 was zero, because there were no such creatures at the time; the term itself had yet to be invented.

"You look doubtful, Gideon," Rafe said. "The age determinations—you think they're a bit more specific than the evidence might warrant?"

"Could be, yes."

"A pitch pond," John was saying. "What is that, like the La Brea Tar Pits?"

"Much the same, I imagine," Rafe said. "Although, alas, we have yet to turn up a dinosaur. In fact, its official designation, in the parish land record books, is the rather grandiose 'Carlisle Tar Pits.' You can imagine the extent to which that has embellished the family name. But it's simply an area into which a slow, steady stream of oily gunk seeps and bubbles up from crevices in the underlying rock and sits there stewing in the sun until the oily elements eventually sink to the bottom and you're left with a great sticky, blobby puddle of pitch, or asphaltum, or tar, or bitumen—all one and the same."

"Sounds messy," Julie said.

"It is that. Nasty stuff. Smelly too. But commercially viable, very much so. In fact, the bones were discovered by workers in the process of extracting the pitch, you see, and as you might expect, the police came up with a dozen theories about how they'd come to be there. Naturally enough, foul play was assumed, with good reason, I might say, although there were no indications of it on the bones. But then, there wasn't much left in the way of bones. Only fragments, and not too many of those."

"Tar *pits*?" Gideon said. "More than one, then?"

"Not really, no, but the pond is shaped something like a pair of spectacles, only with one lens larger than the other, and with the two of them connected by a small stream that runs from the larger to the smaller—the nosepiece of the spectacles, you might say. As I understand it, they were commercially worked at different times, so people have always thought of them as two separate ponds. But they're not."

He paused to offer more wine all around but got no takers—everyone had already had two cups—so the little that was left remained in the bottle. "And so, Gideon, if you would deign to give it a try, I'd be glad to put you up—to put all of you up—for a few days at a nice Saint Helier hotel in which I keep a suite for just such a purpose: sitting room, small kitchen, and two bedrooms, both en suite. And even a valet's room, should anyone want to iron a tuxedo. Please. Do come and have an island holiday on me. I think you'd enjoy it. There's plenty to see."

"Oh, I think I just might deign," Gideon said, "as long as there's a valet's room." Julie and John readily nodded. They were game too.

"Wonderful!" Rafe's round face was alight. "In fact, if it's convenient, I would love to have you all there as early as tomorrow."

Their exchanged glances, followed by nods, indicated that it was convenient. "Excellent. You'll want to book an early flight. They're not terribly frequent, you know, and all of them require a stopover somewhere—Gatwick, Paris, Exeter—which can add quite a bit of time. I'm catching one later tonight, at three fifteen. Oh, I say, why don't you join me on it? I believe there are still seats available."

"No kidding, I wonder why that is," John said. "Three fifteen *in the morning*? Are you nuts?"

Gideon and Julie expressed similar if less blunt opinions, and Rafe laughed. "Ghastly hour, I know, but unfortunately for me there's States Assembly business that has to be attended to tomorrow."

"States Assembly?" Julie said. "Is that the Channel Islands' legislature?"

"No, the two bailiwicks, as we call them in our ever-so-quaint and colorful dialect, are quite separate. Guernsey has its own government. This is Jersey's. I'm a senator, one of twelve."

"I'm impressed," Julie said.

"Please, don't be. My grandfather cut quite a figure in Jersey politics in his day, you see—he was president pro tempore of the legislature at one point—and it was expected that I would run for election simply on the strength of the name. I did, and I won . . . simply on the strength of the name, I'm afraid. The job is nothing very important, I assure you; nothing at all like being a US senator. I'm never on the telly, and people don't run up to me on the street to ask for my autograph. I doubt if one out of a hundred people even knows I am a senator. And all it requires is attendance at three or four extraordinarily dull meetings a month, for which the endurance of tedium is the primary requisite."

Coming from most people, these conspicuously self-effacing protestations would be evidence of false modesty, but from Rafe, with his odd mixture of diffidence and self-assurance, Gideon thought they were genuine.

While Rafe was speaking, Julie had used her phone to get seats for herself, Gideon, and John on a 10:15 a.m. flight the following day that would have them at Jersey Airport at 3:35 p.m.

"Why, that's perfect," Rafe said. "I'll be free by then, and I'll drive you to your hotel—oh, and naturally, the flight's on me." The first offer was gratefully accepted, the second politely declined.

Rafe began to insist, but Gideon gently sidetracked him. "Why do you keep a suite for visitors to Jersey, though? Don't you live in York?"

"York? No. My laboratory is in York, at the university, but I'm only there a few days a month. I don't run the place, I just endow it," he said with a smile. "Well, and run a small project for them now and then, such as the one I'm doing here. No, no, I live in Jersey. Always have. I consider myself a farmer first and foremost, you see, a dairy farmer. That's what got me interested in genetics in the first place, and raising dairy cows is still my primary occupation. It's what I do for my living."

"Must be a heck of a living if you can afford to endow a DNA lab and keep a two-room suite at a hotel just for company," said John, who wasn't known for his subtlety but who had a wonderful knack for saying this sort of thing without giving offense.

"Well, yes, I suppose you might say that," Rafe said, and then made a clucking noise. "Oh, I don't know why I should be coy about it. Silly how embarrassed people are about wealth these days. The fact is that Carlisle Dairies are the largest dairy enterprise in the islands by quite a lot. We have four different farms totaling fifteen hundred acres—two square miles, almost five percent of all the land there is in Jersey."

"Wow, how many cows is that?" Julie asked.

"Three thousand, and every one of them prime Jersey stock. And then we have the dairy itself, the processing plant, in Grouville. I inherited the whole thing from my father, you see, and he from his, so it's nothing in which I can take any personal pride. The Carlisles have been, shall we say, prominent in Jersey for a long time, and, if I do say it myself, our Jerseys are right up there with the finest milk producers in the world: 4.9 percent butterfat content. Even among Jerseys, the accepted standard is only 4.84."

"The skeletal material," prompted Gideon, whose interest in dairy cows, Jerseys or otherwise, had been sated and then some. "What's the story on it? You said—"

In turn, he was interrupted by Rafe. "Gideon, could you hold your question for a bit? It's ten past seven. I think we'd best make our way to a restaurant."

"Second that," John said, raising a hand.

"But won't they be jammed?" Julie asked. "All those cruise passengers?"

"Not at all. No more crowds. Look around." Rafe gestured toward the amphitheater's public overlook, behind and above them on Calle Alcazabilla. It was the street they'd taken to get there, and it had been as jammed as Julie had predicted; they'd practically had to fight their way through the hordes. Not anymore.

"What happened?" she asked. "Where did everybody go?"

"Most of the passengers have to be back on their ships in time for a five or six o'clock departure. And the ones that don't have to leave until later have usually had enough—and spent enough—for one day and are more than ready to return to the ship, especially to their no-additional-cost dinners. As for the locals, however, they're barely up from their siestas and aren't nearly ready for dinner yet, as you know. So between now and, say, nine o'clock, finding a table couldn't be easier."

"And I think I know a place everybody would like," Julie offered, "right on the Plaza Mayor. It couldn't be too far from here."

"The Plaza Mayor?" Rafe said. "Only a few streets over. Shall we go?"

CHAPTER 8

Every city in Spain has its Plaza Mayor, its "main square," where the seminal events of its history are likely to have taken place: proclamations, celebrations, rebellions, and executions. Málaga is no exception. The handsome old square is still there, still the heart of the city, and still ringed by sixteenth- and seventeenth-century governmental mansions and palaces. But it's been a while since anybody got hanged there, and the upper floors of the buildings have been broken up into holiday apartments. At street level, there are restaurants, cafés, *taperias*, and boutiques, easy and pleasant to access because the square is now a pedestrian area paved with handsome slate blocks of an eye-soothing rose-gray color.

In name, however, and unknown to Julie, it hadn't been the "Plaza Mayor" for two centuries. Since 1812, it had been the "Plaza de la Constitución." Ask for the Plaza Mayor in Málaga, and you will be directed to the gigantic shopping mall of that name out by the airport.

The best-known restaurant on the square, mostly on account of the prime people-watching from its patio, is the hundred-year-old Café Central. Julie had had lunch here two days earlier, and it was here she brought them. And even in this long-established hub of city life, as

Rafe had told them, they had no trouble finding a table for four on the awninged patio. Their waiter—a dark, aging Latin-lover type, with hair a little too black and improbably narrow hips that suggested the help of a corset—laid their menus on the table with a bullfighter's flourish, threw a burning, lingering glance at Julie, and sidled away.

"My goodness, I certainly hope that was meant for you and not for me, Julie," Rafe said.

"I was totally unaware of that of which you speak," Julie said in a fluty voice that might have come from a portly Victorian duchess peering down her nose through a lorgnette. "Such things are beneath my notice."

"Probably wasn't anything personal, anyway. Just part of the service," John observed. "The tourists expect it."

Julie dropped the duchess manner and made a sour face. "Thank you so much. I really appreciate that."

Gideon smiled. He loved it when her nose wrinkled.

John shrugged. "Just sayin'."

As they began to browse the menus, Rafe turned to Gideon. "You had a question you were about to ask."

"I did, yes. You described it as a murder case. You said there was good reason to suspect foul play."

"Indeed, I did."

"But why, if there's no evidence on the bones?"

"Well, when the two of them had disappeared a few years earlier, the circumstances had been somewhat suspicious, to say the least."

"Wait a minute, are you saying you know who these people were?"

"Certainly, I know who they were. One of them was my father, after all—"

"Your *father*!" Julie exclaimed.

"Yes, of course, Roderick Carlisle," Rafe said, as if surprised that they hadn't figured it out for themselves. He frowned for a second and then looked blankly, pleasantly, at them. "Oh, dear, did I neglect to mention that?"

"If you did, I sure missed it," John said.

"That is to say, I *think* they're my father's remains, but I've never been a hundred percent certain." He glanced curiously from face to face. "Why in the world are you looking at me like that?"

It was Julie who replied. "It's just that you don't seem very upset about it—about your father being murdered and the case never having been solved. It seems a little . . . cold, as if it's just some kind of academic exercise for you."

"Oh, I see. But you have to understand, that's what it is, in a real sense. Naturally, I'm very interested to know what happened, but it's true that I don't have a great deal of emotional investment in it. It's been almost half a century, after all, and I feel very little personal connection to the man. I have only the vaguest memories of him, you understand, and I'm not certain that even those are real. When he disappeared I was barely three years old. And then, as I said, I've never been sure that those bones really are his. Not *completely* sure."

"But I thought you said you had access to them," Gideon said. "You never ran a DNA analysis at your lab?"

"I did try, but the material was unusable. They'd been in the pitch a long time, you see."

"Huh," Gideon said. "I would have thought that, if anything, the tar would have acted as a DNA preservative."

"As would I, but as it turned out, that wasn't the case. It was too degraded to yield any usable results. Ah," he said, spotting their approaching waiter, "Don Juan slithers back."

He was there for their drink orders. Rafe asked for some more Rioja, but red this time. Gideon and John were both pleased to learn that Guinness was on tap and ordered it. As most Americans did, they enjoyed beer in Spain (but not necessarily Spanish beer) because it was typically served ice-cold, a rarity in Europe. Julie ordered a lemonade, which earned the waiter's smoldering, dark-eyed approval, as if she'd given the sexiest, most brilliant order he'd heard all week.

"Now. What else would you like to know?" Rafe asked amiably.

"A lot," Gideon said. "First, you said that when your father disappeared there were suspicious circumstances. Such as?"

"And what about the other guy that was found with him?" John asked. "In the pitch pond. Who was he?"

And from Julie: "What exactly did the police think happened? A double murder?"

The questions threw Rafe off his stride. "My word. It's a bit more complicated than I realized. Perhaps I'd best go back a little and set the stage for you. A few background details." With his forefingers steepled at his chin, he took a few seconds to arrange his thoughts. "First, it occurs to me that I might also have failed to tell you that at the time my father disappeared, he himself was the subject of a murder investigation."

"That might have been worth mentioning, yes," Gideon said.

Julie stared at Rafe. "Your father was . . . ?"

"A murder suspect, yes, I'm afraid so," Rafe said calmly. "He still is, I suppose, if a nonliving individual can be a suspect." He shook his head. "Oh, a wretched affair from start to finish. Now, the man he was suspected of killing—George Skinner was his name—was a cousin to my father, but not in the usual sense. That is to say, *his* father, George's father, Willie, was the husband of Rose, who was the sister of Grace—"

"Uh, Rafe?" John said quietly.

"—who was the wife of *my* father's father, Howard, my grandfather that would be, but he—not my grandfather but George's father, Willie—married again after Rose died, so that—"

"Rafe?" John said a little more loudly and succeeded in getting noticed. "You think maybe you're giving us a few more background details than we need? At this point?"

"Ah, right, yes, very true. Right, then. George Skinner and my father, Roderick Carlisle, known by one and all as 'Roddy,' were cousins—their mothers were sisters, don't you see—and they'd been friends to some degree all their lives, and perhaps that's as much as need be said on the matter."

John rapped his knuckles on the table. "Hear, hear."

"Now then," Rafe went on, "the two of them, my father and George, also had business relationships, in that George had been an employee of my father's. He'd served as sales manager of Carlisle Paving and Road Construction and—"

"Paving and road construction?" Gideon echoed. "I thought you said your father was in the dairy business too, like you. Carlisle Dairies."

"Well, yes, he was, but he had the road-construction company as well. That had been in the family since the 1870s, when asphalt came into its own as a paving material, and the useless, smelly stuff that was bubbling up turned into a giant moneymaker, the only source of pitch for more than two hundred miles in any direction. My father inherited both businesses as a very young man and ran them quite successfully. For a while—until we lost access to the pitch—Carlisle Tar Pits proved more profitable than all the dairies combined."

"Lost access?" John asked. "How'd that happen?"

"It was the trials, the suits—we were forced to sell the rights."

"Trials? Suits?" said Gideon. He was starting to wilt. This was a lot to take in, especially after a few glasses of wine.

"Yes, I'll come to that in a moment. In any event, we were able to hold on to the land, you see—in fact I continue to live on the property today—but Inter-Island Road Construction bought the rights to the pond and had them for some years, until the pitch ran out, and that was the end of that."

"So the pond isn't really there anymore?" asked Gideon, who'd been thinking it would have been helpful to have a firsthand look at the site.

"Correct. We—that is to say my mother; I was still a child at the time—had it cleaned up and turned into a lovely freshwater pond, with a charming little gazebo beside it. A good thing too, because it's only thirty meters from the house. I still remember the stench when the wind blew the wrong way. Whew."

He wrinkled his nose to emphasize the point. Not as cute as Julie's, but it was one hell of a wrinkle, more like a full-fledged twitch that a rabbit would have been proud of. The man didn't have much going for him in the way of overall musculature, but his *nasalis* and *dilatatores naris* would have been something to see.

When their waiter came back with their drinks and a pen and pad at the ready for their dinner orders, Julie asked for the seafood tapas platter, Rafe the *plato de carne* mixed grill, and Gideon the *paella Valenciana*—Café Central was one of the rare Spanish restaurants that didn't require a two-person order for paella. John, breaking with his red-meat tradition, went for fish: *boquerones fritos*, a beautiful, heaped pile of whole, golden, deep-fried, fresh anchovies, which he'd seen on its way to a nearby table.

They clinked glasses and took their first sips, and Rafe carried on.

"It pains me to tell you that there was yet a third person involved, other than George and my father, whom you need to know about to understand it all. And that is a young man named Bertrand Peltier, who was married to George's wife's younger sister, which would have made him George's brother-in-law, if I have it correctly, or would it have been—"

A second gentle finger wag from John got him off that particular track.

"Thank you, John, I needed that. Well, whatever else he was, young Bertrand was apparently a whiz kid when it came to maths; he was the assistant bookkeeper at the paving company, although quite youthful for such a position, but unfortunately—unfortunately for *him*—not overly endowed with moral fiber."

"I'm guessing this Peltier would be the other person who wound up in the pitch pond with your father?" Gideon said. "The younger one?"

"You guess correctly. It was he who performed the hands-on work necessary to the embezzlement until . . . ah, you're all looking rather confused."

"*What* embezzlement?" Julie asked, speaking for the three of them.

"Jesus Christ," John said. "Help, somebody."

"I'm coming to it, I'm coming to it. We do seem to have gotten a bit ahead of things, though. Don't despair, all will become clear."

"Knock on wood," John said. And did, following it with a lusty swig of beer and using his napkin to swipe away the mustache of foam that resulted.

"Now, back to Carlisle Paving and Road Construction itself . . ."

The company had grown ever more successful under Roddy's adaptable and forward-looking management philosophy, to the extent that by the early 1960s, Carlisle Paving had a virtual monopoly on road construction throughout the Channel Islands and was making inroads in building construction as well, to say nothing of the business they did in England.

Until it turned out that there was more at play than vision and adaptability. In January 1964 the government had begun an investigation into "a culture of corruption" at Carlisle Paving.

"My father, believing George to be at the bottom of any disreputable activities—and I have no doubt that he was—dismissed him from his employ, despite their relationship and their long friendship. By June it was an ill-kept secret that Roddy and George would both be charged as coconspirators in the crimes of intimidation (of competitors) and bribery (of government officials)."

"And this Peltier guy, when does he come into it?" asked John.

"Right now. One day my father and George both disappeared and, surprisingly, Peltier as well. Simply vanished, the three of them, leaving not a trace behind."

But nobody had needed traces. What had happened was obvious. With indictments imminent, Roddy Carlisle and George Skinner had fled the island, and Peltier with them. This suspicion became a virtual certainty when rapidly compiled company audits showed that £990,000 of Carlisle Paving's money had disappeared with them.

"Were there charges pending against Peltier too, then?" asked Gideon.

"Not at the time. Only later was it shown that it was most assuredly Bertrand—and this is one of the few certainties in the entire affair—who had used his position as assistant bookkeeper to help them extricate that million pounds. Very likely, that was why he was put into the position in the first place. How he came to end up in the pitch pond with my father is one of the many mysteries that was never resolved. In fact, I have yet to hear a credible theory."

But by the next morning, the certainty was no longer a certainty, not even a virtual one. They hadn't gone anywhere after all, or at least George hadn't. His body was found twenty meters from his house, at the foot of a cluster of craggy outcroppings. He had been shot to death, and the police were able to establish that the bullet that killed him—killed him instantly—had been fired from atop the crags.

Suspicion now fell on Bertrand Peltier and Rafe's father, then quickly focused entirely on Roddy when it was discovered that the murder weapon was a gun that belonged to him. The motive for the killing, it was now thought, probably had more to do with their recent estrangement than the coming indictment, a squabble between thieves who had fallen out. It was believed at the time that Roddy and Peltier had probably made off to some distant corner of the Commonwealth—Canada, Australia, Singapore, God knows where—and then separated.

And with nearly a million pounds to split between them, they weren't expected back anytime soon.

As a result, the murder case was never pursued with much vigor and eventually faded away, as did the investigation into the embezzling. The corruption case against Carlisle Paving, however, was carried forward, ending in a conviction and in criminal sentences to two government officials for accepting bribes. Afterward, there were half a dozen civil suits, resulting in years of wrangling and in the sale of Carlisle Paving to its chief competitor, Inter-Island Road Construction, in 1965. The Carlisles' dairy business, happily free of legal troubles, remained in the family and was successfully managed by Roddy's highly efficient wife—Rafe's mother—until it was handed over to Rafe when he was in his twenties.

"Back up a second, Rafe," Gideon said, putting down his Guinness. "The police said George's death was instantaneous. How did they determine that, do you know?"

"Yes, I do know. The bullet went through his heart, right through the left . . . what is it, atrium . . . and, er . . ."

"Ventricle."

"Yes, ventricle and atrium. 'Shredded his heart' was the unnecessarily graphic phrase they used. I shouldn't think death would be very long in coming, would you?"

"Ah," murmured Gideon. "Hm."

"Hey, Julie?" John said. "What do you think he means when he says that?"

"What do you mean, what do I mean?" Gideon said. "I didn't say anything."

"No, you said, 'Hm,' loud and clear."

"I did? I wasn't even aware—"

"But first you said, 'Ah.'" This from Julie. "Coupling those two, one right after the other—now that's *really* suggestive."

"Of what? What is it with you people? 'Hm' is just a way of . . . what . . . I don't know, just acknowledging that you're hearing something somebody is saying, that's all. And 'ah'—I don't know what the hell it means, it's just a . . . a figure of speech, a nonliteral interjection that, that . . ."

"Right," said John, nodding soberly.

"Right," said Julie. "Absolutely."

And then they both said, "Hm."

Gideon rolled his eyes. "Pay no attention to these people, Rafe. They seem to be under the impression they can read my mind. I really don't—"

He was interrupted by the return of Don Juan, who skated out from the interior, showily bringing four large, plentifully loaded plates without the help of a tray: one on each palm, one on each forearm. The tricky process of getting them onto the table without loss of contents was accomplished with the flare of a flamenco dancer.

The prettily arranged food looked good and smelled wonderful, and the four of them dug in. After they'd made a little progress, Rafe, apparently deciding not to pursue Gideon's "hm," picked up where he'd left off.

For five years, progress on George's murder and Roddy and Bertrand's disappearance remained where it was: in limbo. Then, in 1969, came the discovery of the bones, made by workers engaged in harvesting the pitch for Inter-Island Construction, the company that had held the lease to extract it. "They were quickly determined to be my father's and Peltier's."

"Based on the age determinations?" Gideon asked.

"Yes. None of the other missing-persons searches that were open at the time fit those ages. Oh, and I should mention that my father's wedding ring, engraved with his initials, came up with the bones. That pretty much settled it, as far as the police were concerned."

"But you're not convinced," John observed.

"I shouldn't say I'm not *convinced*, but none of it is exactly what one would call proof positive, is it?"

"Proof positive, no," John said, "but awful damn close. You'd have to come up with a pretty weird scenario to explain how your father's wedding ring got mixed up with somebody else's bones."

Julie looked up from a cheese-stuffed salmon roll. "Unless somebody put it there exactly for the purpose of confusing the issue."

"Yes!" Rafe chimed in. "I've thought and thought about that."

"Yeah, I think I've seen it on TV about a dozen times," John said. "Just never in real life." His brow knitted. "Well, you know, I *have*, actually. Something like that, where the guy wanted to make the cops—and even more, the insurance company—think he was dead when he wasn't."

"Exactly," Rafe said. "Given the strangeness of everything else about this, I'd say that's a real possibility, wouldn't you?"

"I'd say you got a point, I admit."

"And what would you say, Gideon?" Rafe asked.

"I'd—"

"He'd say, 'Hm.'" Julie said.

Gideon laughed. "That's about right."

Rafe smiled uncertainly. "Er, I'm not altogether sure I understand this 'hm' business."

"It means," Julie explained, "that something we said woke up one of his seven gazillion gray cells, but he's not about to let us in on it until he's good and ready."

"What can I say?" Gideon said to Rafe. "I think they do know me better than I know myself, which, I have to say"—he arched an eyebrow in John and Julie's direction—"is a damned irritating thing." Back to Rafe: "Look, it's not that I'm keeping any secrets to myself or that I've come up with some amazing new insight. It's more as if I'm taking mental notes about what to look for when I get started in Jersey.

And it certainly doesn't mean that I disagree with what the police came up with."

"Oh, no," John muttered. "Excuse me. Perish the thought."

"Or that I agree with them either. Carry on, Rafe, will you?"

"Well, there's little else to tell. Exactly why and how Father and Peltier *had* ended up in the pond, and who was responsible, was never officially determined, although it's hard to argue that it was the result of anything other than foul play."

"Had to be," John agreed.

"What if they'd fallen in accidentally?" Julie asked. "I wonder, could you crawl out of a pitch pond, or would you be stuck for good?"

Rafe shrugged. "No idea."

"Well," said John, "those dinosaurs at La Brea didn't make it out, so how easy could it be?"

"Actually, there aren't any dinosaurs in the La Brea Tar Pits," Gideon said. "The tar pits are only about forty thousand years old. Dinosaurs had been extinct for sixty-five million years by then. What they do have are mammoths, sabre-tooths—"

He stopped, recognizing a look from the others that he ran into a lot. Nothing overtly impolite, but something along the lines of: *And how are these ever-so-interesting little factoids of yours pertinent to what we are discussing?*

"It's not his fault," Julie said pleasantly to the others. "He can't help himself."

"Well, I did let it go by the first time," Gideon mumbled in his own defense, "but I felt I had an obligation to say something when it came up again. Anyway, dinosaurs aside, the idea that *two* men fell in accidentally is just a little improbable, in my opinion."

"Yeah, I'll buy that," said John. "So what exactly did the police say did happen?"

Rafe shook his head. "As I said, there was no formal conclusion. One theory, the one that seemed most popular, according to the press of the time, was that Peltier and Father had gotten into a fight over the money and ended up killing one another. There are plenty of rocks lying around the area, God knows. Easy enough to pick one up in a fit of anger . . ."

John was dubious. "They brain each other with rocks? And then both of them fall into the tar pit, beside which they happen to have been fighting?"

"I know, it seems unlikely to me too. The other theory, and it's the one I prefer to believe, is that someone else killed them both. And very likely killed George as well."

"Some other person killed George . . . with your *father's* revolver?" Julie asked, to make sure she had it straight.

"Yes. I'll admit, it sounds a little, ah . . ."

"It sure does," Julie said. "I can certainly understand why you'd like to think it, but now *you're* starting to sound like a TV mystery."

Rafe laughed. "The entire thing sounds like a TV mystery, wouldn't you agree?"

No one disagreed.

"They come up with any suspects?" asked John, sounding more by the minute like the FBI special agent he was.

"Yes, there were suspects. The bribery and intimidation for which Carlisle Paving was convicted—rightfully, I have to admit—had injured a good many people. Two competitors had been put entirely out of business. Several had sued the company, and one old gentleman—well, he's old now—had been particularly vociferous in his denunciations. The investigation concentrated on him, and it went on for months, I understand, but to no good end. I still see the old fellow from time to time, and, believe me, he doesn't let me forget it. In the event, however, no one was ever brought to trial. Nearly five years had passed since they'd been killed, after all; credible evidence was harder to get. Memories had begun to fail." Rafe sighed. "And now it's been a dead issue for more than forty years."

"A long time," said Gideon. "Let's be realistic about that, Rafe. I'd be happy to have a try at this, but what do you think getting me into it now could accomplish? The case isn't going to be reopened, even if I come up with something, not after all this time. Chances are, whoever killed them isn't even alive anymore. What's the point of it?"

"It's a personal thing with me, Gideon. Academic exercise or not, I do want to know—in my position, you'd want to know too: Are those really my father's remains? How did he die? Who killed him? Did he really shoot George? Was he—"

Gideon was shaking his head. "Rafe, there's no conceivable way I'm going to come up with all that. At most—"

"Whatever you come up with would be more than I know now. And if you don't come up with anything, well, I'll appreciate the effort. And I'll have the pleasure of having the three of you in Jersey for a few days."

"Oh, he'll come up with something," John said. "He always does. Problem is, and I'm quoting my boss here, 'I appreciate what he does, but why can't he ever even once come up with what you *wanted* him to come up with?'"

Gideon smiled. "I boldly go where the facts lead me."

"I'll take the risk," Rafe said. "I just want to *know*." He settled back in his chair and returned to spearing the few tidbits of sausage and skewered lamb that remained on his platter. His recounting was obviously finished. No one was interested in dessert, but on the recommendation of the waiter they all ordered *Carajillo con coñac* (brandy-laced coffee), which came, steaming, in clear tumblers.

It was while they were quietly, slowly absorbing this innards-warming drink, along with what they'd just heard, that Gideon said, "Rafe, do you happen to know *which* bones were found in the pond? Any parts of the skull?"

Forensic anthropologists always hope for a skull. As any textbook will tell you, there is likely to be more information there about the decedent—about how he lived and how he died, and who he was—than anywhere else in the skeleton. More than that, although you won't find this in the textbooks, there is a connection, an empathy, with the once-living person that you feel when gazing into the hollow eye sockets of a skull that you just don't get from staring into the obturator foramina of a pelvis.

"Yes, there were. Two, I believe. A piece of parietal, was it? And the occipitus? Is that a name? Sorry, I don't remember. My skeletal anatomy's a little shaky. Altogether, there are something like a dozen fragments, all of them relatively small. Well, small, period."

A dozen? Gideon thought. That was it? Twelve *fragments*? Not even one whole bone? He'd understood that there wouldn't be much material, but twelve fragments, and all of them "relatively small"? Like the anthropologist he was, he'd been looking forward to opening a standard "archival skeletal-remains container"—a miniature coffin, three feet long or so and made of heavy cardboard—and having his first look at the contents. But for these bones, a shoe box would more than do the job.

And those impressive conclusions from the 1969 postmortem were suddenly even more suspect.

"And to tell you the truth," Rafe went on, "I don't remember how many of them are my father's and how many are Peltier's and how many of them couldn't be identified, but it's all in the postmortem report. I have a copy somewhere, and even if I can't find it, I'm sure the police would—"

"Hold up a second, Rafe. Why is it that you have Peltier's bones as well as your father's? I would have thought they'd have gone to his family. Didn't you say he was married?"

"I know only what I've been told, and what I've been told is that when Miranda saw those few broken, blackened pieces of bone, she wanted nothing to do with them, refused to accept the idea that they could be her handsome young husband's. I understand she actually ran screaming out of the police station. So the police kept them with my father's and with the ones they couldn't identify for sure. They'd all been found together, after all."

At that point, John threw back his head, turned aside, and covered his mouth with the back of his hand but couldn't quite stifle a yawn, which set the rest of them to doing the same. They'd all consumed too much food, and too much wine, and too much Carlisle history to keep things going. And the warm cognac had them practically asleep.

"I sense an approaching end to this delightful evening," Rafe said when his own discreet yawn ended. "Shall we head back to the hotel? I know I could use a few hours' sleep before my flight."

"Three fifteen a.m.," John said. "Sheesh."

CHAPTER 9

WELCOME

Seyiz les beinv'nus à Jèrri

The sign was prominently stenciled on the windows of Jersey Airport's baggage area, and it stopped Julie cold. She tried mouthing the words, then shook her head. "Now that is really strange. Look at that."

John was surprised. "You didn't know? The Channel Islands, they're like Canada. A lot of the signs, they're in English and French. This used to be part of France."

"I do know that, John. But that isn't French—not exactly. Either that or someone doesn't know how to spell."

"You're right, it isn't French, but it's close," Gideon said. "They're welcoming us in Jèrriais, the local version of medieval Norman. It's been spoken here for a thousand years. Came to Britain with William the Conqueror in 1066, but the Channel Islands are the only place it hung on."

"Well, sure," John said. "Hell, everybody knows that."

Gideon was undeterred. "Practically right up until the twentieth century, it was what everybody spoke here. Then it started fading out, and the German Occupation pretty much wiped it out. English was fine with the Nazis, but French, they didn't want to hear. Now only a few hundred people speak it at all, and probably none of them are under seventy. Over on Guernsey, they have a slightly different variant, Guernésiais."

John cocked an eyebrow at him, looked as if he was about to ask a question, but then turned to Julie. "Julie, tell me something. Your honest opinion. Does he really *know* stuff like that? I mean, do you think he really carries it around in his head, or does he just bone up on it the night before, so he can toss it out like he knew it all along?"

"That's something I've never been able to settle for myself, John. I haven't ever caught him sneaking in any prepping, but I have my suspicions."

Gideon huffed. "The fact is I certainly did know it. It was unnecessary to 'bone up' on anything." Then the laugh he'd been keeping in check broke through. "Well, okay, except for the last part, maybe, about Guernésiais. But it *is* all true, and the difference is I was looking it up to enlarge my own store of knowledge about the place I was coming to, not to impress you two sluggards, who don't bother with such things."

"'Ey," John said, "I resemble 'at remark."

"Hullo, all." Rafe had come up behind them. "Talking about the sign, are we? About our poor, disappearing Jèrriais?"

Julie laughed. "Well, Professor Oliver here was. We were listening."

"Speak for yourself," John said.

"Do you ever hear it spoken at all?" Julie asked Rafe. "I'd love to hear what it sounds like."

Rafe shook his head. "No, you would not. Even spoken correctly, it sounds like an Englishman from Liverpool endeavoring to speak French from a book that neglected to provide any guidance in pronunciation. A nerve-jarring experience, in my opinion. You have your baggage? Shall we head for Saint Helier? My car's just a few steps away, in the car park."

Rafe's car turned out to be a boxy black SUV, scruffy, beat-up, and splattered with mud. In the United States, someone would have finger inscribed "WASH ME" in the road grime by now.

"Hey, a Range Rover," John said.

"It is that," said Rafe, "the 2008 edition. It's what country squires are expected to drive, you see, and since I am a country squire of sorts by Jersey standards, I thought it only right that I act like one. Don't worry, once you get inside it's quite clean, and comfortable too. I let the exterior go only to prove that I'm the genuine article, not some jumped-up parvenu trying to show off with his shiny, spanking, brand-new estate car."

The interior, as he'd said, was nothing like the decrepit exterior, its fabrics and dove-gray leather upholstery spotless and unmarred. The original passenger benches in the rear had been replaced with bucket seats like the ones up front. Julie got in front next to Rafe, with Gideon and John behind.

"Now tonight I'm afraid there's States business I need to attend to," Rafe said as they buckled up, "but I'd like to have you all to the manor for dinner Wednesday—if that's agreeable."

"The manor?" Julie said.

"My home," Rafe said with a smile. "Ridiculous, isn't it, but that's what everyone calls it—Le Fontant Manor, in honor of the Norman family that built it in the seventeenth century."

"Impressive."

"No, not really. There are a good two dozen places that go by 'manor' on the island. As you'll see, Le Fontant is one of the smaller, plainer ones. Just an old farmhouse, really, with a few mod cons added over the years. I'll have a car come round and collect you at your hotel at six Wednesday evening, all right? We'll have cocktails first." He turned the key in the ignition. "Well, let us go."

And so they drove in comfort out of the parking lot and into a pleasant, rolling countryside of farms and pastureland populated with small, coffee-and-cream-colored cows that seemed even more placid and content than the usual bovines.

"Are those Jerseys?" Julie asked.

"Yes, mine as a matter of fact. Pretty things, aren't they?"

"Very," Julie said. "Look at those *eyes*! And the calves—oh, look at them, they all look like Bambi!"

The day was warm and sunny, and Rafe had the windows open. For a while they drove in easy silence, taking in the roomy, tranquil landscape and the mixed fragrances of grassland, farm, and barn. They drove down country roads with French (not Jèrriais) names—*Avenue de la Reine*, *La Route de Beaumont*—but were reminded that they were on Dominion soil when they turned onto the more stodgily named, solidly British *A2*, which soon became the even more definitively British *Victoria Avenue* as it ran beside a sweeping bay edged by a smooth white-sand beach with clumps of sunbathers here and there.

"Saint Aubin's Bay," Rafe told them, and a very few minutes later: "And here we are, our metropolis, Saint Helier. Population, thirty thousand, the largest city on Jersey. Largest city in the Channel Islands, for that matter."

"Looks like a nice place," John said politely as they turned into it.

That was about right, Gideon thought. Not splendid, not squalid. Not poor, not rich. Clean, modest . . . nice. Not particularly ancient by European standards, nor up-to-the-minute modern.

On an island just offshore, there was a massive fortress (Elizabeth Castle, according to Rafe, in which Sir Walter Raleigh had lived when he was governor of the island and in which the future Charles II had holed up during the English Civil War). But the town seemed solidly nineteenth century, with many middle-class, two-story Victorian residences, a few graceful Regency crescents, and even fewer late twentieth-century apartment blocks. Anything that went up more than two stories was a rarity.

There were a very few seventeenth- and eighteenth-century buildings to be seen as well, and the Revere Hotel, to which Rafe drove them, was one of them. An old coaching inn, from the look of it, Gideon thought, or maybe a post house. It had obviously started out with two stories, but a third floor had been added in the last fifty years, an unfortunate development from an aesthetic point of view. The hotel was on the east side of town, on Kensington Place, a quiet street of guesthouses and restaurants. Like many of the older buildings nearby, it had been stuccoed over in white, but at street level the stucco had been peeled away to show the rough, handsome granite blocks underneath.

Cozy and charmingly quaint, with wing chairs, fireplace, and library shelves, the lobby area was staffed by Glenda, a bubbly bleached blonde in her fifties, whose fussing and fluttering over Rafe gave the impression that, from the Revere's point of view, he was a top-of-the-line VIP. But then he would be; in a small, middle-of-the-road hotel like this, how many clients would they have who kept a suite year-round?

"I imagine this place must have a lot of history," Julie said, looking around as they checked in.

"Oh, I should say so!" Glenda enthused. "Loads! The Beatles stayed here once, and so did John Denver! And Sean Connery! Mr. Connery sent us an autographed picture after. And we even have a *movie* of the Beatles showing when they were here, larking about, right in our pool! And Ringo, all by himself, reading a magazine, sitting right in our lobby, right in that chair there, where that old gentleman is sitting. You could sit in it too if you want to."

"Thanks, Glenda, I just might do that. I think I'll wait till he gets up, though."

Glenda clapped a hand to her mouth to hold back a giggle. "Oh, aren't you the funny one!"

"And what about before the Beatles, Glenda?" Gideon asked. "Anything interesting ever happen here before then?"

"Not that I ever heard of, sir," was her thoughtful reply, "and I've been here fourteen years."

Rafe interjected politely, "Glenda, if the registration's done, do you suppose you could have the luggage taken up to the suite, please? My friends and I are going to take some refreshment in the bar."

This had been agreed to during the drive, and in they trooped to the adjacent hotel bar, a room that seemed little changed in four hundred years, although, judging from its length and narrowness, it had probably been a passageway back then. The plastered walls were lumpy and irregular, the ceiling was supported by adze-carved wooden beams, and along the sidewalls there were stone archways opening into the various little alcoves and niches that these old places had. The four of them sat on a couple of sofas that were set up to face each other over a coffee table, Julie and Gideon across from Rafe and John.

It wasn't much after four, and none of them were ready for anything alcoholic, so Rafe asked for an afternoon tea service. From the reaction of the barman who took the order—"Did you want tea sandwiches? Would you care for sweets? Shall I include some scones?"—Gideon could see that afternoon teas were not part of the regular menu, but this being Rafe Carlisle, everything he asked for (which was everything that the barman had suggested) was gracefully accepted as a matter of course. As was his request for coffee instead of tea.

"Well, now," he said while they were waiting, "I assume everybody would like to relax for a day or two—find your bearings, see some sights—so why don't we put off any forensic work on Gideon's part until . . . well, until you're ready."

"Actually, Rafe, speaking for myself, I'd really rather go ahead and get started—tomorrow, if that's possible. You've gotten me intrigued, and I'm kind of chafing at the bit. I'll fit in some sightseeing along the way, don't worry."

"And I'm fine doing something on my own," Julie said. "Is there a local history museum in Saint Helier? I always like to start with that."

"There certainly is, a good one, and it's only a ten-minute walk away. Neanderthals, Celts, Romans, Normans—they've all been here, and they've left bits behind, many of which you'll find in the museum. Modern people who lived here too: Victor Hugo, Lillie Langtry—they've got her rather amazing toiletries case, which is worth a visit in itself."

"But nothing from the Beatles?"

"Alas, no," Rafe said. "Not to my knowledge."

"Darn. Well, what the heck, I might go anyway."

"I'll probably mostly hang with you, Doc," John said, "if that's okay with you."

"Sure, it's okay; I'll appreciate the company. But you already know what I do; there's not much to see. Basically, it's just sitting around, looking at bones and thinking about them."

"No, I always like watching you talk to them." And to Rafe: "That's not something you see every day."

"And do they talk back?" Rafe asked.

John waggled his hand. "Hard to say."

"No," Gideon said. "They do not talk back. And I don't talk to *them*, I talk to myself."

"Which, you'll admit," Julie said to Rafe, "makes all the difference."

"Whatever does the job," Rafe said.

The barman returned with a tray holding the coffee things: busy little blue-and-white cups and saucers and a matching porcelain pourer, creamer, and sugar bowl. All very fancy.

"Ah, the old Wedgwoods, I see," Rafe said.

"Of course," said the barman, "for you, sir."

"Thoughtful of you, Paul, I appreciate it. And now that I think of it, perhaps we'd better have a little sherry to accompany the hors d'oeuvres."

"Yes, sir, the Fino?"

"Mmm . . . perhaps something not quite so dry as that."

"Manzanilla?"

"Perfect."

Once Paul had laid out the coffee service and filled the cups, Rafe took the conversation up again.

"So, Gideon, if you like, we'll get the bones out for you tomorrow morning. I'm all for it."

"Great, where are they? Do the police still have them?"

"Not at all, they returned them to my mother when they more or less gave up on the case. In 1970, I think. They're still in a carton in my garage."

Julie looked up from pouring cream into her coffee. "Your father's bones have been in a box in your garage for over forty years?"

Rafe laughed, a closed-mouth chuckle. "It does sound rather hard-hearted when put like that, but yes, that's exactly where they've been. I was only an infant at the time they came to us, but Mother was terribly upset with him. The paving company indictments had come as a complete surprise to her, you see. And then, with everything that followed from them—the scandal, the police investigation, George's murder, the years of waiting without knowing what had happened to him—well, with everything he'd put her through, she was no longer very kindly disposed toward him, shall we say. And when the remains were to be given to her, she couldn't face the idea of having a funeral for him—or of not having one. And so she put it on hold. And time simply slid by, the way it does. And eventually, she died, without ever having done anything more."

He took his first slow, thoughtful sip of coffee. Talking about these long-ago events had sobered him. "For me, from the time that I was a child, that dusty old carton on the top shelf in the garage was just another fixture, no less so than the nineteenth-century farm implements piled on the shelf below or the ancient horses' yokes on the walls. I have no memory of a time when it wasn't there." He spread his hands. "And so, other than my unsuccessful try at testing the DNA, I simply never got around to doing anything about them either. And now that you're here, I'm glad I didn't."

"So what's the plan, exactly?" John said.

"I had the carton taken to our dairy plant in Grouville this morning and asked the plant manager to set up a work space for Gideon in an unused storeroom. It's not a bad place: modern, clean, well lit. I think you'll be comfortable there."

"And Grouville is where?"

"Out in some very pleasant countryside, but only a ten-minute drive from here." He smiled. "But then, ninety percent of Jersey is within a ten-minute drive." And then, after a beat: "The remainder can be as much as fifteen, if the traffic's heavy."

The barman was back with the rest of their tea, set out on a silver three-level plate holder: crustless, triangular little sandwiches on the bottom level; crumpets and scones, along with jam and clotted cream on the middle plate; and sweets on the top one.

"Now, doesn't *that* look good!" Rafe enthused. "What do we have there, Paul?" He was pointing at the sandwich tray.

"Cucumber, tomato, sardine, curried chicken, and egg," the barman rattled off. "Oh, and the ones on dark bread are gravlax and cream cheese—your favorites."

"Marvelous. Thank you, Paul, and please express my appreciation to Annie. This should certainly do for us."

"For about the next three days," Julie said with a laugh.

"Ho ho, I think not," Rafe said, reaching toward one of the gravlax sandwiches with the tongs provided. But he changed his mind midway and laid them down. "First, a toast," he said, pouring an ounce or two of sherry all around and lifting his own glass. "To new friends made and old mysteries solved."

"New friends made and old mysteries solved," murmured the others. Glasses were clinked, and sips were taken.

"And let the chips fall where they may," added Rafe, his glass still aloft. "Now, Gideon, may I have any tools or equipment gotten for you? Measures? Calipers?"

"Not at this point, no, and probably not at all. You understand, I'm not going to be doing a full-scale analysis here."

"Right. Just a look-see."

"Right, see if something jumps out at me. Whoa, crumpets." It had been a long time since he'd had a real English crumpet, and he took one now, warm and satisfactorily butter drenched, put it on his plate, and toyed a little with it, but then let it sit there. His mind wasn't really on the tea. "Rafe, there's something I've been wondering about."

Rafe looked up expectantly. The tiny sandwich had been a two-bite affair, and having finished it, he dabbed at his lips. "Yes?"

"How did they establish that the gun that killed George was your father's?"

"Oh, they *found* it. It was weeks later, and only by accident. It was stuck in an overgrown hedge near his house, which is to say, my house now. It'd been brought back from the Great War—the First World War—by my grandfather—that would be Howard Carlisle—and it'd been in the house ever since."

"Yes, but I mean, how did they establish that it was the same gun that killed George? Did they find the bullet?"

"Yes. Oh, Lord, did they find it! It was lodged in George's hip, near the base of his spine. They matched it to the gun, however it is that they do that sort of thing. Grooves and such, what?"

John pondered for a few seconds. "Rafe, this crag they said he was shot from—how far away was it, do you know?"

"The distance the bullet had to travel, is that what you're after? Fifteen meters, I should say. Call it fifty feet."

"And would you happen to know what kind of gun it was?"

"Yes, I do. Certainly. It was a . . . oh, dear, a Something 1895—an Avant, or a Gavilan, or . . . damn it, it's on the tip of my tongue . . . made in Belgium or Luxem—"

"A Nagant 1895?"

"That's it, yes, very good! Oh, but of course. FBI! You know all about ballistics, don't you?"

"Not even close to 'all about,' but, yeah, I do know a little about Nagants: seven-shot Belgian revolvers, used by the Russians up into the Second World War. Not produced since then, and never too popular because the emptied cartridges don't get expelled when you fire. You have to take them out by hand."

The chicken salad triangle he'd selected a moment ago was now put down on his plate without his having taken a bite. And he was leaning intently forward. "Look, tell me what else you remember about the gun, will you?"

He was onto something, Gideon could see, but what, he didn't know.

John's intensity put a dent in Rafe's self-confidence. "Well, you have to understand, I know next to nothing about guns myself, but I do remember that when they found it, only one of the cartridges was empty, indicating, so they said, that only a single bullet had been fired." He shrugged. "I don't know what else I can tell you."

"The cartridges," John said. "Do you know what caliber they were?"

"Mmm." He shook his head slowly. "It was something unusual, nothing I'd ever heard of. Not simply .32 or .45, or anything like that. More complicated."

"How about 7.62 by 38 mm, that sound right?"

"Why, yes, I believe so."

"That should be it. It was the Nagant's original ammo, and extremely unusual. Also no longer produced. Now—"

"John, where are we going with this?" Gideon inquired.

"Hey, do I rush you when you're taking a million years to get to the point?"

"Yes, all the time."

"Okay, well, now you know what it's like being on the other end. Rafe, was your father any kind of a marksman?"

"Roddy Carlisle a marksman? Not at all. He hated guns. They made him nervous. Mother told me he didn't even want that one in the house. It was there only at her insistence. She was always a bit, er, paranoid, you see, and she wanted to have it there for protection when he was away overnight, in a little table by the front door. Not that she would have known what to do with it, you understand."

Now John sat back, finally popped the sandwich into his mouth, chewed for about two seconds, swallowed it down, and rubbed his hands together. "O-*kay*," he said with satisfaction. "The cops said the shot came from up on the rocks, right?"

Nod.

"Well, if that's true, then I'll tell you right now there's no way in hell your father fired it."

Rafe blinked and opened his mouth to say something, but nothing came out.

"How can you be so sure?" Julie asked. She refilled the coffee all around.

John helped himself to some of it and to another sandwich before explaining. "Okay. The fact that you had to take the cartridges out by hand wasn't the only reason the Nagant went out of favor. The sights were nothing to brag about, and it had a real heavy trigger pull. I've fired those puppies, and I can tell you, it ain't easy; you really have to *squeeze*. Put those two things together, and it's not going to be the most accurate gun in the world. Rafe, you happen to know whether it was single action or double action?"

"Single action, I believe is what they said, but I'm afraid I don't know what that means."

"Doesn't matter, except that it makes the gun even harder to aim right and harder to use. I'd say anything farther than ten feet away, it better be the size of a barn if you want to hit it. So then, what's the chance of anybody, especially a guy like your father—afraid of guns, no experience with them—killing someone with one shot, a single, perfect shot on the first try, right through the heart, from on top of a rock fifty feet away, or whatever? And using dicey, fifty-year-old ammo, besides? I'd say zero. I'm surprised the propellant even ignited. Doc, you agree with me?"

"Gideon's a scientist through and through, John," Julie said. "You're never going to get him to agree to zero probability about anything."

Gideon nodded. "That's true enough, but this one has to be way down there, right around .001. I'll buy it."

"But . . . but that's wonderful!" Rafe exclaimed, still blinking away. "What you're really telling me is that it couldn't have been my father! You've essentially cleared him—ha-ha!—just like that. And you haven't even had to look at any of the evidence yet!"

"Well, you know, I've been at this awhile," said John with a modest shrug.

"I can't believe it! If only I'd gotten the two of you involved years ago! You have no idea—John, old man, could you pass that lovely clotted cream this way? Ah, thank you, thank you."

He sliced a scone in half, lathered on the thick cream and a layer of cherry jam, and went to work. "Nothing in the world like Jersey cream," he said, looking up happily. "And this is from Carlisle cows—the very best!" But he caught a fleeting shadow crossing John's face, and his elation visibly withered. "John? Is there something else? Is something wrong?"

"Nah, nothing wrong. I was just wondering if you've told the police that Gideon's going to be working on the bones."

Rafe let out a soft, unvoiced "Whoo." *Oh, is that all.* "No, I didn't see the need. I can't imagine there being any interest. We're talking about a case that hasn't been active for forty years. And anyone who worked on it back then has been gone from the department for at least twenty of them, probably more."

"Yeah, that's all true, but I still think it would be a good idea—*before* Gideon gets to work. A courtesy, you know? They'll appreciate it, trust me."

Rafe looked unconvinced, but he shrugged his acquiescence. "All right, if you think it's best, certainly, I'll let them know. The head of the CID is a friend. I'll ring him tonight."

"I don't mean to push you, Rafe, but I think what you really ought to do is bring Doc over to meet him."

"I agree, Rafe," Gideon put in. "In case I do come up with something that they need to look into—not that I expect to, but if it did happen—it'd be nice not to spring it on them as a surprise."

Rafe inclined his head. "Gentlemen, I yield to your superior knowledge and experience. I'll stop by headquarters on my way home to arrange it, for tomorrow morning, if possible, and I'll ring you later to let you know." He finished off the scone, took one more obviously final swig of his coffee, and got to his feet. "Well, then . . ."

"One more question before you go, Rafe," Gideon said. "How exactly did the police *know* the bullet came from that crag? Did they find some evidence up there? A cigarette? A footprint?"

"Oh, no, as I understand it, it was a simple matter of geometry. The entry wound was just above the collarbone, after which the bullet traveled down through his heart and lodged in his hip bone, well below where it entered. Ergo, its starting point had to have been somewhere well *above* his collarbone, and the only such place in the vicinity would have been up on the crags."

"Ah, I see," Gideon said.

"And now," Rafe said, "I think I'd better be on my way. I'll see you all at dinner Wednesday, if not before. John, thank you again for those remarkable insights, and thank you all for being so good about coming here."

"We appreciate the hospitality, Rafe," Julie said. "We're all looking forward to seeing something of the island."

"Yes, do. Oh, I should mention that we're extremely proud of our bus system. Frequent busses, clean, not too crowded, and you can get absolutely anywhere. There are cars for hire as well, of course, but honestly, if I were new to the countryside, I'd put myself in the hands of the public transportation system rather than deal with our narrow, tricky, nameless little lanes on my own—especially with hedgerows hemming you in and cutting off your vision on every side."

"Particularly when everybody's driving on the wrong side of the road," Julie said.

"Amen to that," said Gideon, who tended to be an abstracted driver and had had a close call or two when driving on the *right* side of the road when his mind was elsewhere. Busses suited him fine.

CHAPTER 10

They remained in the bar for a while, then walked half a block back down Kensington Place to Casa Mia, a cozy, busy little restaurant they'd seen from the car on the way in. The tea at the hotel seemed to have stimulated their taste buds rather than satiated them, and the aromas inside the restaurant got their salivary glands going. They ordered tricolor salads and two pizzas: a Margherita—the simple, basic archetype of all pizzas—and a more elaborate pizza *pescatore*, with artichokes, shrimp, and clams. And a bottle of the house Chianti (wicker basket and all) to drink.

While they were waiting for their food, they sipped wine and chewed contentedly on slices of Italian bread dipped in olive oil and salt.

"Red wine and bread," John said. "I could make a meal of just this."

"You and Omar Khayyam," said Julie. "And me. Gideon, what was that about, when you asked Rafe how they knew the shot was fired from the crags? I could see you had something on your mind."

"I did, yes, and I was afraid that he was going to say what he did say—that they figured it out from the trajectory. But he was so thrilled by what you told him, John, that I didn't have the heart to bring him back down to earth."

"Why wouldn't he be thrilled?" John demanded. "What do you mean, 'bring him back down to earth'? What I told him was right; there's no way his old man—"

"What you told him *was* right, and it was good thinking. But it was based on false assumptions."

John put down his bread. "Hey!"

"No, not your assumptions, the police's—back when it happened."

"Like what, for instance?"

"Like thinking they could figure out where a shot came from by tracing its trajectory through the body. It enters at the collarbone, takes a downward path through his body, and lodges in his hip bone. Ergo, it came from *above* his body."

"And that's *wrong*?" Julie said, her eyebrows going up.

"Yes, it is."

"But—"

"Oh, jeez!" John said, loudly enough to turn heads at nearby tables. "Of *course* it's wrong." He sighed. "I guess I was so impressed with how brilliant I was that I didn't even think to ask about how the cops came up with . . . I can't believe I didn't . . . damn." He sounded like an old-fashioned vinyl record winding down, slower and slower, deeper and deeper, until it just faded away.

"I know the feeling, John, believe me," Gideon said. "It's—"

"Quit it, you two," Julie said. "I'm totally in the dark. Are you really both saying that a bullet's path doesn't tell you what direction it came from? Sorry, but that's—"

"The path it took through the *air*, yeah, that would tell you something," John explained. "But, see, Doc's point is we don't know what that was; nobody does. All we know is the path it took through his *body*, and based on that, you can't . . . Doc, maybe you should explain this."

"Yeah, Doc, maybe you should explain it," Julie said. "I'm still in the dark."

"Well, think about it," Gideon said. "What the trajectory of a bullet through a body does give you is the placement of the gun barrel relative to the body, and that's all—not where the shooter was and not where the victim was. A shot like that could have come from absolutely any direction at all: maybe from above him, maybe from alongside him, even from *under* him."

Now even John looked uncertain. "I know you're gonna turn out to be right, Doc, but I have to say I'm having a hard time seeing how that could be. From *under* him?"

"Look—either of you have a pencil? Not a pen—a pencil, with an eraser."

John produced a mechanical one, and Gideon used a paper napkin to draw two stick figures, one on a small rise, the other one standing what would have been a few feet below him. A crude gun was then put into the upper figure's hand and a straight line drawn from its muzzle through the lower figure's torso, necessarily taking a downward track. "This is essentially what the police said happened, right?"

Nods all around.

"Well, the crag must have been a lot higher than that, but, essentially, yes," Julie allowed.

Gideon now erased the rise and drew a straight line down the shooter's back, as if he were standing against a wall. "All right, presto-chango—" He rotated the napkin ninety degrees, so that the line was now at the bottom of the drawing, and scrawled, "This is the ground" under the line.

"Now we have a new scenario. They've been fighting, wrestling. The shooter—that is, the one who's about to be the shooter—has been thrown to the ground onto his back. He's managed to hold on to the gun, though. The victim, standing at his feet, launches himself onto him, hoping maybe to get a hand on the gun. He flings himself full-length through the air, okay? Like a swimmer diving into his lane. And just as he gets himself airborne and roughly horizontal, and his head even with the shooter's waist, say, the shooter manages to get off a shot . . . from underneath. The shot enters under his collarbone—"

"Of course!" Julie exclaimed. "Horizontally or vertically, the relationship between the gun and the body is the same. The bullet goes *downward* through his body, even if it goes *upward* through the air."

Gideon bowed his head and spread his arms, the magician waiting for his applause.

"Oh, hell," John said with a shrug, "it's pretty obvious, really. I don't know why you had to go through that whole rigmarole to explain it."

Gideon sighed. Magicians had it better than forensic anthropologists, he thought. Anthropologists had to *explain* how they did it . . . with predictable results.

"So what you're saying," Julie said, "is that, based on nothing but that trajectory, there's no way of telling *where* it came from."

"Right. You can't rule anything out . . . or in."

The pizzas came then, and they each put a couple of wedges on their plates. "I see why you thought this might depress Rafe," Julie said as she applied knife and fork to a slice of Margherita. "It doesn't help his father's case, does it? If the bullet had come from up on the crag, that would have essentially let Roddy off. He never could have made that shot; John made that very clear. But from close up—the way you've drawn it, for example—he'd be just as capable of doing it as a marksman would."

"You gonna bring this up with Rafe?" John asked Gideon.

"I don't know. What do you think?"

"I think you have to. You can't let him keep thinking that I got his father off the hook, when I didn't."

"Julie?"

"I don't agree, Gideon, not entirely. You're not saying Roddy *did* do it, you're only saying that it's *possible* he did it. I say wait a day or two, let him stay up there on his cloud. Who knows, by then you might have something more definite to tell him that does absolve Roddy."

"That's true. I think I'll hold off for the moment and let him be happy. Once we get into the skeletal remains themselves, there's no telling what'll come out of them. There's almost always a surprise or two."

"Especially with you working on them," John said with a honk of laughter.

Afterward, back to the Revere for their first look at their suite, which John found a little dowdy but for Gideon and Julie was welcome, especially after the depressing postmodern hotel they'd stayed at in Málaga, with its straight-line, right-angle, minimalist decor and its eyeball-scorching excess of ultrabright primary colors.

Here at the Revere, there were earth tones; clean if slightly tired carpets; soft, comfortable, unfashionable chairs; and, in each bedroom, a handsome four-poster bed. A sizable sitting room with an up-to-date TV set was between the two bedrooms, and there was a small, open kitchen and a plain, uncarpeted little room off to one side as well, the old valet's room that Rafe had told them about. All in all, a welcoming, homely place, just about what you'd want from an old coaching inn.

They listened to a telephone message from Rafe, who had arranged a 9:00 a.m. meeting for John, Gideon, and himself with the detective chief inspector in charge of the police's criminal-investigation department. Police headquarters were only a few blocks from the Revere, and Rafe would show up at the hotel at eight thirty so that they could walk over with time to spare.

Winding up the day, they read or worked individually for an hour, after which the three of them grew sleepy watching a *Blue Bloods* episode, until Julie and Gideon said good night, leaving a dozy John in front of a *Hawaii Five-O* rerun—not the new series but the original 1970s version.

"Jack Lord," he'd muttered, nodding his approval of the original McGarrett, "now that's my kind of cop. 'Book the fucker, Danno!'"

Julie smiled. "Um, I'm not sure you got that quite right, John."

CHAPTER 11

Rafe showed up at the hotel at eight thirty on the dot, just as Julie left for the museum. He was still elated over John's conclusion the day before that, whoever pulled that trigger, it wasn't Roddy Carlisle. Gideon was a little uneasy about it but couldn't bring himself to spoil things yet. And Julie was right: Who knew what he might turn up in the next day or two?

"Rafe," he said as they left for police headquarters along with John, "any problem if I use someplace else to look at your father's remains?"

"Oh? Won't the dairy plant work for you? I can have someone take you there and back whenever you like, if that makes it easier."

"No, it isn't that, but that little valet's room would be a perfect place to lay out the bones. There's already a table in it. Much more convenient than the dairy, especially if I get an idea in the middle of the night that I want to check out. Which does happen."

"Just ask Julie if you don't believe it," John said.

"All right, then," said Rafe, "that's what we'll do. I'll have the bones brought to the Revere this very morning."

They walked up Kensington Place toward the Parade, Saint Helier's closest thing to a boulevard, after crossing which Kensington became

Elizabeth Place for a few hundred yards, then underwent another of those name changes between English and French when, for no discernible physical reason, it changed to Rouge Bouillon, meaning *red broth*. A few hundred yards along this queerly named old street was a plain, two-story, brown brick building that couldn't have been more nondescript, except for the distinctive blue-and-white-checkered sign on the sidewalk in front. *States of Jersey Police Headquarters*.

A fast walker, Rafe had easily kept pace—sometimes even setting the pace—with John and Gideon, even though he had to take almost two steps to their one. As a result they were fifteen minutes early. They weren't made to wait, though. In the tiny, cluttered lobby, the woman at the "Enquiries" desk recognized Rafe at once and reached for a telephone. "He's expecting you, Senator. I'll—"

"Don't bother, Marie. We'll just go on up."

"Certainly." She pushed a button that buzzed and opened the waist-high gate into the interior. "I assume you know the way?" It was meant as a joke, and Rafe laughed accommodatingly.

As they passed her, John and Gideon were handed visitor badges. Rafe apparently didn't need one. They walked into an open work area with five or six people sitting at desks, most of whom looked up with pleasure to see Rafe and called greetings.

"Hullo, Senator!"

"How are you, Mr. Carlisle?"

"Nice to see you, sir."

"I thought nobody even knew who he was," John murmured.

"Modest guy," said Gideon. "Nothing wrong with that."

As they walked through, Rafe responded in kind to the calls, sometimes with surprising intimacy. "Elmer, old man, glad to see you looking your old self. . . . Hullo there, Bea, give my best regards to Charlie. . . . Why, Johnno, you old miscreant, I thought they'd sacked you long ago." His shining face made it obvious that he enjoyed the exchanges.

Toward the rear was a stairwell with a placard on a stand beside it. *Criminal Investigation Department*, it said, and in case anyone should miss its intent, a prominent arrow pointed up the stairs.

"So what's he like, this detective chief inspector?" Gideon asked as they climbed the steps.

Rafe replied with an amused but otherwise enigmatic smile. "Let's save it for a surprise, shall we?"

The upper floor could have been the upper floor of just about any police station in the world: a slightly tacky corridor smelling of disinfectant (but less so than the ground floor), with flickery, buzzing fluorescent tubes above, linoleum flooring below, and office cubicles with shoulder-high walls that were glass from waist-level up and scuffed, colorless fabric below that. The surfaces facing the hallway were blanketed with tacked-up, dog-eared official notices and lists a dozen deep, scrawled Post-it notes, newspaper cartoons, and one big, plastic-coated grease pencil calendar and schedule.

Gideon had been in enough places like it by now so that he was feeling right at home. At the end of the corridor was the lone "office" in its traditional sense—walls you couldn't see through all the way up to the ceiling and an actual, genuine, closable door made of real wood: the throne room, obviously, the lair of the Boss.

With the door ajar, enough of the office was visible to see that it was a sizable, airy, high-ceilinged place with windows that must once have looked down on the avenue below. Now, however, they stared straight into the dense foliage of the trees that had grown up out front, the ends of the upper branches close enough to touch. Not an unpleasant prospect, really, restful and somehow removed from both the nastiness and the humdrum routine of police work. But the room itself was so neat compared to the cluttered hallway that there was something cold about it. If there was anything on its walls besides another schedule—a bit fancier one, on whiteboard—Gideon couldn't see it. Two small tables were also bare of anything but paperwork and its accoutrements. The closest thing to decoration was a limp standing flag in one corner: the simple red diagonal cross that was the emblem of the States of Jersey. None of the usual plaques or commendations or pictures taken with VIPs or family photos. Nothing personal, nothing to suggest the tastes or values or interests of the entity that lived here.

"This guy," John whispered, taking it in, "is gonna be all business. A hardnose. Rotsa ruck, pal." As an Asian, a Chinese Hawaiian, John felt he could get away with that kind of thing. He was usually right, but it had gotten him in trouble more than once. Being John, he was unaffected by this.

Rafe, preceding them to the open door, rapped on it. "Mike? We're here."

There was a grunt from inside. Rafe stepped out of the way and gestured for Gideon to precede him, which he did.

CHAPTER 12

Gideon found himself looking across the office to a large, battered corner desk with a large, battered man behind it. About sixty, thick necked and thick chested, with a meaty face and a nose like a slightly smushed zucchini, he wore a crisp, spotless white shirt with its sleeves folded neatly back over thick, hairy wrists. The shirt was buttoned to the top to allow the fastening of a sober blue tie around his eighteen-inch neck. He looked like a dockworker uncomfortably—and unwillingly—decked out in his Sunday best and itching to get back into his worn-out old cords and flannels. He was looking straight at Gideon with a broad, pleased grin on his slab of a face.

"Hullo, there, lad. Here to boggle the minds of us poor, benighted coppers, are you?"

"Surprise" didn't begin to cover it. For a couple of seconds, Gideon just stood there with an incredulous grin on his own face. "Mike Clapper! What in the world are you doing here? The last time I saw you—"

"I was an old relic of a constable sergeant in the Isles of Scilly, yes."

"And now you're an old relic of a detective chief inspector in Jersey. How did that come about? *Detective chief inspector*, wow. Congratulations!"

"Amazing, is it not? The Home Office continues to leave no stone unturned in its efforts to keep me the hell off the British mainland, and this struck them as one of the safer places for me to eke out my few remaining years of employment without doing too much damage to the reputation of our police services. Ah, and this, I presume, is the gentleman from the FBI?"

"John Lau, Detective Chief Inspector," John said.

Clapper waved that off. "'Mike' will be fine, thanks." He got up and came around the desk, welcomed the three of them with handshakes—Gideon got a vigorous two-handed one—and seated them all at a grouping of a few weathered and mismatched leather armchairs around a low table at the other end of the room.

"Now, then," he said, squeezing between the arms of his own chair.

But Rafe held up a finger. "A note before we proceed. As usual, gentlemen, Mike is selling himself short. The reason he's here is that we *asked* for him, because—"

Clapper's chair creaked as he shifted in it to the extent he could. "Ancient history, Rafe. I don't see the need to—"

"No, before we go any further, I insist on setting the record straight." He turned slightly to address John and Gideon. "And I speak whereof I know, being a member of the chief minister's appointments commission. The gentleman you see before you is in this office because our CID had, for several years, been moving in a . . . a softer direction, shall we say, with increasing attention to internal diversity, team building, community relations, and so forth and a resultant lessening emphasis on traditional police work. Now, it goes without saying that diversity and community outreach and police morale are good things, but not if they put at risk the primary function of a police force, which, in my increasingly unfashionable opinion, is the enforcement of the law."

He paused to see if John and Gideon agreed with him. They did and so indicated with nods. Clapper looked a little out of sorts, uncomfortable with the plaudits that he sensed coming. He fidgeted with opening a pack of cigarettes and getting one lit. Still loyal to the Gold Bonds he'd smoked in the Scillies, Gideon saw.

"And so we created a new position of community resources liaison, packed the then head of the CID off to it—where I daresay he finds himself better suited and much more at home—and petitioned the Home Office for their recommendations of experienced officers who knew police work from the ground up, who could apply rules and discipline firmly and fairly, who had the ability and self-discipline to implement serious change and to see it through, and whose reputations and comportment were likely to command the respect of colleagues, subordinates, and the general public."

John laughed. "Is that all? They must have come up with thousands of possibilities."

"Of course they couldn't find anybody like that," Clapper said, "not in this world, and so they settled for me instead." He had gotten his cigarette lit and flapping at the corner of his mouth while he spoke, and he no longer looked quite so crabby. No matter how much people might resist hearing themselves praised, there aren't many who are impervious to it.

"On the contrary, we found the *perfect* person," Rafe insisted. "We thought ourselves lucky at the time, and we think so even more now, a year later."

Gideon didn't doubt it. If there was anybody in England who could come close to meeting that formidable set of criteria, Mike Clapper was the man. He had applied to be a policeman to the Devon and Cornwall Constabulary late, at forty, having newly retired from the army as a regimental sergeant major—the very top of the noncommissioned pile. He'd been accepted and then graduated first in his class from the National Police Training Center in Hampshire. Only two months after that he'd received a chief constable commendation for actions over and above the requirements of the service, the only one of its kind ever awarded to a probationer. Off duty, out of uniform, alone, and weaponless, he had broken up an armed robbery, subduing the two perpetrators and sitting on them (literally, in the case of one) until a couple of police cars could get there.

More citations and awards followed. He became the first three-time recipient of Devon and Cornwall's Officer of the Year Award. The BBC featured him in a television special (*England's Finest*). In less than ten years he'd become a well-respected detective chief inspector and one of the most famous cops in England.

But then came the one adversary he couldn't handle: political correctness in all its many forms. There were in-house complaints against him from the Gay Police Association and the Diversity Enhancement Task Force: his unit was "disproportionately" male, white, and straight, and he showed little interest in changing things. That was the point at which circumstances—and modern times—had begun to turn against him, but he had thoroughly sealed his doom with his heartfelt but impolitic response at the last of his three hearings. One question, one accusation, one straw too many, and the camel's back had snapped. Clapper's reined-in frustration had burst through:

"Look, what I want in my people is intelligence, drive, and ability. I don't give a rat's arse if they're white or green or yellow, or Mr. bloody Fred Bloggs himself, and I sure as hell don't give a rat's arse whether they wear knickers, or Y-fronts, or no flipping underpants at all."

It made him famous all over again but infamous to the brass who made the decisions. Steps were begun to get rid of him, but the Police Federation—the police union—came to his defense, even though, as a department head, he was not a member. Eventually, a compromise was reached: Clapper would be transferred from the large port city of Plymouth to the obscure, virtually crime-free outpost of the Isles of Scilly, thirty miles off the southeast coast of England, where he could harmlessly serve out his time without getting into trouble or offending anyone. The compromise consisted of his rank being downgraded to constable sergeant but his grade for pension purposes remaining that of chief inspector.

Gideon, working at the time on some bones discovered on a deserted Scillies beach, encountered him not long after Clapper had arrived at his new post. The relationship had started poorly. Gideon found Clapper arrogant, plodding, and narrow-minded, while Clapper thought Gideon was a modern version of some carpetbagging Old West "professor" going from town to town using long-winded academic speak to peddle his miraculous nostrums. More than that, he was treading, without invitation and not any too lightly either, on Clapper's own turf.

But circumstances had forced them to work together, and before long not only had they gotten to like each other, but their initial views of one another had been turned upside down. Gideon, Clapper saw, was a real scientist who had useful skills to offer and offered them generously. And Clapper, Gideon realized, was as thoroughgoing, knowledgeable, and resolute a cop as he'd ever met. An old-fashioned flatfoot in the very best sense of the word.

A perfect fit, Gideon thought, for the job they'd brought him to Saint Helier to do.

"Senator, have we finished with the bloody encomiums?" Clapper asked now.

"Unless you'd like to deliver one in my behalf?" Rafe suggested.

"Well, let me think." He cogitated for a few seconds, then cleared his throat and turned to John and Gideon. "Rafe's a bit of all right," he said, "a long-winded chappie, but a pretty good bloke in spite of it. Will that do, Senator?"

Rafe laughed. "And there you have Mike's one failure. An unfortunate tendency toward hyperbole."

"It's a terrible thing to live with," Clapper said. "I just can't help myself. Now then, Rafe, I looked over those case files this morning, and

I have some idea of what was involved. But will you tell me one more time just what it is you expect Gideon to do for you?"

"I've asked him to have another look at my father's remains to see if modern forensic science can tell us anything that couldn't be determined in those ancient days. Is it really my father, for one thing; are there any indications of the cause of death, for another? What was it that really happened back then?"

"Well, as the man's son and the owner, so to speak, of those remains, you don't need my approval or anyone else's to have them looked at." Clapper took a long drag on his cigarette and blew out a haze of thready smoke. He wasn't a chain-smoker, but when he smoked, he really smoked, sucking in great lungfuls of air and staying with it right down to the filter tip. "But tell me this: What role do you expect the CID to take in this matter?"

Gideon knew what was troubling him. Even Mike Clapper wasn't immune to the natural mind-set of cops toward closed cases: *Let 'em stay closed. Leave 'em be.* In their defense, there was something to the attitude. Partly it was because reopening an old case never failed to mean a flood of paperwork and explanations, but mostly because it was the nearest thing to popping the lid off a can of worms. Not only couldn't you get the things back in, but once out they were likely to crawl into crevices that you preferred to leave unexplored.

But before he could say anything, John said it for him. "Mike, we don't expect to involve you at all. This is strictly a courtesy call, my suggestion. We just thought that if we were poking into old police affairs, you would want to know about it and you'd prefer to hear it from us first. I know that's the way I'd feel."

A mollified Clapper nodded. "And I do, John, I do, indeed." The Gold Bond was ground out in an oversize pub ashtray that held the mashed butts of four or five earlier ones. *The Rousted Seaman*, read the logo circling the rim, inside of which a grizzled, gap-toothed old salt in a sailor's cap and a red-striped shirt merrily hoisted a tankard, although he was in for trouble if he didn't get the pipe out of his mouth before it got there. "And if there is anything I can do—"

"Actually," Gideon said, "now that you mention it—"

Clapper rolled his eyes. "Blimey, I've gone and put my foot in it this time, haven't I? I knew it before the words were out of my mouth. You'd think I'd have learned by now."

"Nothing to put you to too much trouble, I promise, but if you could let me have a copy of the medical report on those remains—"

Clapper nodded.

"And if one on George Skinner still exists, that'd be good to have too."

"Skinner, Skinner," Clapper said. "Isn't that . . ." he hesitated, trying to remember who George Skinner was. He had, after all, become familiar with the case only this morning. "Oh, yes, the other one, the first one found, the one who was shot in the heart."

At this point an alarmingly young-looking police officer with stiff, corn-colored hair and black-rimmed glasses appeared at the door and stood waiting, not quite at attention, military style, but close.

"Coffee, anyone?" Clapper said. "Tea? No? No takers, Constable. Oh, hang on there, Tom. That file you got for me earlier? There's a postmortem report in there. Will you make a copy for me? And then if you can find one on a man named George Skinner—another homicide—I'll want that too. That would have been a bit earlier . . ." He looked at Rafe.

"Nineteen sixty-four," Rafe told the officer.

"Right away, sir." The young cop looked as if he didn't know whether to salute or not and decided on a halfway gesture that could be interpreted as one if necessary but didn't look too ridiculous if it was out of place. He turned smartly and went in search of the files.

"Gideon, I've just had a thought," Rafe said. "Would you be interested in seeing the actual remains? George Skinner's remains?"

"Sure, I would, but do you have access to them?"

"I just might."

"Jesus Christ, Rafe, don't tell me *they're* in your garage too," John said. "Mike, I'm starting to think you better have someone go out and see what else he's got in there."

Rafe burst out laughing. "No, no, I don't have George's bones. They were returned to his family, and I've always assumed he was cremated, but now it occurs to me that he may have been interred instead. George's son would certainly know, and if he *was* buried, I believe Abbott might agree to have him exhumed for Gideon to examine. He wants to know what happened as much as I do. Well, almost."

Gideon was shaking his head. "I don't know, Rafe, having a body exhumed is a complicated undertaking that's bound to take some time, and I won't be here that much longer. Besides, it's not cheap. Are you sure Abbott—"

"Oh, I'd pay for it, of course, that goes without saying. But if he approves, you'd be willing to examine the remains, wouldn't you?"

"Sure, I'd be glad to, but are you sure—"

"That's settled, then," Rafe said, jotting a note in a small, leather-bound pad he'd taken from the inside pocket of his suit coat. "I'll pop in on Abbott and find out. Today, if possible. Haven't seen him for a while anyway."

"Abbott Skinner," Clapper said reflectively, tapping his lower lip. "Would that be the same Abbott Skinner that was involved in the Mumbai Global prosecutions?"

"Yes, it would. That's Abbott, all right—George's boy." He thought it necessary to elaborate to Gideon and John. "He wasn't the *subject* of the prosecutions, you understand, quite the reverse. He's a banker himself, and he assisted the Crown, serving as one of their witnesses at the trials."

"Their prize witness, I'd be inclined to say," Clapper said approvingly. "The one that made all the difference. You'll have to get a permit from the Health Department, you know."

At the round of puzzled looks, he added, "For Mr. Skinner's exhumation."

Rafe frowned. "That's right, we will, won't we? That'll throw a spanner in the works. Health is notoriously slow about such things. I suspect it'll take a fortnight to process. Do you have that much time, Gideon?"

"Two weeks? No, I'm sorry, can't stay anywhere near that long."

"Not to worry," Clapper said. "Let me take care of it. I'll see if I can't accelerate the process."

"It won't make much difference unless they get going on the digging tomorrow—the next day at the very latest," Gideon said. "I figure the exhumation itself is bound to take at least one more day after that, and four days are about all I have before we have to get going. Can you really get it through as quickly as that?"

"Not ordinarily, no," Clapper said with a smile. "However, I am not above the occasional exploitation of my position to, ah, move things along in a propitious manner when required. I'll get it started this afternoon. Assuming the son approves, you're in business. If not, no harm done."

They bantered a bit longer, mostly about the Scillies, which Rafe knew from a visit the previous January, until the constable returned, empty-handed.

"They're quite busy, sir. They've asked if you can wait an hour for the Carlisle postmortem report, but if you need it now . . ."

Clapper looked at Gideon. "Do we need it now?"

Gideon shook his head. "No, I want to look at the bones themselves first anyway."

It was a principle he stressed to his students and one that he stuck to himself (which wasn't true of all of them): the law of expectancy applied to anthropologists as much as to anyone else. You see what you expect to see. The fewer expectations you have, the more objective and open-minded you're going to be. And so if you are about to examine a set of skeletal remains for which you are lucky enough to have an autopsy report available, or perhaps the results of an earlier forensic examination, go ahead and read it—but not until you've examined the remains for yourself and come to your own conclusions. Then compare.

"And the one on Mr. George Skinner?" Clapper asked Tom. "Also an hour?"

"I'm afraid the Skinner report is, er, unavailable, sir."

Clapper cocked an eyebrow. "Unavailable," he repeated, or rather growled.

"Missing, sir," the constable replied and then went nervously on. "There's a removal card in its place, signed by a Sergeant Lavoisier in 1964, but no indication of its ever having been returned."

"Well, get back out there and see if this Sergeant Lavoisier is still alive, and if he is, you tell the flipping—"

"I've already done that, sir. He passed away in 2004."

"Oh," Clapper said. "Ahum. Well, that's good work, Tom."

"Sir." Another tentative, sort-of-kind-of-almost salute and he turned smartly and escaped.

"Isn't that Tony Vickery's son?" Rafe asked.

"Yes, there have been some doubts about his being quite cut out for the job since joining the force, and Minister Vickery asked if I wouldn't do what I could to look after him, so I made him my adjutant, as you might call it." He shook his head. "A nice enough lad, certainly bright, and he does try his best, but . . ." A minute shrug. "In any event, Gideon, at least we can have the report on Rafe's father sent along to your hotel as soon as it's done. But it looks as if Mr. Skinner's is out of our reach."

Rafe put his hands on the arms of his chair and set himself to get up. "We may yet get the actual remains for you, though, Gideon. Speaking of which, we'd better get going, Mike. Many thanks for your help."

"You're welcome here anytime, you lot. And it's always a pleasure to have the Skeleton Detective on the scene." He laughed. "It never fails to mean things are going to get exciting. One way or another."

Gideon reacted with a determined shake of his head. "Not if I can help it."

CHAPTER 13

It was ten forty-five when they left Clapper's office, and because none of them had eaten yet, they stopped in at the first place that offered food, the Parade Gardens Café and Takeaway. They were hoping for either sandwiches or full English breakfasts but had to settle for coffee and pastries—"Sorry, gents, no breakfast menu after ten, no lunch menu till eleven thirty." Their meal had a slightly frantic feel to it, not only because Rafe had a meeting at the States Building within the hour and kept checking his watch, but because anytime he wasn't chewing, he was on the telephone, first leaving a message for his dairy manager, arranging to have his father's remains taken from the dairy to the Revere, and then trying to reach Abbott Skinner, getting through only on the third try.

"Well," he said, finishing with Abbott, "luck is with us. They didn't cremate his father, after all. It seems he's buried in Surville Cemetery at the north edge of town. But if I want to see Abbott about it today, it has to be either at one o'clock or not at all, for God's sake. And me with a meeting with the chief minister at eleven thirty. Crikey."

Clearly flustered, he made another call, instructing his secretary to put together a packet of the forms required for an exhumation. And then he was on his feet, the harried government official, stuffing the last of a prune tart into his mouth and sending it on its way with a gulp of coffee. But he hesitated before leaving.

"Gideon, I was wondering . . . would you like to come with me to speak with Abbott? You can explain things to him better than I can."

Gideon mulled this over. "I *would* like to talk with him, yes, but maybe not at this point. I'd say it'll go better if you keep it in the family for now. But if you'd be more comfortable with me there—"

"No, no, just a passing thought. If I find myself in rough seas and I need you to rescue me, I'll ring you, but I don't anticipate that. No, you two stay and enjoy the rest of the repast. Gideon, a carton from the dairy should already be waiting for you by now. I'll check with you later about it."

They took his advice, ordering more coffee and working through the remaining pastries, or rather John did. Gideon had had all the sweets he wanted after a single maple syrup scone that had enough sugar on it, and in it, to furnish a dozen doughnuts.

After finishing off the last of them, John blew out his cheeks and said, "Damn, you should never have let me have those two treacle things. I don't even like treacle."

"My apologies, John."

"Yeah, you *should* apologize. If you could've just ate one of them, I would have just ate one too."

"John, what can I say? I was remiss."

John pushed himself up from the table. "Ah, never mind," he said charitably. "I'm gonna walk around town a little, you know, get the feel of the place, walk off this stuff. No point in asking if you want to come along, not when you've got a box of bones waiting for you."

"Is no thought of mine safe from you?" Gideon said with a smile. "You go and have a good walk. See you later." And off he headed to the hotel to see if his carton had been delivered yet.

John had his number, all right. He really did love working with bones.

The carton that awaited Gideon at the reception desk wasn't a shoe box, but it wasn't a whole lot bigger than one; an ordinary grocery carton, probably the original container in which the police had stored them. Its corners were softened and collapsed from its many years in Rafe's garage, and it had been taped and retaped multiple times. On the sides were printed *Patum Peperium, the Gentleman's Relish, Delicious on Hot Toast, 12 ct.*

Not much of a final resting place for anyone, but then there wasn't very much to rest. He carried the carton upstairs to the suite and took it into the old valet's room. The first thing he did was to move the table over to the window, to take advantage of the slanting light from the afternoon sun. Texture and detail were going to be important, and an oblique, raking light brought them out more clearly than even the brightest direct illumination.

After that he went to the pad of white easel paper he'd bought at a stationer's on the way back from the café and covered the table with sheets of it to provide a better background than the dark, marred wooden tabletop.

"So," he murmured with the anticipation of a skilled workman contemplating the task that lay ahead. Despite the paucity of material to look at, he was stirred by what he was about to do, as he always was. In his view, forensic anthropologists had a unique and immense responsibility: they were the last representatives of the dead, their final voice, and all too often in forensic cases, their last chance at receiving justice, in this world at any rate. It was a responsibility he took seriously. He breathed in, breathed out, and peeled off the sealing tape yet one more time.

When he had carefully extricated the contents from the time-soiled windings of cotton wool in which they were packed and laid them out on the white surface, he found that they were a kind of smutty, blotchy gray brown, a color he'd never run into before. But then he'd never before examined bones that had been submerged in pitch for five years. Altogether, as Rafe had said, there were twelve fragments.

His usual first step would be to lay the remains out in their anatomical positions, but with this meager assemblage that part could be skipped. Instead he began with step two, which was a general scan of the material, not looking for anything specific but letting his well-honed instincts tell him what they would. Twenty minutes later he had concluded that nine of the twelve fragments, all of which from arm or leg bones, held no information other than that four of them were male, two of which were definitely adult. The other five held no information at all. There was nothing to indicate that there was more than one person represented here.

He moved those nine fragments to the far end of the table, leaving plenty of room for the ones that had caught his attention: two roughly triangular cranial fragments, the larger one about three by four inches, the smaller one two by three, and the medial or central half of the left clavicle, the collarbone. Picking up the big, Sherlock Holmes–style magnifying glass he'd bought along with the easel paper, he reached for the larger of the two cranial fragments, and . . .

. . . felt his stomach rumble.

The single pastry he'd had with John and Rafe, all that he'd eaten that day, had achieved his sugar-tolerance level, but that was all. He was hungry, and he realized he was also feeling dull. Slow. Sluggish in mind and body. And no wonder, he'd had nothing that could pass for exercise for three days now. It had been a mistake not to have gone on the walk with John.

Standing there with the magnifying glass in one hand and the skull fragment in the other, he was seized by a colossal gawp of a yawn. That did it. What he needed, and right now, was a vigorous thirty-minute walk of his own around town to get his blood moving again, and then a quick sandwich somewhere. The bones had lain awaiting his attentions for half a century. They wouldn't mind waiting another hour.

CHAPTER 14

As Gideon stepped out of the Revere and onto Kensington Place, Rafe Carlisle was approaching the door of Abbott Skinner's three-room flat in one of the new multicolored but otherwise uninspired condominium blocks on Saint Helier's harborside. His meeting with the chief minister had run longer than he'd hoped, so he was going to be late for his appointment. Which would get them off to a bad start. Abbott was a stickler for punctuality. Abbott was a stickler for everything, come to that, a trait in which he took a conspicuous and morally superior pride; he was a bit of a prig, in other words. The trait did nothing for his personal relationships but was largely responsible for his reputation for uncompromising rectitude in Jersey's most important industry and, as Clapper had said, for his sterling assistance to the Crown in the successful prosecution of Mumbai Global Private Bank.

"International financial services"—in the common parlance, offshore banking—had replaced agriculture as the number one driver of Channel Island economy in the 1990s and had never stepped down. By the beginning of the twenty-first century, this tiny, out-of-the-way dependency of the British Crown had become one of the world's top tax havens, right up there with Switzerland and the Caymans. (The very term *offshore banking* derives from the location of the Channel Islands—offshore from the United Kingdom.) It had brought a lot of benefits to the islanders, but as with any place that becomes known as a tax haven, there was a shady side as well, and a few of Jersey's multitude of financial institutions had been party to dubious, sometimes criminal activities. One such had been Mumbai Global's Jersey branch, where Abbott had been an accounts representative for six years. In 2012, however, he had discovered not only that the taxable monies in numerous accounts had been underreported to the clients' home countries but also exactly how the cheating had been executed and then covered up. Being Abbott, this brazen violation of rules and procedures had deeply offended him. Laden with his records and his calculations, he had gone to the police in high dudgeon.

A huge investigation had followed, resulting in the criminal convictions of four Mumbai bankers. Throughout the trials, he had served as the prosecution's most effective witness. His whistle-blowing was praised by most, but it had brought him enemies too—even a couple of death threats—but Abbott was no coward; Rafe would say that much for him. In fact, such things seemed to charge him up. What was right was right, Rafe had heard him say more than once (*many* times more than once), and he would do what had to be done. And so he had. Rafe respected him for that too, although it would have been nicer if he were less smug about it.

His actions in the Mumbai case had also earned him a reputation for steadfastness and detail mindedness, two traits in newly high demand in Jersey's shaken financial sector. Even while the trials were underway, two other banks had offered him higher-level jobs, and a year ago he had accepted the position of vice president of International Services at Jersey Bank and Trust. Knowing a little about banks himself, and their tendency to spread around impressive titles in lieu of impressive salaries, Rafe doubted that he was earning much more than he had as a bottom-feeding accounts rep. Still, as far as Rafe knew, he was highly regarded at his new bank, and so he should have been. There was, in fact, plenty to admire in Abbott.

But that didn't make him any less a prig.

"It's ten minutes past one," was his priggish, testy greeting when he came to the door to answer Rafe's buzz. He was a little taller than Rafe, but narrow shouldered and bent, as thin as a chopstick except for a hard little belly that looked like a cantaloupe he carried around under his shirt.

"Sorry about that, Abbott," was Rafe's amicable reply, "the chief minister wanted to sound me out on a number of things, and, as you know, the chief minister gets what he wants."

Abbott couldn't have been less impressed. "Yes, well, come along."

In the small, neat parlor, two people waited, already seated. "Well, hello, Aunt Edna. Hello, Miranda," Rafe said. "How very nice to see you both."

Not strictly true, not even loosely true. He had anticipated meeting only with Abbott, and the presence of Abbott's Alzheimer's-stricken mother, Edna, and Edna's younger sister, the maddening, constitutionally obstructive Miranda, was not going to make things any easier.

He could see no legal reason for either of them to be there. As George's widow, Rafe's "aunt" Edna would ordinarily have been the one to say whether her husband was to be exhumed or not, but she was much diminished. Abbott, her only child, now held power of attorney in her behalf. It was up to him to decide on the exhumation. As for Miranda, she'd been given no such formal powers, but she was Edna's sister and the only other living blood relative she had on the islands. As such, apparently Abbott felt that she too should be party to the decision making.

And perhaps she should have been. Miranda might have no legal standing in the matter, but there was a reasonable basis for her concern with the events of 1964. As Edna's sister, she'd been George's sister-in-law. More important, she'd been married to Bertrand Peltier at the time of his disappearance, the twentysomething widow who, according to the police report, had run from the building five years later when confronted with a collection of bone fragments, some of which were purported to be her husband's.

Or, now that he thought about it, maybe none of that figured in Abbott's reasoning. More likely, it had to do with techniques Abbott had been exposed to in a management-training workshop at the University of Kent to which Jersey Bank and Trust had sent him not long ago. Abbott had come away from it with a fervent faith in team building, especially something called Consensual Decision Making, and had eagerly begun putting their techniques into practice.

This had astonished Rafe, because Abbott was not by nature what anyone would call a team player; he needed to get his own way too much. But after Rafe once saw him put CDM into action, he understood. For Abbott, Consensual Decision Making meant getting his "team" to go along with whatever it was that he'd already decided on, while making them *think* it was their idea. Even at that, he wasn't very good, but he thought he was, and it had become a fixture in his private dealings as well as those at the bank.

Rafe was guessing that Abbott, who didn't get along all that well with Miranda (who did?) was eager to try out his new Svengali-like methods on both women. Edna, poor Edna, was too far gone to be aware of being manipulated (or to care) and would have little impact on how things went, but Rafe was curious to see how Miranda would deal with it. Not to Abbott's satisfaction, he guessed.

A peremptory nod from Abbott motioned Rafe into a chair, so that they all sat facing each other around a coffee table. The coffee table held neither coffee, nor tea, nor anything else other than a vase of silk roses, and nothing was offered now.

"I know we all have things to do, so let's get right to it," Abbott said. "Rafe, suppose you lay out for us what it is that you have in mind. Give us something to chew on." He leaned back with a sober, I'm-listening look on his face, his elbows on the arms of his chair and his hands loosely clasped on the firm little shelf of his belly. A facilitator's posture, a moderator's posture, much practiced, no doubt. *I am not here to express my own opinions,* it said, *but to help clarify and resolve issues and differences so that we can reach a decision on which we all concur.*

"Right, then—" he began.

Miranda wasted no time getting in the first blow. "Abbott, if you want to give us something to chew on, a proper luncheon would have been a nice touch, but since it doesn't appear we're going to get one, how about a few bloody biscuits? Is that too much to ask? And some tea to wash them down with?" Then, to Rafe: "Whatever has happened to civility in this country?"

When Abbott came back, Rafe waited to see if Miranda had something else to get off her chest. When she didn't, he briefly and delicately explained who Gideon was and why it might be beneficial to all if he were permitted to examine George's remains.

By the time he'd concluded, Abbott had laid out the tea makings and a tray of shortbread cookies. For a few moments after Rafe finished, there was silence, and then, in a bit of a surprise, it was Edna who spoke, with a barely audible, "Well, I'm sure I don't know." Not directed at anybody in particular and not replied to by anyone.

Abbott waited a couple of beats, then said, "No, well, you know, I do think it might be a good idea," which was about par for the length of time it took him to get around to expressing the opinion he wasn't there to express. But it was the one Rafe was hoping for. His optimism increased. It was looking to be, as his American friends might say, a done deal.

Not quite yet. Miranda was slowly, firmly shaking her head while the last of her biscuits was on its way down. "I disagree. I don't like it. No, I'm very sorry, but it feels wrong to me."

"Oh, really? Why 'wrong'?" Abbott asked. He leaned forward, cupping his bony chin in his hand, the image of unbiased, dispassionate inquiry.

"Because it's revolting. Digging up a rotting corpse, having strangers root through it." She offered a histrionic shudder. "Besides that, the man has suffered enough: murdered, cut off in the prime of his life. Isn't that enough? I'm surprised at you, Abbott. Your own father. Leave the old blighter in his grave in peace."

"I see your point, Aunt Miranda, and I do respect it," Abbott said, laying on Training Technique Forty-Seven, or maybe it was Sixty-Two, "but don't you want to find out what really happened? Who killed him? He was your brother-in-law, after all."

Here, Rafe broke in. "Now, that's something we can't promise. Dr. Oliver made a particular point of saying as much. What we *might* learn—"

"We already know who killed him," Miranda said coldly, glaring at him. There was no mistaking her meaning: *Your father. Roddy Carlisle.* "The police made that quite clear in their report."

As inoffensively as he could, Rafe declined to pick up the gauntlet, responding with no more than a polite, neutral smile and a small shrug. But Abbott jumped right in.

"I understand what you're saying, Aunt Miranda, I really do, and there's a lot to be said for it, but shouldn't we remember that that was their *first* report, a good five years before they learned that Roddy himself was killed the very same night? And not only Roddy, but er . . . ah . . ."

"Er, ah, mmm, hum, *Bertrand*," growled Miranda. "Bertrand Peltier? My husband?"

"Aunt Miranda, I'm so sorry, I forgot for a moment."

Forgetting Bertrand's name wasn't that surprising, since Miranda made a point of not talking about him. Whether this was because it pained her or it bored her or she just wanted him in her past and not her present, Rafe didn't know. What he did know was that for the first two decades following her husband's death she had lived a private and restrained widow's life, unbroken except for another brief foray into marriage, this time to an older man named Atterbury, who owned two markets, one in Saint Helier and a smaller one in Saint Brélade, as well as a pub in Rozel. That had lasted only two years before Mr. Atterbury made a run for it, but she'd kept her second husband's surname as her own. Legally, she had been Miranda Atterbury since 1990.

Then, in 1999, something extraordinary happened. A onetime English teacher, she had taken a stab at writing the romance novel she'd always said she could write and, to everyone's surprise except her own, had landed a contract with Tatting & Nivens, a London publisher of historical romances. Under the pseudonym Tennessee Rivers, she had since written nine novels, all set in 1840s California, about a beautiful, gunslinging gold prospector named Belladonna "Red" O'Higgins, revered and feared around the Old West as "Two-Gun Bella." They had quickly found an enthusiastic and ever-growing readership, especially in the United States.

She was quite well-to-do now and had become something of a celebrity and a jet-setter, flying off to England or the United States several times a year to do book signings or television interviews and frequently showing up in feature articles in the Jersey and Guernsey papers. Her sizable income had enabled her to buy and completely refurbish Dechambeaux Manor, a moldering, once-grand manor house, and to purchase the fifty acres of open land around it, all of which she christened Belladonna Park. Currently she was in the process of cranking out number ten in the series: working title, *Vein of Blood*. The word was that Hollywood had already optioned it.

At sixty-nine, she acted and looked fifteen years younger, with the same rangy, big-boned, outdoorsy good looks that Rafe remembered from his childhood. She bred horses at Belladonna Park now, mostly for her own pleasure, and when she was mounted on one of them, as assured and elegant in the saddle as she'd been at thirty, she could make him shake his head in admiration.

Her personality hadn't changed much either, but that wasn't anything to celebrate. Generally speaking, Rafe's friendly looks and pleasant manner reflected the man within. He took people on their own terms and liked almost everyone he met. Oh, he saw others' faults as well as anyone else did, but he looked on them with tolerance and often with amusement; he was well aware that he had plenty of his own. Even Abbott he found reasonably congenial when his foibles weren't actively driving him mad. But Miranda was another matter.

Once upon a time they'd been close, or at least in his child's mind they had. She had been his funny, irreverent Aunty Mandy then. She'd always had a sharp tongue, but she'd been witty too, and as a youngster he had often giggled at her barbs. Not so much anymore. Now they were flung about in greater profusion but with much less wit. Rafe had concluded some time ago that it wasn't so much that she'd become more mean-spirited with age (well, maybe a little) but that her celebrity—and in Jersey terms she was a superstar—awed and intimidated people enough so that few had the nerve to do anything but laugh when she insulted them or nod thoughtfully when she said something patently inappropriate. Apparently, it had gotten her to believing that her particular brand of blatant disagreeableness was droll and that anything that might come from her mouth was, ipso facto, worth saying. But to Rafe, these careless, side-of-the-mouth throwaways seemed to have little point other than wounding.

"You forget a lot, don't you, Abbott?" Miranda said now. "You also seem to have forgotten that by no means do we *know* that they were all killed on the same night. It's nothing more than conjecture."

Abbott's above-it-all veneer was beginning to show cracks. He persevered but with a slight tinge of desperation. "Aunt Miranda, I don't have all the answers. I'm simply going along with what the authorities eventually concluded. I don't really see how we're in a position to dispute the conclusions of a competent, professional—"

Miranda jerked her head. Her own tiny store of patience was about gone. "Oh, for heaven's sake, Abbott, if it's the conclusions of the police you want to prattle on about, then what about their conclusion that it was Rafe's father's gun that killed him? Let me hear you get around *that.*"

Abbott was getting increasingly tight-lipped. "Let me put it this way, Aunt Miranda. What you're suggesting simply doesn't hold water. The idea—"

"You know, there must be something wrong with my hearing, because I could have sworn I heard you say only a few minutes ago that you weren't going to be expressing your opinion. Am I wrong, Rafe?"

Rafe jumped. "Ah . . . what? Well . . . no, I don't believe he explicitly, ah—"

"I have a few questions for Rafe too," Abbott said abruptly. "Just who's supposed to pay for this exhumation you're talking about? It won't be inexpensive. And he'd have to be reburied, that would cost money too. And I doubt if Gideon Oliver is working for nothing. And—"

"He is, as a matter of fact."

"And most important, how do we know they'll treat my father's remains respectfully?"

A last-ditch technique brought back from Kent? Demonstrate to the recalcitrant (Miranda) that there was a common enemy (Rafe) in the room? That things were still up in the air, that you haven't made up your mind yet? No matter, Rafe had been expecting this particular parry, had been waiting for it, in fact.

"Naturally, I'd pay all costs," he said. "I'm the one who's pressing for it, so it's only fair. And so I've already looked into the matter." He produced from his inside pocket the envelope containing the papers his secretary had prepared. "I spoke with the people at Bonnard and Sons this morning. They'll arrange for it to be done, they'll hold the body at their facility for Gideon to examine, and they'll rebury him with all propriety and even hold another memorial service if you like. You'll need a new coffin for the reburial, and I know you'll want a nice one. Bonnard can supply that as well, and I'll be happy to cover the cost."

"I don't care for Emil Bonnard, never have," said Miranda. "The man is *flashy*. Funeral directors should not be flashy. That ridiculous funeral coach, like something from the Royal Mews? No, Collett's Funerals are far more circumspect. More dignified. If I were to agree to your proposition, which, frankly, I can't imagine doing, I would never select Bonnard."

There was Miranda in a nutshell: you say something—anything—and before the words are out of your mouth, she's come up with a way to disagree, even while removing herself from the issue being considered at the same time.

"I can certainly understand why you'd feel that way, Aunt Miranda," Rafe said and barely managed to check a sudden laugh; he was starting to sound like Abbott. "And so I thought the best thing would be simply to write out a check and let Abbott—let you and Abbott—decide where and exactly how to spend the money. Bonnard told me he'd charge nineteen hundred pounds for their services and that their 'Prestige' coffin for the reburial would be another thirteen hundred. That would come to thirty-two hundred, and additional fees would likely bring it to thirty-five hundred, so I've made it out for four thousand pounds to cover anything unexpected as well. I've also gotten the necessary governmental forms filled out for you and brought them with me. All you need do is sign them, and whichever funeral director you choose will take care of submitting them. Is that a satisfactory arrangement?"

Miranda barked a laugh. "Are you asking me? What for? Obviously, Abbott has already made up his mind and will do as he chooses. My presence here seems to be no more than ornamental."

"No, that's not true, Aunt Miranda," Abbott protested. "I haven't made up my mind at all. I value your opinion enormously. I would never make a decision like this without your input."

It was said with a great show of sincerity, and it occurred to Rafe that the man might actually believe what he was saying. It was possible. For someone with an indisputably keen eye for inconsistencies and ambiguities in financial matters, he could be amazingly obtuse when it came to self-perception. *But then, who couldn't?* he thought charitably.

"Abbott . . . Aunt Miranda," he said, "would it be helpful if I had Professor Oliver come round and explain a little more fully what it is he'd be doing? He could do that far better than I can."

"A bit late for that," Miranda said. "Why didn't you bring him with you in the first place?"

"I thought it would be best to treat it as a family matter, without outsiders present," he said. "Apparently, I was wrong."

"Apparently, you were," said Miranda.

The slightest of grimaces marred Rafe's amiable countenance for a split second. I am *really* starting to dislike this person, he thought.

"Well, why don't you go ahead and give him my number?" Abbott suggested with a complete lack of enthusiasm. "At least we can hear him out. It won't take long, I hope."

"I will. The sooner, the better. Later this afternoon all right? He'll be here only a few more days."

"No, I've got to get back to the bank. And, honestly, this is a very bad time for me. I'm going to be terribly busy for the next several days."

Rafe was struck with the belated perception that Abbott didn't really give a damn about any of this. He'd laid the whole affair permanently to rest. He was cooperating now because he had no good reason for refusing Rafe's request and because it offered him another chance to hone his Consensual Decision Making skills. But Miranda wasn't cooperating, and Abbott was clearly tired of the whole thing and thinking about a face-saving way of throwing in the towel.

Well, why wouldn't he be? Abbott had even less connection to his father than Rafe did to his. When Roddy died, Rafe had been three, and his earliest memory was of falling into a little inflatable swimming pool and landing on his back. It was only a few inches deep, but water had gotten into his nose, and he lay there, hysterical and sobbing, limbs waving like an overturned beetle's. Out of nowhere had appeared his father's smiling, reassuring face, and Rafe had been swept affectionately up into his strong arms and into safety. It was his warmest memory from infancy, although he was no longer sure whether he really remembered it or he'd just heard his mother tell the story. Abbott, on the other hand, had been born a few months after George had been killed. He couldn't have any memories of his father, not even imagined ones.

All of which made it more important than ever to get them together with Gideon in a hurry if anything was to come of it. "This evening, then?" he suggested. "He says he'd need to get started no later than Friday. Assuming the exhumation itself will take—"

"No, no, no, tonight is out of the question. Tuesday is my sunset hiking group."

"Yes, Rafe, you wouldn't want him to miss that," said Miranda. "How else do you suppose he maintains that magnificent physique?"

"How frightfully amusing, Aunt Miranda," Abbott said crossly.

Actually, Rafe did find it funny, although he was no longer in a mood to laugh. Abbott's "hiking" group called themselves the Over-the-Hill Gang, a dozen bankers and a few other businessmen, some aging and the rest aged, who put on jeans or fatigues and sturdy shoes and met once a week to stroll the coastal or forest paths for an hour. For Abbott, even this mild exercise was overdoing it. It was an open secret, the subject of jokes out of his hearing, that somewhere about the twenty-minute mark, he would find some appealing spot from which to admire the view or meditate to the sounds of nature or simply not be up to par that particular evening. The hikers would then pick him up on the way back, and all would repair exhausted to the nearest pub to restore their strength with a classic British evening of pub grub and pints.

"Tomorrow morning, then?" Rafe pressed. "Early?"

"I suppose so," Abbott said, loosely lifting one hand, palm up, in a clear *whatever* message. "But no, not early. I should be able to get away at ten, though, if he promises to keep it to half an hour. But have him ring me earlier—between seven thirty and eight—to confirm that he'll be here. You can make yourself available, Aunt Miranda? Ten?"

"I wouldn't miss it," she said drily. "Indiana Jones himself. Will he wear that splendid hat of his, do you think?"

Rafe's responding smile was on the weak side. Maybe getting Gideon together with them wasn't such a good idea after all. Abbott wasn't exactly keen about it, and Miranda was digging in her heels, a warrior salivating for battle.

"But I warn you, Abbott," she continued, "I'm not likely to be swayed. Besides, I would much rather have this settled today."

"Well, it would be, if you would only—"

"I would also like to have my sister Edna's views, if she'd care to offer any."

This last sentence was directed somewhat threateningly at Edna, who snapped to frightened attention. "May I go home now?" she ventured. "Teatime at the Hamlet is at two thirty sharp, and they're awfully prompt about it."

"In a minute, Mum. Miranda's right, this is important," Abbott told her. "Try to concentrate."

"Edna, they do *not* have tea at two thirty. That's ridiculous," Miranda said. Even with her mind-destroyed sister, she could find something to dispute. "You must have forgotten."

"Oh yes, they do too. They have a lot of old people there, you know, and old people like to eat early. And on Tuesdays—isn't this Tuesday?—they have apricot tarts, but if you arrive even five minutes late, they're all gone." She scrabbled nervously at her sleeve. Her eyes welled. Her lip began to tremble.

"I'll get you there by two thirty, Aunt Edna, I promise," Rafe said tenderly. "It's on my way." He knew perfectly well that she wasn't his aunt any more than Miranda was, but from his earliest childhood he had called her that, and this wasn't the time in the old woman's life to tell her otherwise.

Not that it would have made any difference. She smiled brightly at him. "Thank you, young man."

Rafe's heart contracted. Once she had been the warmest and most delightful of his supposed relations, and he'd been her favorite so-called nephew. "You're welcome, ma'am," he said.

"Mum, this is your husband we're talking about," Abbott said forcefully. "Do we have your approval to exhume him or not? That's all we're asking you. Just tell us, yes or no, and you're on your way home."

"But I still don't see how any of this concerns me," Edna said, on the edge of desperation. "I don't believe I know the gentleman to whom you're referring." She appealed to Rafe: "Shouldn't we be leaving now, young man?"

"Mum, we're talking about your husband!" Abbott exclaimed. "*George*—your *husband*!"

"Oh, no, not mine. I don't have a husband, never did."

"You—"

But Edna had reconsidered her words. "I don't *think* I have a husband," she said slowly, scowling with the effort to remember. "Or maybe . . ." Behind her eyes, a dim light flickered. "Maybe years ago, I did. Oh, yes . . . now, what was his name?"

Miranda's exasperation broke through. "His name was *George*, for Christ's sake, Edna! Your husband. Abbott's father. Can't you just, for one minute, *try*—"

Rafe jumped to his feet and held out his hand. "Come along, Aunt Edna. Let's get you to the Hamlet on time."

Edna took the hand and rose with a beautiful smile. "Get me to the church on time," she sang softly.

"I'll leave it to the two of you to sort out," Rafe told the others. "As for myself, I really don't give a damn anymore what you decide, or *if* you decide. Just leave Aunt Edna out of it." It had been a long time since he'd had an outburst like that, and he was immediately embarrassed by it. "Sorry about that," he said stiffly. "I seem to be a little touchy this afternoon."

"I'll say," Miranda said.

"I do apologize, and I appreciate your giving me the time to talk with you. I hope you see your way to approving the exhumation."

They couldn't have been more unreceptive, both of them looking at him with dull stares.

Well, consider that a mission blown, he thought glumly. A surprise, really. He'd expected no trouble. But then, he hadn't anticipated the presence of the impossible Miranda. Perhaps he needed some training in Consensual Decision Making himself. Too late now, though. With a sigh, he gave up the ghost and bestowed his most winning smile on Edna. "Come on, dear. Tea and tarts wait for no man. Or woman."

"I say, Rafe?" Abbott called after them. "Look, why don't you leave that paperwork here? Aunt Miranda and I will talk it out for a while longer."

Miranda rolled her eyes, and from deep in her throat came a low warning rumble. "A *little* while longer," she said. "Randy's probably waiting for me downstairs right now."

"Oh, and you might as well leave the check too," Abbott added offhandedly to Rafe. "So you don't have to come back if we decide on doing it."

Rafe's world brightened. Maybe he hadn't blown it, after all.

CHAPTER 15

Miranda was right. There was Randall Campion, across from the building's entrance, waiting for her on a bench along the waterfront walkway. He was sprawled like a teenager, half-lying, half-sitting, weight on the base of his spine, legs stretched out in front of him, and arms spread casually across the back of the bench. Not a care in the world.

Campion was the latest in Miranda's string of what the media called "boy toys," although "man toys" would have been closer to it, since most of them were at least as old as she was. This behavior on her part started when she'd become a member of the "avant-garde celebrity community," another term from the media. Rafe knew of at least three of them, a succession of shiftless reprobates who came to live with her (and sponge off her) until she got sick of them and threw them out, which was usually a matter of five or six months.

The latest, Campion, was showing more staying power. He'd shown up with her when she'd come back from a publicity trip to London two years ago, and he'd been with her ever since. Like the others, Randall was a past-his-prime Lothario, good-looking in an oily, lounge-lizard sort of way. Indeed, he claimed to have been a nightclub singer who had once opened for Jerry Lewis and for Liberace at the Palladium. Maybe he had, who knew? Who cared? Rafe had met him a number of times and had been put off by his slick, smug manner. Smug about what? he wondered.

"Hullo, there, Senator, Edna," Randy called, smashing any hope Rafe had of making a getaway without being spotted.

"Ah, good afternoon, Randall," he said brightly. "Didn't see you there. I say, that is what I call a handsome mustache. I wish I could grow one like that." He had his arm linked with Edna's, and with his other hand he gently patted her forearm. "What do you think, Aunt Edna? Doesn't he look nice with that mustache?" In fact, it was a ratty-looking thing, tobacco stained.

"I always liked David Niven's mustache," Edna said, smiling. "But when he didn't wear one, his nose was too big."

"Oh, I used to have one like this in my singing days, don't you know." Randall spoke with one of those accents that was impossible to place; British at base, Rafe thought, but with Continental shades and nuances as well, and American too. "Thought it might bring back my distant youth, but it's come in all gray, as you see. Mandy wants me to keep it, though. She says it makes me look distinguished."

Mandy, Rafe thought. *Mandy* and *Randy.* How cute. Surprising, though, that Miranda permitted it. Even as a young woman, she'd disliked the nickname (Rafe had been forbidden from using it when he was barely old enough to say it), but it had been what her mother and Peltier had called her, and so she went along with it. But the day of her mother's funeral, a few years after Bertrand had disappeared, was the day she made it clear, in an uncomfortable scene at the ceremony itself, that no one (very explicitly and publicly including the officiating minister) was to call her "Mandy" any longer. And as far as Rafe knew, no one had, not until this slippery old coot came along.

"It does, indeed," he said. "Extremely distinguished. Well, it was nice—"

"I say, what in the world is going on up there? How much longer will she be? Long enough to pop in at the pub there for a pint, would you say?"

Rafe, uncomfortable with shouting back and forth across the street, steered his aunt over to him.

"Hard to say," he said in response to Randall's question. "You might make it if you drink fast."

"I can do that." Randy stretched and stood up. Between two fingers of his left hand was the nub of a dead cigar, the last slimy, nasty gobbet, which he waved a few inches from Rafe's face. "You wouldn't have a light, I suppose?"

"I do, yes." Rafe smoked the occasional after-dinner cigar himself (but not with others present or to the revolting extreme that Randall took it). He produced a leather-encased lighter from his jacket. "Try not to let the smoke get blown in Aunt Edna's face."

"Smoke gets in your eyes," Edna sang.

Randall took the lighter, made an unsuccessful effort to get the stub going again, and gave it another try.

"No, wait a moment," Rafe said. "I would hate to see that superb new mustache catch fire. Here, have a new one." From a matching leather case, he extracted one of the three cigars it held and extended it.

"Why, thank you, Senator." The repulsive stub was dropped into a flower bed (Rafe forced himself not to notice) as Randall read the band on the new cigar. "Montecristo Reserva Negra," he said. "My, my, thank *you*."

The paper band followed the stub into the flower bed while he got the cigar lit, carefully exhaling the smoke away from Rafe and Edna. "Ah. This calls for more than a pint to do it justice. I believe I'll have a good brandy with it, a cognac. No, a whiskey, I think. Would you and the lovely care to accompany me, Senator?"

Edna tugged at Rafe's sleeve. "Two thirty," she said anxiously.

"That's right. I wish we could, Randall, but Aunt Edna has to get back to the Hamlet, and we can't be late. Awfully sorry."

"Apricot tarts," Edna explained with a friendly smile.

CHAPTER 16

Gideon's plan for a long walk and a quick lunch lasted exactly two blocks, at which point it turned into a quick walk and a long lunch. He started by turning off Kensington Place onto the Parade, which took him down one long flank of the Parade Gardens, the eighteenth-century regimental parade ground that was now a park with benches, colorful raised gardens, a children's play area, and acres of lawn.

And that was as far as he got. This being the early afternoon of a pleasant, sunny day, a good many people—local workers, families, travel-stained backpackers—were spread out on the lawns enjoying picnic lunches, some out of brown bags brought with them from home, others from boxed snacks provided by the cafés alongside the park. In the window of one of these cafés was a display of lunch suggestions, among which was a classic ploughman's lunch: a six-inch chunk of crusty baguette, a good-sized wedge of crumbly, blue-veined Stilton and a slice of cheddar, a pickled onion, a hard-boiled egg, a dollop of pickled-vegetable relish, and a few pear and apple slices.

It was too much to resist, and five minutes later, he was in the park too, sitting on one of the benches that circled the plinth of a nineteenth-century monument to an early lieutenant governor. He had the box on his lap and a bottle of lemonade beside him. The sun felt good, the breeze felt good, and the food, as humble and basic as could be, was terrific. He took his time with it, simply soaking up the lazy ambience of the place and content to have his mind amble about on its own for a while, free from considerations of skeletons and murders.

He might even have dozed a little, because when his cell phone gently clunked (it was the most unobtrusive call tone he could find, something like what you'd get if you used a rubber mallet to softly tap on a metal pipe), it made him jump despite its muted tone, and he fumbled getting it out of his pocket.

"Gideon, it's Rafe . . ."

"Rafe, hello."

"I wondered if you'd had a chance to look over those remains yet."

"Barely, just got them out of the carton, nothing to report at this point."

"Ah." Only one syllable but clearly a let-down one. "Well, look, that's not what I've called you about. Listen, I've just come from Abbott, and, unless I've misread the signs, he's willing to go ahead with the exhumation, but he hasn't made it official yet. He'd like to talk with you about it tomorrow morning at ten, if that's convenient for you, and I think your silvery tongue might be just what's needed to get him to commit."

"Sure. Be better if it was today, though. We need to get started."

"Unfortunately, he's tied up for the rest of the day, but I think we're still in reasonable shape, as long as Mike can live up to his promise to hurry things along."

"That, somehow, is not something that worries me."

"Ha-ha. Just a minute, let me . . . ah, here it is, Abbott's number: one, five, three, four, six, one, two, one, one, two. He wants you to ring him a little before eight in the morning to confirm."

"Will do," Gideon said, writing the number on the lid of the box. "And where does he live?"

"In the harbor area, right on the marina, on La Route du Port Elizabeth. I forget the address, but it's in the ugliest one in that row of condominium buildings there, and the only one with a tangerine facade."

"Ugliest one. Tangerine facade. Got it."

"Yes, you can't miss it. But we should probably strategize a bit first. I want to clue you in on Abbott a little. And perhaps even more importantly, on the dreaded—and dreadful—Miranda."

"Now you're scaring me. Who's the dreadful Miranda?"

"I'll tell you when I see you. I'm tied up here at the States Building at the moment, but should be free in half an hour. Let me come over to the hotel then."

"Why don't I come there instead? The States Building is in Royal Square, right? It's on my agenda of places to see: the seat of government, correct?"

"It is that, from which all power emanates. All right, that will be fine too. Use the States Chamber entrance. It's at the south end of the building."

"I'll head over now, give me a chance to look around the square a little first."

"Good, I'll meet you in the entrance foyer."

Royal Square was Saint Helier's version of the Plaza Mayor in Spain, the heart of the town both geographically and historically. On the French half of the bilingual street signs it was still identified by its original name, the *Place du Marché*, Market Square.

It wasn't square, however, but triangular, perhaps five hundred feet long and not much more than a hundred feet wide at its base, with shade trees and benches attractively spaced at regular intervals. Gideon had taken a pocket guide with him on his walk and had read a little about it in the park. As expected, it was a sort of open-air historical museum of the last few centuries. At the wide end (in front of a couple of old pubs with lively terraces) was a blindingly gilded statue of George II, erected in 1751. Not far from the statue was a worn granite plaque:

The Battle of Jersey was fought in the Royal Square formerly the Market Place on the sixth of January 1781.

There were more up-to-date markers as well. On what had once been the public library:

On May 8th 1945 from the balcony above Alexander Moncrieff Coutanche bailiff of Jersey announced that the island was to be liberated after five years of German military occupation.

The long, two-story States Building, which formed the western border of the square, was its most prominent feature. It had been cobbled together from two adjoining structures—the library (with its original 1878 designation—*Biblioteque Publique*—carved into the stone lintel above its doors and still encrusted in gold) and the old Royal Courts building. An addition had been tacked on at the south end of the building and was christened as the States Chamber in 1887, on the fiftieth anniversary of Queen Victoria's accession, and still served in that capacity. (The pocket-sized guide was chock-full of facts.)

The entrance he'd been told to use was easy enough to find, and there was Rafe, waiting inside, hands clasped behind his back and looking his usual bright-eyed, chipper self.

"Welcome to my castle," he said with a wave that took in the entire anteroom.

"Thank you. Nice place you have here."

Nice, but surprisingly small. It wasn't much bigger than an ordinary, good-sized living room, but the carpeting was a richly patterned burgundy, the wainscoting and the stairway that led to the upper floor were of dark, richly glowing wood, and the three groupings of three chairs each were burgundy-red wingbacks of lush-looking leather, most of which were occupied by sober, suited, whispering men who looked as if they were deciding on the final fates of nations. On the walls were at least two dozen oil portraits of the statesmen of previous eras, and one of a contemporary stateswoman, the young Elizabeth II, in full royal regalia. An unlit crystal-teardrop chandelier, handsome but too big for the room, hung from the ceiling, but the restfully soft lighting came from wall sconces.

"Not exactly your typical governmental establishment," Gideon said. "It makes me think of one of those posh old clubs on Pall Mall or Saint James's Square—or on upper Fifth Avenue, for that matter—full of rich old guys who rule the world but never stop complaining about it, and this is where they come to hide out."

Rafe smiled. "I don't know that I've ever heard a more incisive description of the Assembly. Come, the Chamber's not in use this afternoon, so let's talk there. We legislators do have offices, but they're tiny, and they're at the other end of the building, miles from here."

Like the anteroom, the intimate little States Chamber was resolutely Edwardian, with lots of dark, richly carved wood. Other than the wood, the color of choice was, again, a regal burgundy. At the front was a dais with two formidable, high-backed leather chairs on it, facing a double horseshoe of wooden benches.

"Might as well be comfortable," Rafe said, leading Gideon up to the front. "Whose chair would you like, the bailiff's or the lieutenant governor's?"

"Who ranks higher?"

"The bailiff. She's the president of the Assembly, the person who calls the shots. The lieutenant governor is more the Queen's man, a ceremonial figure, neither seen nor heard from very often."

"I'll take her chair, then."

"What a gentleman you are," Rafe said, taking the lieutenant governor's chair himself. "Now then, strategy."

"Wait. This terrifying Miranda person—what is that about? When I go, should I be carrying?"

"Couldn't hurt," Rafe said. "Miranda is Edna's sister—"

"Sorry, Rafe, who's Edna again?"

"My apologies, old man. Edna Skinner is Abbott's mother, George Skinner's widow. A grand old lady. Under ordinary circumstances, it would be her permission we'd need, but she's quite old now, and her capacities are . . . well, not what they were. As her sole offspring, Abbott has the legal authority to act for her, but he seems to feel it's appropriate to consult Miranda on this particular matter."

"Miranda the Dreadful."

"Yes. She's the only one left who was indirectly involved in those old doings; by the way, she was Bertrand Peltier's wife at the time—"

"She's the woman who wouldn't accept his bones?"

"Precisely. She refused to acknowledge the idea that could really have been him in the pond."

"She must be pretty well along in years now."

"Not so much as you might think. She's quite a bit younger than poor Edna—sixty-nine, I believe, but a young sixty-nine, if such a thing exists. And she's . . . let's say, not inclined toward being helpful. She's the most consistently, unyieldingly negative person I know. And one of the most forceful, a dismaying combination. And she's very much used to having her way, and she speaks her mind all too readily, and—"

"—that's why she's Miranda the Dreadful."

"Exactly. And she's our essential problem here. She doesn't want George exhumed—mainly, I believe, because Abbott *is* willing to have it done."

"But you said he doesn't need her consent."

"Yes, that's so, but . . . well, *he's* the problem too. He's not against having it done, no. I don't think he cares much one way or the other, really. And so my concern is that whereas she is something of an irresistible force, he is not so much an immovable object, especially when it comes to her. I'm afraid she'll wear him down just to get her way, and he'll give in, simply to get away from her."

"Okay, and what am I supposed to do to get her to be reasonable?"

Rafe chuckled. "How would I know? I've never been able to do it. I simply thought you ought to be forewarned, that's all." But then he gave it some more thought, staring out at the empty rows, stroking his chin. "Do everything you can to avoid antagonizing her, and try not to let it affect your behavior when she becomes antagonized anyway. Those would be my suggestions. If you can get her on our side, it's a fait accompli. If you can't—well, I'm not sure which way things will go."

"I'll do my best, Rafe. Don't look so worried. Even if it doesn't work out, what I came here for is to look at your father's remains, not Abbott's father's. And that I can and will do. That's the important thing."

"Yes . . . Uh-oh . . ." Rafe was looking toward the double doors, one of which had opened to show a formidable middle-aged woman peering disapprovingly at them.

"Is there something scheduled in here, Henrietta?" he asked.

"Yes, and in ten minutes. You lot had best clear out right now. You shouldn't be up there in the first place." Henrietta, a large, scowling woman built along the lines of a Laundromat washer-dryer combination, looked like someone who was used to being obeyed.

"Certainly, my dear," Rafe said. "Just give us another second."

"Lieutenant Governor Phillips will be attending, Senator. If I were you, I'd get out of that chair rather in a hurry."

"My God," Rafe said, jumping up, "he'd skin me alive, the brute."

Gideon took that as his signal to get up as well, and they hurried out, past a censorious Henrietta. "The Chamber schedule is posted for a reason, Senator," she informed him. "You'd do well to consult it once in a while. This," she added, her voice laden with portent, "is not the first time."

He hung his head. "You're right. I consider myself well and truly rebuked."

"And *you* are expected to be in attendance."

"Of course. And I'll be here."

"*Not* at the front."

"Of course not."

"Ten minutes," was her parting valediction.

"The bailiff?" Gideon asked when they were out of earshot.

"Oh, no, a much more important figure than that, a person whose good offices one is well advised to cultivate. Henrietta Scaliffe is the bailiff's *secretary.* I don't know the way it is in the United States, but here—"

"It's the same in the States," Gideon said.

In the anteroom, Rafe paused alongside one of the portraits, pointing to the brass plate below it:

Howard Francis Carlisle

Senator, 1937–1962

President pro tempore, 1961–1962

"Ah," said Gideon. "This would be . . . let's see, your grandfather, Roddy Carlisle's father."

Rafe nodded. "The brightest light of our long genealogy. Unfortunately, he was gone long before I was born."

Gideon studied the portrait, that of a handsome, florid, robust-looking man in his midsixties, dressed in a dark, midcentury-style business suit rather than in the ceremonial robes most of the other subjects wore. His left hand rested gracefully inside the opening of his suit coat as if it were an admiral's tunic.

"Looks like a competent guy. And I love the Napoleonic pose. Very magisterial."

"Oh, there was a reason for that. He had a disfigured hand that he preferred to hide. An injury from the First World War, I understand."

"Not at all," said a scratchy voice from behind them. "Howard's hand was not 'disfigured,' except in his own mind. Nor was it the result of an injury in the Great War or in any other war."

"Why, hello there, Senator," Rafe said brightly. "Senator, this is my friend Dr. Gideon Oliver, an esteemed professor of forensic anthropology from the University of Washington. Gideon, allow me to introduce my learned colleague Wilton Goldsworthy, our longest-serving assembly member and an invaluable asset to our ancient and sadly enfeebled institution."

Senator Goldsworthy was a sturdy, square-shaped man in his mid-seventies who projected a hard-to-miss air of authority. His thick gray hair was longish but beautifully barbered and blow-dried. He'd have had no trouble passing for an American senator.

"Eh? What's that?" he said, cupping a hand to his ear and stiffening in mock indignation. "Did you just refer to me as an ancient and sadly enfeebled institution, Senator?"

"Certainly not, Senator."

"I should hope not, Senator."

Pretty lame as banter went, but fun to listen to, anyway—except that Gideon thought he detected a trace of artificiality to it, as if they were working too hard at being convivial, putting on an act for his sake.

Goldsworthy and Gideon shook hands. "Long-serving enough to have worked alongside your granddaddy in the last years of his life, Rafe," he said. "Even when I began, merely as an awestruck messenger boy, a lad of fifteen, he was very kind to me."

"And there wasn't anything wrong with his hand?" Rafe asked. "Then why the pose?"

"Oh, the two middle fingers on that hand were—how would one put it?—were fused together so that they looked almost like a single thickened finger. You know the old Mickey Mouse films? The creatures all wore puffy white gloves, and their hands had only a thumb and three fingers, but no one would call them unsightly. They look right somehow."

"Does Mickey Mouse have only four fingers? I never noticed," Gideon said.

"He does, indeed. As do Minnie and the quacking duck chap and the rest of that crew. But you see? You never noticed. Well, that's what

Howard's hand was like. It didn't call attention to itself. It was symmetrical, you see. I certainly wouldn't call it misshapen."

"Syndactyly," Gideon said.

"Sir?"

"Syndactyly. That's what the condition is called. From the Greek, *syn* meaning—"

"*Syn* meaning *together*, and *dactyl* meaning *finger*," Goldsworthy said testily. "Or *toe*. I may not be up on this 'forensic anthropology' of yours, Professor, but when I was a schoolboy, the classic languages were still being taught. And learned."

"And remembered, I see."

But Goldsworthy didn't care for the flattery. He frowned. "I'd best be getting along." He nodded curtly. "A pleasure meeting you, Professor." And he continued on his way to the Chamber.

"Something wrong between you two?" Gideon asked.

Rafe looked surprised. "Why would you ask that?"

"Oh . . . I don't know. I had the impression there was something a little, well, theatrical about all that hearty good fellowship. Not my business, Rafe, I don't know why I mentioned it. Probably misread it anyway."

"I'm afraid so."

As they talked, Gideon was fighting to keep from looking too obviously at Rafe's hands to check them, but Rafe caught him at it anyway and held them up, laughing. "Nope, not a webbed finger among them. Why, is it something that's inherited?"

"It tends to run in families, yes."

"Well, then, I've lucked out. It died with Granddad. My father didn't have it either, or at least no one's ever told me about it. I gather it's not very common?"

"About one in four thousand, I think it is. But if you've got the autosomal dominant variant, which is the most common one, then there's a fifty-fifty chance you're going to pass it along to your offspring. And it can skip a generation or two and then show up again, and—"

"Yes, I see." Rafe glanced at a clock on the wall. "Well . . ."

"I know, you've got a meeting to go to, so I'll leave you to it. Thanks for the heads-up on tomorrow. I'll call Abbott in the morning."

"Right. Good." He paused, looking uncharacteristically sheepish. "Ah, Gideon? I was being untruthful a moment ago. Do you remember my telling you about a man who'd been put out of business by my father's . . . ah, irregular business practices? The prime suspect in his death at the time?"

"Sure. You said there was still some bad feeling there."

"That's right. Well, that man—"

"—is your esteemed fellow senator Wilton Goldsworthy. Yes?"

"Yes," Rafe said with a grin. "Not much gets by you, does it, old man?"

Gideon laughed. "Old fellow, you'd be surprised."

CHAPTER 17

Energized, alert, and pleasantly filled with Stilton and sourdough, the Skeleton Detective was once more ready to ply his trade. Standing at the table, he examined the bones again, and it was one of the cranial fragments that caught his attention; he saw now that it was a piece of the right parietal. He turned it in his hand for a moment, then laid it, interior side up, on the white paper, which was smudged now with pitch residue. With the magnifying glass held just a few inches in front of his eyes, he leaned over the fragment . . .

It was half an hour before he fully straightened up, and that was only because John had walked in.

Startled, Gideon unbent a bit too quickly. "Ow. Damn."

"Yeah, I'm glad to see you too," John said.

"No, it's only that I've been leaning over for too long." He stretched backward, pressing his hands to the base of his spine. "Getting old, or at least my back is."

"Ha," said John, "tell me about it." He was forty-three, a year older than Gideon. He waved a manila envelope he was carrying, the kind you tie by wrapping a string around a couple of flat paper buttons. "Cop was delivering it downstairs when I came in."

"Probably Carlisle's autopsy report."

"Yeah, you want it?" He held it out.

"Not yet, no."

John came up to the table and looked down at the fragments. "Not a whole hell of a lot there. Is that all there is?"

"That's it." Gideon stretched himself backward even more and then relaxed. "Ah, that's good, my lumbar spinal extensors are starting to unknot."

"Yeah, you gotta watch those lumbar spinal extensors." He picked up a fragment and turned it over. "Parietal, right?"

Gideon nodded. "Very good."

John shrugged. "Nothin' to it; you just have to have the knack."

"Which side?"

"Left."

"Try again."

"Right."

"Excellent. You *do* have the knack."

"So, anyway, tell me," John said, "what do you know now that you didn't know before? Anything?"

"Um, well, yes, a few things, I guess you could say."

"Uh-oh, now he's getting coy. That usually means I better get ready to get my mind blown. How did Clapper say it? 'Boggle the minds of us poor coppers.'"

"Of you 'poor, *benighted* coppers' is what he said. Not that I would say it."

However, Clapper was basically right, and so was John. One of the more enjoyable rewards of forensic work—and this was another thing not to be found in the textbooks—was the guilty (but not terribly guilty) pleasure you took in watching a cop's face when you pulled the occasional rabbit out of a hat right in front of his eyes.

But Gideon didn't quite have his rabbits ready yet. "Tell you what, John. I have a few more things I need to tease out first. Why don't you take the report out into the living room and read it, and by the time you finish, I should have my act together."

Within seconds he was in the highly focused, almost trancelike state he fell into at such times, so that he was once again startled when John poked his head into the workroom.

"Didn't want to read it, after all?"

"Doc, it's been almost twenty minutes. It's two lousy pages. I read it three times. You need some more time? I could always memorize it if you want."

"Nope, I'm ready. Got ourselves a few surprises here, my friend. Come on in, I'll go through it with you. We can begin with just how many people we have represented here."

"Not two? Peltier and Carlisle?"

He shook his head. "Just one. Carlisle. No evidence of anyone else."

"No kidding." He moved closer to the table. "Show me."

Show me. That was one of the many things that made John fun to be with, the pleasure he took in hands-on forensics. He was a good learner, too. He'd sat in on a three-day seminar of Gideon's at an earlier Science and Detection conference, and he'd taken away—and retained—more information than some of Gideon's students got from a quarter's instruction.

"Sure, but first I'd like to know what made the guy who did the autopsy think there were two people in the first place."

John scanned the report. "Okay, the guy that wrote it is named Dr. Victor Graydon, MB, ChB, blah, blah, blah, Office of the Coroner, Viscount's Department. Hey, I love that—Viscount's Department. That's what we need at the Bureau, a Viscount's Department. Anyway, he says they have to be from more than one person because the bones, they're from two different-aged guys."

"Oh, that's right, a twenty-five-year-old or above and a . . . what, a nineteen-year-old or below?"

"Twenty."

"Twenty and twenty-five. Yes. And what exactly made him think . . . wait, let me guess. It wouldn't have anything to do with epiphyses, would it?"

"Yup, you got it. The good old epiphyses." John had been around Gideon long enough to know exactly what an epiphysis was and how it was used in skeletal age determination.

The body's "long" bones—legs, arms, clavicles, and ribs—grow not only by getting longer from the center outward but by laying on new cartilaginous material at both ends: these are the epiphyses. (*Epiphysis*, from the Greek *epi* "on, in addition" and *phusis* "growth.") With time—a lot of time—the cartilage ossifies and becomes permanently fused to the shaft of the bone, at which point the bone has finished growing. And when the last epiphysis has fused to the last shaft, which for all but a couple of them is somewhere in the midtwenties, that's when we've finished growing too. Alas, from then on, after a pathetically few years in our "prime," we get going in the other direction: we start getting shorter. Happily, the process is a lot slower and less drastic than when we were coming the other way.

The time between the start of epiphyseal attachment and full union and ossification varies from bone to bone, but for each individual bone, the general chronology is known. Obviously, then, the state of epiphyseal union in the various bones is helpful in aging a skeleton anywhere from childhood up through the middle or late twenties.

"So what does Dr. Graydon have to say about them?" Gideon asked. "It's the clavicle he's talking about, right?"

"The clavicle and the humerus."

"The humerus!" It was one of the nine fragments he'd set aside as not being of any help.

"Yeah, the humerus." John scrutinized the table and laid his finger on the humeral fragment. "Here, it's this one."

"Oh, really," Gideon said. "So that's a humerus. What do you know."

"A left one."

"Thank you."

John read aloud. "'Epiphyseal union of the head of the humerus begins at the age of sixteen and is completed by the age of twenty-five. In this particular specimen, fusion has been fully achieved. Thus, a *minimum* age of twenty-five can be associated with it. On that basis it is reasonable to conclude that this bone is part of the remains of Roderick Carlisle.'" He looked up. "That's not right?"

"Let's have a look." Gideon picked up the six-inch chunk of bone, the largest of the twelve fragments, and tapped the humeral head, the near-spherical upper end of the arm that nestles into a deep, concave hollow in the edge of the shoulder blade to form the ball joint that connects the arm to the torso. "Now, this part here, the ball—" he began.

"—*is* the epiphysis, right?"

"Right."

"And it *is* fused to the rest of the bone . . . right?"

"Sure is." Gideon ran his finger along the barely visible groove across the base of the humeral head, all that was left to show where the ball had fused to the shaft. "Never going to get any more ossified than that."

"So then," John said, "if Graydon was right about that not happening until you're twenty-five—"

"Roughly right. A little too exact, but close enough for our purposes. So, would you agree with his age estimate then?"

John lifted a skeptical eyebrow. "That's gotta be a trick question."

"Not at all. Why would you even say something like that?"

"Ho. Okay, what the hell. Yes, I would agree with Dr. Graydon. This humerus once belonged to someone who was twenty-five or older. Roughly."

"And you would be right. Roughly. I have no problem with it."

"But I thought you . . . So what *is* the problem, then?"

"The problem is with *this*." The fragment that Gideon picked up now was two and a half inches long, one of the two similar but reversed C-shaped halves of the collarbone that together made up the complete, S-shaped clavicle.

"The left collarbone," John announced. "The inside half, the part that hooks onto the breastbone. The medial half, as we call it in the trade."

Gideon laughed. "You really are getting good at this. Left, right—not so easy with a clavicle, especially half a clavicle."

"Yeah, well, it helps when you just finished reading a report telling you what it is. What's the problem with it, though?"

"What did Graydon say about it?"

"Mmm, lemme see . . . Okay, he says: 'In the case of this specimen, no epiphysis is present. Union has yet to begin. Since fusion at the medial end of the clavicle is known to regularly commence by the age of twenty in males, a maximum age of twenty years can be associated with this bone.'" He put the report down. "Peltier, in other words. And you say what?"

"Well, let's look at this one too." He put it on the table directly in front of them.

John shook his head. "To tell you the truth, Doc, I can't remember what the epiphysis on this thing is supposed to look like."

"Which is completely understandable. It's not anything like the big, round humeral head; it's just a sort of facet that mounts it on the sternum. And he's correct: it isn't there."

John was starting to look confused. "So he's right about this too? This *is* a younger guy?"

"No, he's not right."

John thought for a moment. "It *was* there, but it got broken off? Sure doesn't look like it got broken off." He fingered the end in question. "Smooth as can be."

"Which is exactly what confused him. He figured that because the shaft just ends, nice and smooth, he was looking at a bone that never did develop its epiphysis, a young guy, in other words. But he's wrong."

John sighed. "And are you going to tell me why he's wrong anytime soon, or should I go get some dinner and then come back?"

Gideon handed John the magnifying glass. "Here, check it out for yourself through this."

John took the bone and held it up to the lens, rotating it to see both sides. "Ooh, yeah, I see . . . It's not smooth at all . . . tiny little scratches, little nicks, especially there at the end, tons of them." He put down the glass. "I can see them through this, but . . ."

"Right. You didn't before. You needed the magnification. Well, they're from little crabs, or prawns, or maybe crayfish—something that takes the flesh off a corpse with little pincers, a shred at a time, and puts these characteristic, barely visible nicks in the bone when they reach it."

"So it *did* have an epiphysis, is what you're telling me, but the crabs ate it? So this guy was *not* under twenty or so?"

"No, I can't say that for sure. Maybe he had an epiphysis, maybe he didn't, but with the end of the bone gone, I don't have any way to tell, and neither, really, did Graydon."

"So we don't know which of them it's from, Carlisle or Peltier."

"Literally, that's true, but if the other fragments all fit Carlisle, then there's really no reason, no forensic reason, to put Peltier into the equation at all. As far as I can tell, they're *all* Carlisle."

"Okay, but tell me this. These crabs and things, they chewed off the whole end of the clavicle, but they never touched the humerus. Why is that?"

"Well, since the humerus finishes ossifying several years before the clavicle does, it would have been too hard for those tiny pincers to have any effect on them. But the clavicle, newly fused, would still have been a little soft, which is more inviting to bone scavengers."

"Yeah? I never thought of that. That's interesting." Then, having picked up something dubious about the way Gideon had tossed it off, added: "Is it true?"

"John, I don't have a clue, but I know you always need a reason for everything, so I thought that would sound good. I don't know, it probably *is* true, but the reality of it is, there's no accounting for something like that. Could be a million reasons. Maybe the humerus got stuck under a rock where it couldn't be gotten to, maybe—"

At the sound of the door opening, Gideon started, and when Julie's face and her short, wind-tousled dark hair peeked through, his heart quickened first, then relaxed. After five years of marriage, he was still deeply in love with her, still capable of being thrilled when she walked into a room.

But there was more than that to it. He'd been married before, to the only other woman he'd ever loved, and when Nora had been killed in a traffic accident, it had plunged him into a sinkhole of grief and despair. For almost three years he'd been among the walking dead. It had been lively, lovely Julie Tendler who had brought him back to life. But that old, terrible day had left its mark, so that whenever Julie was out on her own, there was a lingering flicker of worry (for the first couple of years it had been full-fledged dread) that stayed with him until she was back, safe and sound. As she was now.

He smiled. "Hi, Julie."

CHAPTER 18

"Hi, there, fellas," she called back, shouldering her way in, both hands engaged in holding a cardboard drink tray with three cups in it. "Glenda told me you were both up here, so I brought us up some lattes."

"Great, thanks," Gideon said, "I know I can use one."

"Roddy Carlisle and Bertrand Peltier, I presume," she said, looking at the bones as she handed out the drinks. "Boy, not much left of them, is there?"

"Enough for Doc to start screwing around with what everybody thought they knew," John said. "As usual. He's been telling me it's just Carlisle. No sign of Peltier."

"Really?" She smiled. "Well, didn't I say it wouldn't take you long to start standing things on their heads? But how do you know that, Gideon?"

"What do you say we take a short break first?" Gideon said. "I'm ready to sit down for a few minutes."

"His spinal extensors are acting up on him, poor old guy," John said, going into the kitchen. "Hey," he called from there, "I picked up some Figaloos. They'll go good with the coffee."

Julie looked at Gideon. "Figaloos?" she mouthed.

"French Fig Newtons," John said, returning and setting down a packet of cookies. "Only better. Bigger, anyway."

Julie laughed when she saw the label. "Oh, *Figolu*," she read aloud, then repeated it, simply for the tactile pleasure of getting her mouth around those delicious French vowels a second time.

"Oh, *excuse* me," John said. "Feeeguhhlllyieuuww. I tell you what, if you don't like the way I say it, you don't have to—"

But Gideon was quicker, getting to the packet before John could snatch it away and grabbing a couple for himself and Julie. "We like the way you say it just fine."

They each munched one, washing them down with coffee, and Gideon brought Julie up to date.

"Well," she said, "that's really interesting about the crabs and things, but I do see a slight problem there."

"Yeah, so do I," said John. "I was just about to say, when you walked in."

Gideon smiled. "Bravo. I expected no less from the two of you."

"I'm pretty sure crabs can't live in a tar pit," John said. "Or crayfish either."

"Right," Julie agreed, "so what chewed up his bones?"

Gideon nodded. "That's the question, all right."

Julie looked at John. "You are aware, of course, that he's just stringing us along? He's got the answer right there in his back pocket, waiting to astound and flabbergast us."

"Hey, you're telling me? Don't forget, I know the guy longer than you do."

"No, I'm not about to flabbergast anyone this time. The fact is, I don't have a good answer. The only *possible* answer I can think of doesn't make much sense. Someone moved him—moved the bones."

"Moved," echoed John, scowling. He reached for another fig bar.

"Yes, I think Roddy spent long enough in an ordinary pond or river—weeks, months, years—for the little critters to nip away at him enough to get down to the bone, *after* which they got dumped into the tar pit—the bones, not the critters."

"That's crazy, Doc. Why would anybody do that?" John asked. "Moving a body, I could see. But a pile of *bones*?"

"And into a commercial, working tar pit at that?" Julie added. "Wouldn't it be safer and easier to just bury them somewhere? Or toss them into the Channel? Or . . . or . . ."

Gideon shrugged. "Sounds weird, I agree, but if anybody can come up with a better explanation, I'd love to hear it."

They were silent for a while, pensively sipping coffee, and then John said abruptly: "Oh, hey, Doc, there's something I almost forgot. Graydon's got something else he says proves there are two people there." He scrabbled through the report, looking for the relevant section.

"I hope he's got something better than the epiphyses."

"I don't know, you tell us. Here we go: 'The most compelling evidence for the presence of more than one individual lies in the differing and incompatible states of suture closure found in the two cranial fragments.'"

"Oh, boy." Gideon couldn't help rolling his eyes. Graydon had stepped into some really muddy waters here. The idea of using cranial sutures as a way of estimating age had been around for going on two hundred years, and on the face of it, it made sense. The human skull, so solid-seeming, is made up of twenty-two different bones (plus three tiny ones that you can't see—the ossicles, deep in the ears) that, in the first half of life, are separated by *sutures*—hairline "cracks," some squiggly, some relatively straight, lined with dense, fibrous connective tissue. This tissue does a good job of holding the skull firmly together while allowing just enough "stretch" to let the brain keep growing through adolescence and early adulthood, at the end of which your brain is as big as it's ever going to get and your skull might just as well be one solid, immovable hunk of bone. Which is what it becomes. The sutures now begin to ossify and meld with the surrounding bone and slowly start disappearing.

And since the rate at which they ossify is broadly predictable, one would—and did—think they could be used for aging in the same way that epiphyses are used. Hundreds of scientific papers have been published on the subject through the years, along with a steady, seemingly never-ending flood of master's theses presenting yet more "new" ways of evaluating them, of which Gideon himself had (reluctantly) supervised two so far and hoped never to see another.

The verdict had taken a long time to arrive, but now it would seem to be in: They don't work, except—*maybe*, a little—when they're used in conjunction with some pretty abstruse aggregate statistics. Yes, they do ossify in a moderately predictable order, at a moderately predictable rate, but the differences between people are too great to provide anything but the broadest kind of estimate. Are all of the sutures clearly open? This is a young person. Are all of the sutures so thoroughly ossified that barely a trace of them here and there is all that can be seen? This is an old person. And that was about it. But in 1969, when this report was written, the idea still had some life in it.

Gideon's eye rolling had made John hesitate in his reading aloud. "You don't want me to read this?"

"No, I can take it. Read on. The Figaloo has fortified me."

John cleared his throat. "'Fragment *A* comprises adjacent portions of the left parietal and frontal bones. Thus, it necessarily crosses the coronal suture, which separates the two bones. This suture has not completely ossified, but it is well on the way, enough so that these segments of the two bones remain firmly attached. Since ossification of this suture does not begin until the age of twenty-five, it is safe to assume that Fragment *A* comes from an individual of at least twenty-six or twenty-seven years.'" He waited for Gideon's response.

"That would be this one," Gideon said, picking up one of the two cranial fragments, "and I don't really have any major argument with him on it. His description is right, and obviously, he thinks it belongs to Carlisle, and so do I. So then what about the other one, Fragment *B*, I assume? That's an interesting one. What's he got against it?"

"Okay. His reading is . . . here we go: 'Fragment *B*, originally two adjacent fragments, now glued together, consists of a wedge-shaped piece of the right parietal, roughly opposite to the position of Fragment *A* on the left, but slightly more posterior. Two of the three sides of this fragment are the results of fracturing. The third, however, is *not* the result of fracture. What we have instead is the bone's natural border, where in life it would have been part of the parietal rim of the coronal suture.'

"And then he's got a footnote at the bottom. 'It should be noted that Fragment *B* is composed of two adjacent fragments that were glued together.'"

"Right, I was just looking at that when you came in."

"And the footnote also says, 'The small matching discrepancies to be found along the joined borders are the result of the warping of the bone over time.'"

"Oy," said Gideon, in respectful memory of his beloved mentor Abe Goldstein, who would surely have said the same thing. "I don't know where to begin. That is fouled up from the first word to the last."

"Gideon," Julie said, "I know you must be right about all this doctor's mistakes, but what I can't help wondering is why in the world they would have used someone who was so . . . well, incompetent."

"Oh, I wouldn't say incompetent. I'm being harder on him than I should be. Really, his problem was that he was ahead of his time. He was doing forensic anthropology before it existed, before there was a sufficient database, let alone the statistical tools, to make the kind of hard-edged generalizations he makes: coronal closure begins at *exactly* twenty-five, the medial end of the clavicle begins fusion at *exactly* sixteen, and so on. Nothing about human growth is *that* predictable. My guess is that he got his information from his old anatomy texts, for which variation was a nonissue. For them, it still is, pretty much. It's not what they're about."

"All right, fine, he's off the hook," John said. "So let me tell you his conclusion."

"Let me tell *you*. He says that, using the same reasoning, the still-open suture proves that *this* fragment comes from somebody *under* twenty-five."

John nodded.

"And he couldn't be more wrong. The suture's open, all right, but it's not *still* open."

Utterly blank looks from Julie and John.

"I think I'm getting a little overwhelmed here," Julie said.

John put it slightly differently. "Please, somebody put me out of my misery."

"Look, you two, I know you think I'm being mysterious for the fun of it—"

"Nah, why would we think that?" John said.

"—but really, I'm not. Or, well, maybe only just a very little. The thing is, this is pretty complex, and I'm just trying to present it logically. Cogently." Gideon finished his coffee and stood up. "Come on, let's get back in there. Stick with me a little longer, and you'll see what I'm talking about."

At the worktable, he slid the clavicle and the humerus to one side, leaving just the two cranial fragments in the center of the table. "Now. I'm sure you both remember the two parietal bones are the biggest ones in the skull and each one makes up virtually one entire side of the skull. They come together at the top. And the frontal bone—"

"Is the one in front of 'em," John said. "Duh."

"Good man. And the coronal suture, running from temple to temple, over the top of the head, is the suture between the frontal bone and the two parietals behind it. And on this fragment, Fragment *A*, it's closed, as he says. Okay?"

They both nodded. "We're with you, Prof," Julie said.

Now that fragment was swept aside too, leaving the slightly larger Fragment *B* all alone in front of them. "With this one we have a problem. This is the one he glued together from two smaller pieces. Have a look." He gave them time to examine it.

"He's right," John said, "these two edges here are from getting broken, even I can tell that. But this third side *is* different. Not sharp, doesn't look like a fracture. Almost looks like it's from a jigsaw puzzle."

"And that would be the side he says was the border of the suture?" Julie suggested.

"Yes, and about that he's also right. You'd never get a squiggly, curvy edge like that from a fracture. What happened is that he got hit in the head and the blow *popped* that suture open."

"Popped open a suture," John said. "I didn't know that could happen."

"It can happen."

"So he was hit right on top of the suture, is that what does it?" asked Julie.

"No, this crack down here is more likely where he got hit."

"Where he glued the fragment together." Julie again.

"Right."

Julie was running her finger along the glue line. "I don't know, are you positive they really go together? They're a little off. Shouldn't they fit better than that?"

Leaning over beside her, John agreed. "Did he glue two pieces that really don't belong together, is that what's wrong?"

"No, actually, they do go together. But you're right, Julie, they should fit *perfectly*. Remember he mentioned that there's some warping in the bone that throws off the fit a little? Well, that's what we're seeing here."

John stepped back from the table and folded his arms. Willing learner though he was, he could only go so long before his impatience broke through. "Okay, I don't know about you, Julie, but I am *really* ready to cut to the chase. To quote from you yesterday, Doc, 'Where are you going with this?'"

"We're practically there. Hang with me just a little longer." He held up the fragment. "Okay. Warped, yes, but warping *over time* . . . no. It just doesn't happen. Dead bone doesn't warp, not unless you have a one-in-a-million situation—say, an *Australopithecus* skull stuck in a limestone deposit that's been putting it under steady, inconceivably slow pressure for the last three million years. But in five years? No way."

"But live bone does warp, is that where you're heading with this?" Julie asked.

"Exactly. Or rather, it *can* warp . . . although maybe 'bend' is a better term for it."

"Bones can bend?"

"Sure. Mostly, it happens with kids—their arm and leg bones. The ulna or the fibula can get bent *right up* to the point of breaking, but not quite all the way there—and when that happens, sometimes it's bent so far it can't bounce back."

"It's bent forever?"

"No, in a kid it will usually straighten out as the bone grows. But sometimes it does have to be reset."

"But this isn't a kid, this isn't some skinny fibula," said John. "It's a skull. It's *thick*."

"Correct, but traumatic stress can do it in a grown man's skull too, which is what happened here. When Roddy's head was struck, his skull bent inward—gave—at the point of contact. And when that happens, when a semirigid object—stiff, solid, but not a hundred percent inflexible—is forced to bend in one direction, there has to be some *give* somewhere else in the opposite direction to compensate."

"Umm . . ." Julie said, ". . . okay, got it."

"Now most of the time, bone does fracture—shatter—pretty quickly, before it bends too far, so once it breaks, it bounces right back, and you glue the pieces, they fit fine. You'd never know there'd been any give. But if the force is slow-loading enough—it won't happen with a bullet, for example; the force is too overwhelmingly fast—but if it's a rock, or a hammer, say, the bone can bend so much before it breaks that it can't bounce back. It's permanently deformed. That's what happened here. That's why the pieces wouldn't fit together perfectly."

John and Julie were slowly nodding, fully absorbed again.

"And when it's going through that bending phase, just looking for a weak spot to crack open, and it crosses an incompletely ossified suture—"

"The suture pops," Julie said.

Gideon nodded. "It doesn't happen every day, but it happens. It happened here."

"And the suture on the other side, on Fragment *A*, didn't pop because it was . . . well, on the other side, too far away from the blow?"

"Probably so."

John was still thoughtfully fingering the fragment. "So something that did this much damage—would that have been enough to kill him?"

"Oh, yes. Can't say for certain that this was the cause of death, because there's so much of him we don't have. There might have been other wounds. But it sure didn't do him any good. 'Presumptive cause of death'—that's what'll go in my report."

Julie was worrying the gold chain of her pendant necklace. "Gideon," she said slowly, "if the fragments in the tar pit all belonged to Roddy Carlisle—"

"Then what happened to Bertrand Peltier?" John finished for her. "And where the hell is he?"

"That too," Julie said, "but I was going to raise something else: If Roddy wasn't killed in a fight with Peltier after all . . . then who did kill him? *Was* it Peltier?"

"Excellent questions," Gideon agreed. "To which I have not a single answer." Thanks to his findings, all of the conventional theorizing on the case had either been turned upside down or chucked out altogether. A total rethink was required. And that, he had not even begun to try.

"Huh," said Julie.

"Mmm," John grunted.

Gideon laughed. He'd taught more than enough classes to recognize the congealing, glassy-eyed gaze and the slowdown in speech and reaction that indicated his audience had had enough for one day. So had he.

"I'm done for the day," he announced. "It's a little early for dinner, maybe, but I saw a nice-looking steak house this afternoon. 'Fire-grilled T-bones a specialty.' How's that sound?"

"Great!" said John.

Julie was shocked. "Don't tell me they eat those sweet little cows. Oh, no—those kind, beautiful eyes!"

"No, the Jerseys are dairy cows, safe from us carnivores. These, according to the sign, are Aberdeen Angus; aged twenty-eight days. Not nearly as cuddly looking. You need feel no compunction."

"You got my vote," John said. "But maybe you should call Rafe first? He'll want to hear what you found."

"To tell you the truth, I don't really want to talk it all through again right now. I'll write the stuff up and e-mail him, and we can talk about it tomorrow. Give me twenty minutes to do that. Have a glass of wine or something." He opened his laptop. "Or a Figaloo."

"Wine sounds good," Julie said. "What about you, Gideon? Want some? Red? White?"

"White, I think." He began to peck away at the keyboard.

"I think I'll get me a beer if we have any in the fridge," John said. "Hey, Doc, don't forget about Clapper. You probably want to fill him in too."

"Good idea, I'll copy him."

"Did you say 'Clapper'?" Julie said, returning from the kitchen with an opened, cold-frosted bottle of Chablis. "You're not talking about *Mike* Clapper, are you?"

"We are, as a matter of fact," Gideon said. "I was going to tell you. It turns out that the good sergeant is now a high panjandrum in the Jersey police force—not merely a sergeant, not merely a detective or a detective inspector, but a detective *chief* inspector, which I gather is a very high muckety-muck indeed around here. Kind of amazing, isn't it?"

"I'll say," she said, laughing. "Good old Mike. What's the story on that?"

"I'll fill you in later, Julie. Let me get these e-mails off."

"Well, I'm going to get to see him, aren't I? Good old Mike," she said again.

"Good old Mike," Gideon agreed.

Really, neither of them knew him well enough to think of him as Good Old Mike, but Clapper was the sort of hearty, jovial, bluff man that made the moniker a natural—at least if you happened to be on his good side. Whether the criminals he dealt with thought of him as Good Old Mike was doubtful.

"Of course you'll see him," Gideon said. "We'll arrange something in the next couple of days."

"Wonderful. Well, it's cooling down outside. I'm going to get a jacket."

"Good idea, grab one for me, will you? And look, I know all this stuff is pretty complex and you two must still have some questions. The wine is already starting to mellow me, so if you want, we can talk about it some more over dinner."

John nodded. "Or not," he said agreeably.

CHAPTER 19

On this particular Tuesday evening, the Over-the-Hill Gang was undertaking one of its more strenuous walks, along the up-and-down section of Jersey's North Coast footpath that runs eastward along the cliffs from the old stone Priory Inn. Twenty-five minutes into it, conversation had died off, having given way to huffing and wheezing. Thus, it was no great surprise when Abbott Skinner, not one of the group's most robust members, announced to the evening's hike leader that he was calling it quits.

"I'm not quite feeling myself, Nobby. I believe I'll stop here and make use of this delightful bench. You go ahead without me."

"It's a sorry state we've come to," eighty-nine-year-old Granita Ponsonby-Grenville, possessor of two artificial knees and one artificial hip and a decades-long mainstay of the gang, was heard to grumble, "when a nipper like Skinner there can never make it for half an hour without collapsing."

"Damned right about that," said her eighty-five-year-old husband, Gerald (one artificial knee, one double coronary bypass).

But Nobby, wheezing a bit himself, was more sympathetic. "That's fine, Abbott. You do that, you take it easy. We'll come and collect you on the way back." He gazed out over the water, looking as if he might be thinking of giving up the hike himself and sharing Abbott's bench.

Hurriedly, Abbott plumped himself down onto the very middle of the backless stone bench. He wasn't in the mood for company.

Nobby, correctly reading the message, adjusted his day pack onto his sagging shoulders and got ready to continue on. "It is a splendid spot," he said ruefully.

"It is, indeed."

It was, indeed. From the edge of this natural terrace, only a few yards from the bench, the near-vertical cliffside plummeted thrillingly down three hundred feet to a sea cove littered with shattered boulders.

In the far distance, to the northeast, across roiled, foam-flecked waves, France could be seen, the hazy green bulk of the Cherbourg Peninsula; to the northwest, not quite as far, the isle of Guernsey. And close at hand, rolling away into the mists, was the stupendous northern coastline of Jersey itself, so different from the smooth beaches and tranquil seas of Saint Helier and the south.

Along these cliff tops, the undulating footpath dwindled away like an example of perspective in an art primer, with the straggling Over-the-Hill Gang dwindling along with it. Here and there a startlingly bright billow of purple or buttercup-yellow heather popped impossibly out of the rock bed. Fifty feet below Abbott and twenty yards to his left, on a small ledge that jutted precipitously from the rock face, a few prehistoric-looking Manx sheep nibbled at brown, windblown tufts of grass.

This lovely view was quickly being obscured by fast-moving billows of heavy mist washing in from the north. Already beads of moisture were forming on the near-waterproof Aran wool cardigan and the Irish tweed cap that Abbott had had the foresight to put on for the walk. He pulled the rolled collar of the cardigan all the way up so it covered his ears and jammed his hands into the pockets of his corduroy pants. The dank chill felt good; it seemed to cut down the churning of his stomach.

The view was essentially gone now, other than in moving snapshots between the waves of fog, but Abbott hadn't quit the walk for the view. What he'd told Nobby was true: he wasn't feeling up to it. He'd inadvertently arrived twenty minutes early at the group's assembly point, the Priory Inn's car park. Finding himself at loose ends, he'd dropped in for a prehike pint of Guinness, something he almost never did, and it had been a rotten idea. The first moderately steep downhill grade, supposedly made easier by steps cut into the earth and strengthened with old wooden railroad ties, had begun to make him queasy, and then the even steeper upgrade to this viewpoint had finished the job.

No, that wasn't the whole truth, he admitted. (Abbott Skinner took pride in being honest with himself, even when it hurt.) Oh, the down-then-up path had made him queasy, all right, and it was the pint of stout that had surely been the immediate cause, but there was nothing inadvertent about it. He'd gotten to the inn early on purpose, so he'd have time for that pint. He'd needed it; his mind had been churning. But he would have been better off without it. His mind was still seething, and now he was nauseated on top of it.

He knew it was ridiculous to let Miranda upset him the way she had, but there it was. She just had that . . . knack. She'd always had it. Well, it would be the last time. Any future decisions to be made on behalf of his poor mother would be made by him. Alone. Period. And there was nothing she could do about it. But still . . . it was upsetting. His nervous stomach was playing up in a way it hadn't since his testimony at the Mumbai Global trials. And that had been over a year ago.

One would think, surely, that it was impossible to become a writer, a *published* writer, without a certain level of sensitivity, of human understanding, of what the professors at Kent would have called bilateral interpersonal connectivity. But not Miranda. As always, she was blind to anything that wasn't about her. As always, she was excellent at tearing down, awful at building up, and instinctively, contemptuously dismissive of anyone else's ideas.

She'd gotten even nastier and more immune to reason after Rafe had left that afternoon, and they had come to no agreement, let alone a consensual decision. By the time she too had left, Abbott was downright angry, thoroughly upset, and feeling the first signs of bloating. He had chewed up a handful of Bragg's Medicinal Charcoal Tablets, which had helped enough for him to reach a decision on his own.

On his way to the Priory Inn, without having bothered to speak to Miranda again, he had stopped at a funeral establishment to arrange for his father's exhumation. Not her preferred Collett's Funerals either, but Bonnard & Sons, lest she think she had any sway with him at all.

A tiny scraping sound, a shoe on gravel, made him aware that another hiker was on the little terrace. That annoyed him. He'd stopped here to be by himself, and after all, weren't there a hundred other equally pleasant overlooks? Besides, with this mist, what was there to see? Well, if this interloper was expecting to share the bench, which anybody could see could barely fit two children, he was in for a surprise. Abbott planted his forearm firmly on the day pack beside him, spread his elbows to indicate that neither he nor it would be moving anytime soon, and returned to his uneasy reflections.

Arranging the exhumation on his own had been the right thing to do, and he had left Bonnard feeling righteous and decisive. But then his stomach had started rumbling again, and it was still at it, gurgling, too. Choosing Bonnard had been a childish effort to irritate Miranda, and he knew it—the sort of spiteful thing *she* would do. But why would he want to irritate Miranda? No conceivable good came from that. Why hadn't he just—

This was ridiculous; the stupid fellow was still there. Too cheeky by half, if you asked him. What was he looking at, anyway? The fog? Some foreigner, probably, who hadn't bothered to familiarize himself with British notions of personal space, one of those vulgar, presumptuous Eastern Europeans who seemed to find the islands so attractive.

But beneath his irritation, he felt the first small stirrings of anxiety. His neck prickled. He gathered himself together—surely he was in the right here—and began to turn. "Really, sir—*uh*!"

His head snapped back as he was rocketed forward by a ferocious shove against his shoulders that swept him off the bench and sent him sprawling toward the edge of the promontory. With his hands jammed deep into his trousers pockets, he had no chance to use them to break his fall. Instead, it was his face that scraped painfully along the gravel.

Gasping and shocked—What was happening? Was this a robber, a lunatic?—he tried to push himself up, not easy while fighting to get his hands out of the pockets. He managed to pull them free and roll to his knees before the second thrust came. This was not a shove but a blow, a clean, sharp, heavy blow—a kick?—to the small of his back that drove out of his lungs the little bit of air they still held and shot him sliding onto his face again, this time so close to the rim that his head cleared it. He found himself looking straight down at the cove so far below—the rocks, the surf . . .

Dazed, not understanding, his mouth clogged with dirt and gravel, he tried to twist away from the terrible emptiness. "Why . . . what . . . I don't . . . ?"

When his ankles were grabbed and roughly lifted, he knew that this was the end of him. Utterly drained of strength and will, he could offer no resistance as he was swung bodily around to the edge. His left arm fell limply over it. What was left of his functioning mind shut down. He closed his eyes.

And over he went.

"Well, where is he?" Sarah Partridge queried. "Wasn't he supposed to wait here for us?"

"That is what we said," someone answered. "But we did walk a bit longer than we usually do, you know. He's probably gone back to the inn to wait for us in comfort. That's what I would have done."

"That's what I wish I *had* done," Nobby answered. "I'd be well into my second Foster's by now. And," he added sorrowfully as they began walking again, "my feet would feel like feet again."

A hundred yards farther on, they came to the long, stepped incline that had brought on Abbott's queasiness on the way out. Now, dusty, tired, and thirsty, and beginning to get out of sorts, as they usually did at this stage of their hikes, they had to climb it, all sixty-six steps. At the top, breathless and winded, most of them stopped, supposedly to look back and admire what little was left of the view. (Not the Ponsonby-Grenvilles, who continued to plod forward.)

It was one of the younger members who spotted Abbott. "I say . . ." he began, and then pointed back the way they'd come, but to the base of the cliffs rather than the trail. "Down there, on those rocks . . . wait, wait for the fog to clear . . . wait . . . There! Isn't that . . . my, God, is that . . . ?"

It was. Stricken, the rest of the gang stood looking mutely down on the broken body. A few turned away.

"I'll ring 999," someone said quietly.

The Ponsonby-Grenvilles retraced their steps to rejoin the group. "What's the holdup? What the devil is everyone staring at?" demanded Gerald. The Ponsonby-Grenvilles' eyes were not up to the level of the rest of their parts.

"It's Skinner," Nobby told him. "He's fallen over the edge."

"Not dead?"

"Oh, yes, I'm afraid so."

"What a shame," Granita said. "So young."

And then, after a moment, Gerald said, "I suppose this means we won't be going to the inn?"

"I'm afraid not," Nobby said.

CHAPTER 20

"Good morning, Chief Inspector," Police Constable Thomas Vickery sang out from his cubicle as Clapper came into sight down the corridor, heading toward his own office.

"Morning, Tom," Clapper grumbled. The boy was doing his best and trying to impress, Clapper knew, but this business of being at work this early in the morning was too much of a good thing. It smacked of sucking up. The chief inspector himself preferred to be the first one at his desk—it set an important example for his staff—but he was damned if he was going to get there before seven o'clock. Half the year it was dark before seven, for Pete's sake. What did Vickery have to do besides arranging files that was so important it had to be accomplished before—

But on this particular morning there *was* something. By the time Clapper came abreast of Vickery's cubicle, the young man was on his feet and waiting for him in a state of excitement. "Sir, I've been trying to ring you." He was waving the telephone as if to prove it. "Dr. MacGowan has called twice. He's been in the postmortem room with Inspector Lauder for much of the night. The inspector's gone home to get some sleep, but the doctor's still at it. He's very anxious to have you there, but he was reluctant to contact you until, until, well, not before you—"

"Calm down, Tom. Take a breath. Tell me what's happened." Victor MacGowan was the department's forensic medical director. Greg Lauder was their criminalist.

"Yes, sir." As ordered, Vickery drew a breath. "Abbott Skinner was found dead last night—"

"Stop right there. Let's go. You can tell me on the way."

The postmortem room—the autopsy room—is a wing of the police mortuary, which is located in Jersey General Hospital, one of Saint Helier's largest buildings, a five-story structure that takes up most of a full block on the Parade. If one cuts through the Parade Grounds, which Clapper and Vickery did, it is not much more than a five-minute walk from police headquarters, but it was time enough for Vickery to lay out what he knew.

Abbott's body had been discovered by his hiking group the previous evening at the foot of a ninety-meter cliff along the North Coast footpath, on their way back from a walk that he had opted out of less than an hour before, preferring to wait for their return at one of the viewpoints. This set the time of death as being between 6:10 and 7:15 p.m. To reach the body as quickly as possible, the police had hired a private helicopter from London that, by good fortune, happened to be at Jersey Airport. Lauder, MacGowan, and a couple of crime-scene specialists were sent out to the scene by Superintendent Christie—

As I should have been, Clapper thought. But it wasn't young Vickery's fault, so why bring it up to him?

—and the usual protocol had been followed. The body was then flown to the mortuary, where it had been since four that morning, with Lauder and MacGowan in attendance.

That was the end of what Vickery knew, and it had brought them to the front of the hospital.

"Tom, have you ever attended a preliminary forensic examination?" Clapper asked on a sudden thought.

"Only during training, sir."

"Well, then come along with me. It'll be a good experience for you."

"I'd like that, sir," Vickery said and started for the front entrance.

"No, not that way," Clapper said. "Christ, you haven't even ever been to our mortuary, have you? I'll have to have a talk with Training. But come around this way. There's a separate entrance with a separate roadway. They prefer that corpses not be carried in through the main waiting area."

"Or carried out through it, I suppose," Vickery said. "Not quite the image they prefer to present."

Clapper was astonished. Vickery had a sense of humor.

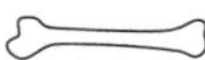

Abbott was lying on one of the two stainless steel autopsy tables, his head propped up with a neck block. His clothes had been cut away and piled on the other table. He was naked and lying on his back, his eyes (surprisingly) still open. He'd been dead between thirteen and fourteen hours, and he looked it, his skin a waxy blue gray, his limbs obviously stiff, and his corneas milky, but the more disturbing aspects of decomposition—the marbling, the bloating, the smells, the skin slippage, the whole ugly panoply of corruption—were still a day away from showing, or would have been if the body hadn't been going into the cooler before the morning was done.

There was plenty of damage, of course: broken teeth, abrasions on elbows, knees, head—all the bodily projections you'd expect to take some abuse on a ninety-meter fall down a rocky cliffside. Except for his face, from which some of the blood had been wiped, he hadn't been cleaned up yet, so there was a lot of dried blood, and his hair was stiff with it. Clapper stole a quick look at Vickery and was pleased to see that he was showing no signs of upset; he'd been afraid the boy might be a fainter.

Dr. MacGowan, a cadaverous, long-jawed man in a green lab coat, got right down to business. "I'm not ready to go on the record with it yet, but between us, I'll tell you right off that we've got ourselves a homicide here."

Clapper's eyebrows went up. Victor MacGowan was a stickler (sometimes frustratingly so) for meticulous analysis, hardly a man given to making rash judgments on the cause of death. And yet here he was, declaring *homicide* mere hours after Abbott had been killed and doing it without benefit of autopsy.

"Explain," Clapper said.

"And not just any simple, run-of-the-mill homicide either. It presents some intriguing questions." He pointed at a white sheet of paper on the other table. "Those little particles you see—"

"Barely. They look like grains of salt."

"Actually, they're grains of stone, and we pulled them out of his face. Five of them."

"Well, he tumbled ninety meters down a rock wall. What's so intriguing about finding rock splinters in his face? Or anywhere else in him, for that matter?"

"It's the splinters themselves. Lauder's already identified them. They're limestone, Mike."

"Yes, and?"

"And the North Coast cliffs are composed of granite, not limestone. Indeed, bits of granite *were* found embedded in his head and a few other places, but in his face—in his forehead and right temple—there were, in addition, these five *limestone* shards. He certainly didn't get them during his fall. Therefore, it would seem obvious he must have scraped his face elsewhere before he came to the cliffs, you agree?"

"Yes, obviously, get on with it."

"The walkers he was with—they swear to a one that his face was unscathed when they left him. Less than an hour later, when they returned, he was dead. With his face full of limestone shards."

"Now that *is* strange," Mike said.

"Not as strange as it gets. Your excellent Inspector Lauder looked into it further in an effort to see where the nearest limestone deposits on the island are."

"And?"

"There aren't any. None in Jersey, none in Guernsey, none in the whole of the Channel Islands."

Clapper scowled. "No, no, we're missing something here, Victor." He picked up one of the shards. He could see now that it was a pale, granular amber. "Is he *sure* these are limestone? They're bloody small."

MacGowan shrugged and crossed his bony arms. "That's what he says. There's a pot of coffee on, Mike. Would you like some?"

Clapper, who knew that until the unit's clerk arrived at nine, the coffee in the pot would be yesterday's, declined. MacGowan, a braver man than he, helped himself to some and gave barely a wince on his first swallow. But then, of course, he was used to it. They stood on either side of the table, looking down at Abbott, trying to make sense of things.

There was the sound of hesitant throat clearing and then, "Sir?"

Clapper had forgotten about Vickery, who had been standing quietly out of the way since they'd arrived.

"Yes, Tom?" he said over his shoulder, still looking at Abbott.

"I believe I can help in this matter of the limestone."

Clapper turned. "Can you, now?"

Vickery cleared his throat again. "During the Occupation, the Germans placed half a dozen resting stops or viewpoints along the path for their soldiers; you know how they love their *Volksmarches*. They found appropriate sites, graded and leveled them, and put down a bed of gravel and a stone bench, or rather their wretched Russian slave laborers did. Well, those viewpoints are still there today, although hardly anyone remembers who built them."

"I didn't know that myself," MacGowan said, "and I've lived here my entire life. I never thought to enquire. I must have used those benches a hundred times."

Clapper was impressed too; it was as long a speech as he'd ever heard Vickery make, but he wasn't seeing the relevance. "Well, that's all very interesting, and if what you're getting at is that the viewpoint Skinner had been sitting at was one of them, I think that's probably so, but where's the significance?"

"The Germans wanted to make everything as much like the trails their homesick soldiers remembered from the Fatherland, and so they paved the viewpoints with gravel as similar as possible to the ones typically used in Germany, and that was—"

"Limestone?" Clapper and MacGowan simultaneously exclaimed.

"Yes, sir, limestone, and so I was thinking—may I continue, Chief Inspector?"

Clapper laughed. "By all means, continue."

"I was thinking that that must mean that Mr. Skinner was injured up above, at the viewpoint itself, before he went over the edge. He must have fallen . . . or been pushed to the ground . . . and scraped his face against the gravel, which suggests even more strongly—"

Clapper's hand went up. He took out his phone and hit a button. "Joyce, is Sergeant Kendry in yet? Good, tell him not to go anywhere, I'm sending Vickery over with some instructions." The phone was slipped back into his jacket pocket. "Tom, I want you to go and see Warren, tell him everything we've been talking about, and have him get those crime-scene people of his out to the site again, and this time I want them to bring their fine-tooth combs and look for . . . well, anything and everything. All right?"

"I'm on my way, Chief."

"Wait, Tom, before you go. The limestone—where did they get it?"

"From Occupied France, sir. They shipped it in."

"Constable," Clapper said, "how is it you've come to know all this?"

"I'm a bit of a history buff, sir. It does come in handy sometimes."

"I'll say so." He slowly shook his head. "We just might turn you into a real copper yet, lad. Blimey, you're looking more like the genuine article every day."

"Thank you, sir," Vickery said, unable to keep back his grin. Without even the semblance of a salute this time, and still grinning, he headed off.

"Smart young man," MacGowan said.

Clapper nodded. "Victor, everything about this certainly *suggests* homicide, but for you to state so baldly that it *is* homicide requires a bit more than we know at this point, wouldn't you say?"

"A bit more than *you* know," MacGowan said with a rare smile that revealed his uneven brown teeth. "I just haven't gotten to it yet."

Going back to Abbott's body, MacGowan used a pair of toothed forceps to trace the track that each piece of gravel had left in Abbott's face and to point out that they grouped themselves into two sets that differed (slightly but unambiguously). While all of them were made in the same general forehead-to-chin direction, the two sets took slightly different paths into his skin. Or, to put it another way, which MacGowan did, Skinner's face had made contact with the ground—which Tom had rightly inferred—from two slightly different directions.

Clapper was nodding along. "He fell twice, then, not just once, before he ever went over the edge."

"Exactly," MacGowan said, "but I think we can go further than that and rule out your young man's 'fallen' to the ground and rule in 'pushed to the ground.' Twice."

Clapper demurred. "I can't see where that came from, Victor. How can we say he didn't suffer a stroke, say, a dizzy spell, an episode of vertigo, and simply fall a couple of times on his own, without any help?"

"Because the idea that a man, even a man struck with a dizzy spell, would fall twice . . . and arise twice . . . within a meter or two of a frightful precipice and still be near enough to the edge to fall over it the third time, is, to put it mildly, unlikely. Wouldn't he have gotten himself farther *away* from that edge after the first fall, and farther still after the second?"

"Well . . ."

"Wouldn't *you* have?"

Clapper allowed that he probably would have.

"And here's something else," MacGowan said. "Those tracks in his face, some of them are ten centimeters long. Would the face of a person suffering a collapse of some sort scrape along the ground for ten centimeters? I think not. I think they suggest strongly that he was *flung* forward . . . twice."

"Yes, they do, but what about this? If he was *flung* forward, wouldn't he have broken the falls with his hands? Shouldn't we have found those shards in his palms too? Or was he wearing gloves?"

"No, no gloves, unless someone removed them after he fell. But that's unlikely. He was at the bottom of a sheer cliff. Not so easy to clamber down there. It took a helicopter for us. Perhaps he was already unconscious when he was thrown down and thus didn't try to break his fall."

"Somebody threw him to the ground unconscious . . . *twice*?" Clapper said dubiously. "Picked him up off the ground and threw him down again?"

"Well, all right, then, I have no answer for that. I'm sure it will come clear."

Or maybe it wouldn't, Clapper thought. As he knew, *knew*, all but the simplest, most primitive murders, no matter how convincingly settled, left behind a loose string or two, an unresolved contradiction, a fact that didn't fit. Good fodder for the conspiracy peddlers; they were still writing books about what or who "really" killed Lincoln, or Princess

Di, or King Tut, for that matter. In all honesty, he doubted that they'd ever find out why Skinner fell onto his face and not his hands.

"Mike," said MacGowan, "I think we'd better get this gentleman in the cooler before any more time passes. I've rung London about getting a postmortem done"—States of Jersey law required that autopsies that were part of criminal investigations be performed by a Home Office pathologist—"but they can't have one here until Friday, the day after tomorrow. I'd like to have the body reasonably fresh for him."

Clapper straightened up. "He's all yours, Victor."

"Thank you. Interesting times, eh?"

CHAPTER 21

Rafe had told them earlier that among their must-sees were tiny Gorey village and its not-so-tiny castle, Mont Orgueil. And, stepping down from the bus in Gorey's harborside parking lot, Gideon and Julie thanked him for it.

Beside the little harbor, filled with bobbing, moored fishing boats and small pleasure craft, "downtown" Gorey itself consisted of a perfect little Victorian waterfront, a single row of small white-stuccoed buildings put up cheek by jowl: pubs, restaurants, cafés, and inns, all of them tidy, conspicuously clean, and inviting. But above this convivial and charming scene, on a rise just behind it, loomed the enormous and somber medieval castle, like a sinister, giant brown spider, hunched and brooding over the defenseless populace below.

So said the guidebook they'd brought with them, but Julie thought otherwise. "It's not 'brooding' or 'sinister' at all. It could hardly be prettier. I feel like we're on a postcard."

"On a bright, sunshiny day like this, yes, definitely," Gideon said, "but imagine it's dark, okay? Ghostly clouds sailing across a pale full moon. Can't you see swarms of scared villagers creeping up that winding path with torches and pitchforks, determined finally to slay the mad doctor and his creature?"

Julie thought about it. "Not really, no. But let's have some coffee before we creep up there ourselves."

"Sounds good."

They were enjoying an unexpected free morning together. Gideon had telephoned Abbott's number at seven forty-five, as instructed, but there had been no answer, and he had left a message. Shortly after that he'd gotten a call from Rafe, who had been most obligingly amazed and warmly grateful for his work on the remains.

"Amazing how much information you dug out of those few bones, just amazing. And what a host of intriguing possibilities it raises. My father met his death from a blow to the head. And Bertrand Peltier, the evasive Bertrand Peltier, was not, after all, accounted for; has never *been* accounted for; has, in fact, disappeared entirely. As has the money. One could be forgiven for assuming that these varied elements might be associated in some way."

"I can see how one could. I'm hoping I can fill in a few more gaps after I get a look at George Skinner."

"Yes, I'm eager to hear what you have to say about him. Have you gotten hold of Abbott yet?"

"Had to leave a message. Haven't heard back from him yet."

"Oh, not to worry," Rafe said. "One thing about Abbott: when he commits to something, he does it. I'm sure he'll be in touch shortly."

But when nine o'clock came and went, and Gideon had tried twice more, his calls still hadn't been returned. "What the heck," he said to Julie over breakfast, "looks as if I have the morning off. Let's go do something interesting."

John, being sensitive to a married couple's need to be by themselves sometimes—one more thing that made the FBI agent such an easy traveling companion—had breakfasted with them and gone off for the day to do his own thing. The Olivers had decided to give Rafe's recommendation of the bus system a try, and that too had worked out well. A short walk to the Liberation Square station, a brief wait for the Number 23, and then a pleasant fifteen-minute ride to Gorey on a bus peopled with chatty, friendly locals.

Apparently, they didn't see much in the way of Americans here, at least not on the busses, because on overhearing them speak, their friendly fellow passengers got a sort of game going trying to guess where they were from. (The winner? South Africa.)

After a couple of caffe lattes in a harbor-front tearoom, they spent an enjoyable couple of hours in the castle, wandering the largely deserted flagstone floors from room to room and taking in the various bits and pieces of architecture and furnishings from its thirteenth-century origin to its takeover by the Nazis. Only when they were leaving did they learn that a map and leaflet had been available to help them find their way around. Lacking them, they had several times wound up climbing the same long, dark stone staircase that they had been on only a few minutes before. In the mood they were in, it added to the fun. They were constantly being surprised by wherever they happened to find themselves.

It was while they were on their way back down to the village, with lunch on their minds, that Gideon's cell phone emitted its unassuming clunk.

"Professor Oliver?" Gideon recognized the tentative voice of Clapper's assistant, the timorous young officer who wasn't cut out to be a policeman. "This is Constable Vickery at the States of Jersey Police. Detective Chief Inspector Clapper wonders if you would find it convenient to come see him at the station."

"You mean right now?"

Julie, listening to his end of the conversation with her arms folded and her head down, sighed. "There goes our nice day together," she said, then added sadly: "It was lovely while it lasted."

"I believe so, sir. If that's convenient," Vickery said. "I don't expect it to take much of your time."

"Sure, I'll be right there . . . well, maybe you'd better give me a little time. I'm out in Gorey with no car. I'll have to find a taxi—"

"I'll have someone come out and collect you, sir. He'll be there in less than ten minutes. You're at the harbor?"

"Yes. Thank you, I'll meet him at the parking lot—the car park."

He put the phone away, a hangdog look on his face. "Dammit, Julie, I'm sorry. Look, it shouldn't take very long, maybe we can still have lunch together. Can you hold out for an hour or so?"

"Sure. In fact, I'll give you an hour and a half. After that, I can't promise."

"Good enough. I'll call you when I get out. I guess Mike's read the report on Roddy. I wonder what the hurry is, though."

"Maybe it's something else. Maybe something's happened."

Something's happened.

The second he walked into Clapper's office, Gideon knew that. This wasn't about any half-century-old case. Not only was Mike's face set and serious, but Rafe was there too, wearing much the same expression.

"What's going on?" Gideon asked as he joined them around the coffee table. "Why am I here?"

"Your meeting with Abbott Skinner is off," Clapper said bluntly. "Skinner's dead."

"*Dead?* How? What happened? When?"

"He fell off a *cliff*, can you believe it?" Rafe said, sounding as if he didn't believe it himself. "Last night, on a walk with his walking group. Ninety meters. Onto a beach full of rocks."

"That's awful."

"Horrible!" Rafe agreed. His usually ruddy face was wan.

Clapper took the next twenty minutes to fill Gideon in on what had happened and the conclusions that he and Dr. MacGowan had reached that morning—with Constable Vickery's very considerable contribution. "Any observations you'd care to make, Gideon?" he asked at the end.

"Me? No, none at all. Do you have leads, any suspects?"

"Oh, yes, we know that his testifying for the Crown in that banking-corruption case—"

"Mumbai Global," Rafe supplied.

"—made him some enemies, and I expect we'll begin there, although . . ." He paused to draw a second Gold Bond from its packet. ". . . my instincts tell me that the solution lies elsewhere."

"Elsewhere?" Rafe's face, which always looked a little surprised, looked more so. "Where? Abbott certainly wasn't the sort of man who went about making enemies, not *that* kind of enemy."

"I don't know, Rafe, but I can't help thinking that we'll find a thread of some kind between the deaths of Abbott and George Skinner."

"That'd be a pretty long thread," Gideon said. "Fifty years long, Mike."

"I'm well aware of that, mate, but I can't seem to get the idea out of my mind. Father murdered. Fifty years later, son murdered—in an island community that for decades has averaged less than three murders a year—less than *one* a year if you exclude the occasional berserker who wakes up one morning and decides to kill his entire family. And I'm supposed to believe that the relationship between George and Abbott Skinner is a mere coincidence? Maybe, but not bloody likely, not in my opinion."

"You just might have a point," Gideon agreed. "What do you think, Rafe?"

"I'm totally at a loss. I'm afraid I'm still a bit stunned at the news. I just learned about it myself an hour ago, from Mike."

"Oh, by the way, Rafe," Clapper said, "we'll need a formal identification of the body for the record. As far as I know, you're as close to him as anyone is, so . . . are you up for the job?"

Rafe made a face. "Well, I wouldn't say I'm chafing at the bit, but yes, of course. Would it be possible to do it now? I'd like to get it over with."

"I don't think that's a good idea. He's still on the table. He hasn't been altogether cleaned up yet. Blood and things, you know. It'd be better if you wait until tomorrow morning. It'll be a good deal less unpleasant."

"Tomorrow, then," Rafe said. "Oh, dear me."

"I suppose that's it for his father's exhumation, then," said Gideon, to whom the thought had just occurred.

"Ah, yes, that's right, isn't it?" said Rafe. "I hadn't thought about that. I don't really see how—"

"No, it's still in the works," Clapper said. "Health was in touch with me last evening. It turns out that Abbott stopped in at Bonnard and Sons late in the afternoon and submitted the request, along with the papers you'd prepared for him."

Rafe blinked. "No! That's astonishing. I can't believe he actually convinced Miranda." He smiled softly. "Either that, or he didn't tell her about it—that's the more likely supposition, now that I think about it. So the exhumation will move forward after all, Mike?"

"With alacrity. Health has already granted the permit. It allows them to begin excavating anytime now. They'll have the body at the mortuary and all ready for Gideon tomorrow morning, they say."

"Already? Unbelievable. Here I am, a feared and powerful senator, and I have never even once gotten them to put through anything—*anything*—in under a week. However did you do it?"

Mike shrugged. "Usual way. Told 'em I'd have 'em killed if they didn't cooperate."

"Now there's an idea for you. I'll have to try it myself next time. Gideon, the papers I prepared for Abbott give you permission to perform whatever procedures you deem necessary. Bonnard will, er, rearrange the remains in a tasteful fashion afterward."

"Good."

"They will simply deliver the casket to the Bonnard mortuary and open it for you. The body itself they will leave untouched. Whatever tools you need will be available to you there. As for cleaning up the body if necessary, and that sort of thing, don't you know, I assumed they would best be done by yourself, someone who knows what he's doing. If you prefer, though, we can have them—"

"No, you're right. Better if I do it. I think I'd better be there for the exhumation itself too."

"Certainly. I'll find out when it'll take place and let you know, and I'll see that they expect you, but—out of curiosity—why would you want to be there for that?"

"Well, Skinner went into the ground almost fifty years ago, and I imagine they weren't preparing concrete vaults for coffins back then."

"I'm sure we weren't."

"And I imagine it was a wooden coffin?"

"I suppose it must have been."

"Then there's a good chance that it's rotted away by now and melded back with the earth. If so, they'll just have to dig up the dirt where it'd been. You can see the casket outlines because the dirt will be a different color. But then getting the body free of the soil is a tricky proposition, easy to make a mistake and stick a spade through a pelvis or a skull, so it'd just be a good idea for me to be on hand to keep an eye on things."

"Really. I had no idea."

"Oh, it happens, believe me. But if the coffin's still holding together, I'll just leave them to it and wait till tomorrow morning to get started."

Clapper, who had been growing restless, ground out his cigarette and stood up. "It's well past lunch hour, my friends. There's a decent fish-and-chips shop a few blocks from here, near Cenotaph Square. A hole-in-the-wall sort of place, but the food's good. Never gotten ptomaine poisoning there, any road. Yet." He clapped his hands. "So—anyone else fancy a nosh?"

Gideon, who'd been heading for lunch in Gorey when Constable Vickery had called an hour before, readily agreed to one. "Let me give Julie a call, though. What's the name of this place? Maybe she can join us. I know she'd like the chance to see you, Mike."

"It's Sully's. And I'd love to see her too."

Gideon called her while they were on their way to the restaurant. She was back in Saint Helier when he reached her, having just gotten off the bus in Liberation Square, only a few minutes away. And no, she hadn't yet had lunch. He told her about Sully's and gave her a quick rundown on Abbott.

Clapper and Rafe had moved a little ahead while he spoke with her, and when he caught up to them, Rafe was shaking his head. "I don't know, a fish-and-chips shop. I haven't been in one in years, decades, perhaps. I wouldn't want my crowd to hear about it."

Clapper patted his paunch, which Gideon now noticed was somewhat more prominent than it had been a couple of years ago. "Well, I'll promise not to tell anyone," Clapper said, "if you'll promise not to tell Millie."

CHAPTER 22

Captain Sully's Fish and Chips—*Quality and Tradition. (Burgers, Chicken, and Kebabs Too! Just Try 'Em!)*—was about as hole-in-the-wall as they came, a tiny, not overly clean place with a one-man counter where orders were placed. Behind the counter, and separated from it by the usual windowed partition, was a small kitchen, from which came the sounds of rap music and the sizzling and spattering of deep-frying. There was room for only four cramped booths, all of which were occupied. On the floor were discarded fish wrappers printed to look like old newspapers, a bent plastic fork, and a few gummy-looking spots that might have been anything before they were stepped on and ground into the linoleum.

A despairing look came into Rafe's eyes as he looked around. "Oh, dear," he said softly.

"Dine in or takeaway?" was the counterman's greeting. A skinny, dark-skinned man with a pitted face, he wore a backward baseball cap and a waist-tied apron that had seen a lot of hand wiping since the last time it had been washed. His eyes had yet to rise from a receipt pad on which he was calculating sums with a pencil.

"Dine in, if we can, please, Sully," Clapper said.

Sully looked up from his pad with mock alarm. "Cheese it, the coppers!" he cried. "I confess, Officer, it was me what done it. Please don't hit me no more." He spoke with an arresting combination of lilting Caribbean and authentic if overcooked Cockney.

Clapper smiled tolerantly. "Sully does enjoy his little jokes," he told the others. "Lucky for him, his chips can't be beat. So, landlord, are we going to be able to find a table, or should we get takeaway and go to the park?"

"No problem, guv. Oy! Baz!" he called to one of the booths, which had two men and a woman in it chatting over three empty plastic hamburger baskets. "Time for you lot to clear out, wouldn't you say?"

The occupants kept talking, but one of them responded with a noncommittal, over-the-shoulder wave.

"Does that mean they'll be leaving?" Gideon asked Rafe.

"I have no idea. It seemed rather dismissive to me. Do you think we might be in luck, though? That they'll refuse to leave?"

Sully, who heard the comment and took it as a joke, disabused him of his wishful thinking. "Not to worry, guv, they'll be on their way. Now, what'll it be?"

Clapper recommended the deluxe cod and chips with mushy peas, and the others followed his suggestion, although Rafe hesitated over the mushy peas before going along with them. "In for a penny," he said, and then, looking up at the sound of chairs scraping over gritty linoleum, his face fell. "Oh, dear, there they go."

"Chalky," Sully yelled back to the kitchen, "give number three a wipe, will you? It'll be ready in a minute," he told Clapper and the others. "You can collect your drinks meantime."

They were at the cooler, choosing their bottled soft drinks, when Julie came in.

Clapper lit up on seeing her, and the two of them hugged and expressed delight. "And how is Madeleine?" Julie asked.

"Millie's just fine. She's back in Saint Mary's right now. Her daughter's had twins, and Millie's there helping out until she's back on her feet. She'll feel terrible to have missed you."

Julie fixed him with a sternly raised eyebrow. "Michael, you better tell me you've made an honest woman of that lovely lady by now."

Clapper laughed. "As a matter of fact, I have. Proud to say she's been the missus since January."

By the time Julie and Gideon offered congratulations and best wishes, their table was ready. They walked to it, drinks in hand, Rafe hanging back a bit, as if hoping for a last-minute reprieve.

"What I keep wondering about," Clapper said to Gideon as they sat down, "is this matter of his body having been moved."

But Gideon heard not a word. He was deep in his own thoughts, and they were not happy ones. Now that it was so near, the examination of George Skinner's exhumed corpse, the analysis he'd so cavalierly volunteered to undertake, was preying on his mind. For, in truth, the celebrated Skeleton Detective was about as squeamish as they came. He had fallen into forensics more or less accidentally, as a result of his expertise in osteology. But he remained at heart a researcher. It was early man and the even earlier hominids that had been, and remained, his chief research interests, and things like maggots or oozing bodily fluids or torn and mutilated flesh or stomach-churning smells or any smells at all weren't things you ran into when dealing with a two-and-a-half-million-year-old *Paranthropus aethiopicus* skull.

Naturally, in his work with law enforcement he had seen, handled, and smelled his fair share of these nastinesses, but unlike most of his forensic colleagues, he'd never grown used to them. Essentially, he was the same wuss he'd been the first time he'd been called into the morgue at San Francisco's Hall of Justice for his views on a fresh body with a truly massive head wound. He'd promptly turned from the autopsy table and thrown up into the nearest stainless steel sink. The episode had made him mildly famous in the field even before his remarkable abilities had made him a true celebrity.

He no longer threw up at massive head wounds or the like, but that was about all the progress he could claim. Things that other forensic anthropologists and pathologists wouldn't bat an eye at still turned his stomach, and among them were exhumed corpses. George Skinner had been there for almost fifty years, so (thank God) at least he'd be well past the horrific early stages of decomposition, but neither would he be anything to look forward to, not to someone like Gideon. Most likely, what was left at this point would be a shrunken, discolored almost-skeleton in a stained, moldy suit. Decayed, dried-out skin and tendons would be stretched across an eyeless, noseless, lipless "face." Bony fingers would protrude from filthy, grave-brown sleeves. Rotting—

He became aware that someone had asked him something. Clapper, had it been?

"Sorry, Mike, did you say something? I was a million miles away."

"At least. What I said was that I'm having a hard time making sense of his body having been moved. Something wonky there."

"His body was moved?"

"According to you, it was."

"According to *me*?" Gideon was still a million miles away. Once focused on something, it could be hard to shake him loose. Was Clapper still talking about Abbott Skinner? "How would I even—"

"Time out, gentlemen," Julie said. "Gideon, I think there's been a slight miscommunication here. Mike's talking about your report on Roddy Carlisle."

"Roddy Carlisle?" Gideon said thickly. He'd forgotten that more or less as an afterthought prompted by John, he had e-mailed a copy of his report to Clapper the previous evening.

"Pater," Rafe supplied somewhat absently. He was busy with something else, having wadded up a couple of the paper towels that served as napkins, and now, tongue between his teeth, going after some of the greasier spots that Chalky had missed. "Move your elbow, Mike, there's a good fellow."

Clapper moved his elbow. "Right," he said to Gideon, "Rafe's father. Now, when you declare that the body was moved—"

"Hold it, I didn't *declare* the body was moved, I said it was the only explanation I could think of."

"—because the little fishies'd been chewing on it—"

"No, I didn't say fishes, I—"

"Well, what the hell *did* you say? D'you mind telling me that?" The bottle of nonalcoholic ginger beer he'd been drinking from was set down on the table with a thump, prompting Rafe to apply the paper toweling to the resulting spatter.

"All right, gents, missus, here we are," said Sully, showing up with a tray of "newspaper"-lined red plastic baskets containing their lunches and setting it down in the center of the table, first shoving aside a collection of salt, pepper, and malt-vinegar bottles. "Enjoy."

"Thank you, looks delicious," Julie told him. The others murmured their agreement, poured on the condiments, and got down to eating, mostly with their fingers. All except Rafe, who was using the tines of his fork to gingerly probe the glistening mound of mushy peas (essentially, a thick purée of mashed peas) as if making sure it wasn't alive. "Damned stuff looks radioactive," he mumbled, referring to its characteristic and, indeed, slightly alarming glaucous-green color.

"What I *said*," Gideon said tersely in response to Clapper's earlier question, "first of all, was that it was crustaceans, not fish, that—"

"Oh, pardon me. Well, now, that changes everything, don't it?"

As Gideon now recalled, Clapper's irritation was not hard to provoke. But then neither was Gideon's.

"I *declared*," he declared, "that the nicks and scratches on the bones were made by crustaceans, and crustaceans aren't known to live in tar. Therefore, I *conjectured* that the body must have been elsewhere for some time before it wound up in the tar pits, in water somewhere, maybe a river—"

"No rivers in Jersey," Rafe pointed out.

"All right, a stream—"

"No streams."

Gideon rolled his eyes, then hung his head. "Will you guys give me a break, please? You have any ponds, maybe? How about puddles, Rafe? I'll settle for puddles."

"We do. Some of both. Not many of the former."

"Fine. Thank you. A pond then. But whatever it was, it was there long enough for the crabs to get down to the bones and start chewing on the damn things." He winced. "Rafe, I'm sorry—"

"And what conceivable reason," Clapper said, "do you *conjecture* anyone could possibly have for taking a bloody pile of old bones—sorry, Rafe, dammit—and dumping them into a tar pit? A body, I could understand, but bones? I can think of a hundred better, easier ways of getting rid of that kind of evidence. Me, I'd pound them to dust and flush them down the loo."

Gideon smiled. "Me too, the old crush-and-flush, that's what I'd do too. But the fact is, they were found in the pitch pond, and all I was trying to do was come up with a theory, a hypothesis, rather, of what could account for their showing signs of crustacean predation. If you have a better one, I'm all ears. But until then—Julie, are you trying to say something?"

"Only for the last five minutes," she said. "Honestly, when you two get going . . . well, never mind. What I'm trying to tell you is that I *do* have another theory, well, a possibility."

Both men turned their attention to her, as did Rafe.

"Now, don't laugh. I admit, it's a little, um, far out, but then so is the whole idea of someone's dumping bones into a tar pit."

"I'll stipulate to that," Gideon said.

"Okay, then." She cleared her throat. "It occurred to me, Rafe, that maybe your father's remains were never moved at all, that they'd been right there all along, right from the moment he was killed."

"But that crab-scavenging—" Gideon began at the same time that Rafe said, "No, that's not—"

"Now give me a chance," Julie said. "At least let me get it out before you start tearing it apart. Just go ahead and eat your lunch and listen for a minute. The thing is, I've been spending some time on the web, researching pitch ponds, and I learned a few interesting things."

The great tar pits of the world, she informed them—La Brea, Carpinteria, one in Venezuela, one in Azerbaijan, a couple in Iran—had been there for millennia and had changed little since they were first discovered. Lesser pitch deposits, like the Carlisle pits, were more common but far more inconsistent. Much like small freshwater ponds, they came and they went. The flow could last decades, or it could peter out a month after first bubbling up from its underground deposit. It could suddenly double or triple in volume one week and go right down to its former level, or dry up altogether, the next.

While she was speaking, she had brought out her iPad mini and was tapping something in. "One of the articles I read really got me thinking. . . . Okay, here. Listen to this:

"'For example, the Pitlochry Tar Pits, near the Scottish village of that name, began in 1924 as an intermittent incursion of bitumen into an old millpond. Within a year, the water in the pond had been almost totally replaced by the tar. Commercial exploitation began and continued into the 1950s, when the tar flow markedly diminished. Extraction ceased in 1954, only to start again in 1970, when the flow of bitumen reappeared in volume so great that the original pit soon overflowed its banks, threatening surrounding farmland and making extraction of the additional bitumen impossible. A channel was then dug from the original pond to a nearby mudflat, where the overflow could be contained and from which it could be extracted. Even this was not sufficient, and soon, two other low-lying areas were similarly utilized. By 1979, there were a total of four connected pits, producing more than—'

"Well, that's enough," she said, flipping down the tablet's cover. "Rafe, I'm sure you can see what I'm getting at. Could I possibly be on the right track?"

"My dear, I'm sorry, but if you're suggesting that our pond may have been freshwater in 1964, when my father was killed, I have to say it wasn't the case. It may well have been freshwater at some time in the distant past—I wouldn't know that—but by 1964 it had been a functioning tar pit for almost a hundred years. And so it remained until Mother turned it into a freshwater pond a decade later." He offered an apologetic smile. "Sorry."

"Yes, I know about all that," Julie said. She was the only one who hadn't yet gotten to her food. She was getting a little frustrated, and Gideon would have liked to step in and give her a hand getting her point across, but he didn't know exactly what it was, and given what Rafe had said, that it could possibly be valid. In 1964, the pond was filled with tar, and had been since the 1870s. End of argument.

But not for Julie. "Let me try again," she said. "Rafe, look, you remember you told us that the pond is shaped like a pair of glasses? A sort of double pond with a channel tying them together?"

"Certainly. I don't know that I'd call it a channel, though. More like a—"

"But you did call it a channel," Gideon said, and when he did, he felt a little glimmer of light break through. He still wouldn't have been able to say exactly what Julie was getting at, but he had the sense of its being on the tip of his tongue.

"Did I?" Rafe said. "Well, all right, 'channel' is good enough, although it makes it sound a little . . . industrial, like something dug by man, whereas it's quite natural and attractive, a gently curving—"

"But that's my point," Julie broke in. "I'm suggesting that maybe it *was* dug by man. What if . . ."

What if, she went on, the original pitch deposit had been a tar *pit*—singular, not plural—in the 1870s, and that it consisted of only one of the two currently linked ponds, the larger one, say, while the other one, unconnected, was still a small freshwater pond in 1964. *And what if*, sometime between 1964 and 1969, when the bones were discovered, the flow in the original pit had outgrown its confines, and a curving, natural-looking channel—the "nosepiece" of the spectacles—had been dug to connect it to the smaller pond. *And what if*, by 1969, the water in that pond had been totally replaced by the incoming tar so—

She stopped when she became aware of Rafe slowly, gently shaking his head.

"Julie, it just won't hold water. Don't you think I would know if it had only recently become filled with tar?"

"I'm not sure about that, Rafe. *How* would you know?"

"Julie, I've lived there all my life. I grew up there. I live there now. I used to sail toy boats in that pond. True, I was only a small child at the time—"

"Did your mother ever say to you that that second pond had been a tar pit all along, before she turned it into a freshwater pond?"

"Well, no, not in so many words, not that I remember . . ."

"Read it in the newspaper? See some kind of official land record? Hear—"

"I don't know. Who can remember how they came to know everything they know? One simply knows, that's all."

Julie smiled. "A lot of the things that one simply knows aren't necessarily true."

"That's so, but in the absence of evidence to the contrary, one can assume . . ." He trailed off, apparently disconcerted at hearing himself use the word *assume*. For a few seconds he sat there, chewing his lip, and then he said, "You know, you're right. How *do* I know that? *Do* I really know it?"

Score one for Julie, Gideon thought. Maybe she did have something after all.

Rafe obviously thought so too, but only for a few seconds. "No wait, even if it *was* a water pond at that time, there's no way a body could have remained in it, unseen. It's very small—perhaps twelve meters in diameter—and quite shallow. Surely, the workers would have seen it when they were digging the channel, if not before—*if* they dug the channel. And it's very close to the manor as well. You almost look straight down at it from the upper floor. You couldn't have a body in there without its being—"

"Tom, yes," Clapper was saying into his cell phone. "I need you to do something for me. Get hold of Andy Scate at Environment and ask to see any record they have—permissions, applications, letters—pertaining to the Carlisle Tar Pits in the years 1964 to 1969. Then e-mail them to me. Yes, all of them, as many as there are. What? No, next January. Of *course* now." He put away his phone, shaking his head and muttering to himself: "Do I want it now . . ."

Like the others, he returned to his rapidly cooling fish-and-chips. "Let's put that on hold until we hear back," he said.

They were just finishing up when his cell phone pinged. He studied the screen for a few seconds and then looked up. "I've heard back from Tom—the boy is quick, I'll give him that. Listen to this. It's from a 1966 approval for a construction project granted to Inter-Island Construction by what was then the Land Use Department.

"'In summation, we conclude that Inter-Island's construction of a lined, open, seven-meter channel, at no place more than one meter in depth, between the foredescribed tar pit on the Carlisle property and a sunken, marshy area from one to two meters deep and approximately ten by ten meters in size, for the purpose of transferring excess tar flow, would have no impact on the area's environment or ecology, other than the elimination of the marsh, which was designated in 1960 and 1963 as a source of mosquito infestation. Inter-Island Construction has given us the results of a geological study that concludes that the subject marshy area and the channel itself will be sufficient to hold overflow for the foreseeable future. Approval is hereby granted.'"

Gideon had to restrain himself from smacking the table. "Good show, Julie, you were right! That takes care of the weirdest question of all right there: Who moved those bones and why? *Nobody* moved them. That tar pit was where Roddy Carlisle's body was right from the start, except that it was a marsh at the time—which was when the crabs did their job."

"And the reason no one saw him there," Rafe contributed, now equally pumped up, "was that what my distressingly feeble memory reconstructed as a clear freshwater pond was in actuality a marshy bog in which you probably could have hidden a cow. Julie, you really are quite brilliant."

"Thank you, Rafe, but all I did—"

Unlike Gideon, Clapper failed to restrain himself and did whack the table, but not with pleasure. He was angry. "And nowhere, dammit, *nowhere* in the case files, is there any mention of this. As far as the record is concerned, it had never been anything but a tar pit. Inexcusable!"

"Oh, aren't you being a little hard on them, Mike?" Rafe said. "The Carlisle Tar Pits' history couldn't have been very widely known at the time. Nobody ever heard of them *until* those bones were found. I'm sure the police—"

"Made a total cock-up of it," Mike barked. "Obviously, the force bollixed the entire thing from first to last." He took a last, long drag on the cigarette he'd lit about two minutes earlier—the burning end of the paper sizzled and sparked—and let the smoke out with what was essentially a sigh. "I'm going to reactivate the case."

"That's good, Mike," Gideon said, "but you don't look too happy about it."

Clapper slowly lowered his gaze to fix Gideon with a baleful glare. "My cup was already overflowing, thank you very much. Another personnel-devouring homicide case is *not* what I was in need of, let alone a 'new' one that's as cold as cold can be." He shook his head. "I should have known this was going to happen the minute you came through my door. I *did* know. After all, I went through it with you before, didn't I? But then I always was a slow learner."

"Hey, I just say what I find," Gideon said. "If you didn't want to know the facts, you shouldn't have asked me, Mike."

"I *didn't* ask you."

"Whatever." Gideon laughed and sat back. Life was good.

Five minutes later, maybe not so good. "Considering that it's now a formal investigation," Clapper said to Gideon, with perhaps the slightest gleam of tit for tat, "I'd better have a more thorough report from you on those bones. Something that could be used in court if it comes to that. We'll pay whatever your usual fee is, of course. Wouldn't want to take advantage."

Gideon wilted. Working on skeletal material, trying to tease information from it about the departed, was unfailingly engrossing, more like adventure than work. Writing it up to courtroom-evidence levels, on the other hand, was tedious, time-consuming, and boring. "Forget the fee, Mike. I assume you'll want to take possession of the bone fragments themselves as well?"

"I do, yes. Rafe, technically, they're your property. Do you have any objections?"

"Of course not, none whatsoever."

"When would you want the report, Mike?" Gideon asked.

"Since you'll be here only a day or two longer, I'd say the sooner the better, wouldn't you? Tomorrow morning? And you can bring the fragments with you when you deliver it."

"Well, it'll take a few hours to write up. And I'm not sure, but I might have to find some equipment somewhere: a pair of osteometric spreading calipers—"

"I'm sure that between our laboratory and the hospital, whatever you need can be found. Just let our resourceful PC Vickery know, and he'll get it for you."

A glum look passed between Julie and Gideon. There went their plans for a morning jaunt to the Durrell Wildlife Park, the famed habitat—emphatically not a "zoo"—for the world's endangered species.

"That's fine, Mike. I'll get going on it early and have it for you by the end of the morning." He spoke with resigned good humor. He'd brought it on himself, after all.

CHAPTER 23

"States of Jersey Police. How may I help you?"

"Is this where I report a robbery?"

"One moment, please."

Four or five seconds of clicks and buzzes followed, and then another human voice came on: "Constable Gray speaking."

"I want to report a robbery."

"And your name, please, sir?"

"Emil Bonnard."

A moment's pause. "That would be Emil Bonnard of Bonnard and Sons?"

"Yes, it would."

"Go ahead, sir."

"Yes. Well . . . what would you like to know?"

"You said a robbery?"

"Yes. Well, a theft, I suppose would be the correct term."

"And what was taken?"

"My coffin van."

"Your, er . . ."

"Coffin van, that's right."

"I see. And you're positive it's been stolen?"

"Positive. Less than an hour ago. My driver came in to report, and when we went out to the car park, where he'd left it, it wasn't there. He'd left the key in it, unfortunately."

"And you're certain that another of your employees didn't—"

"Yes, I'm certain. The vehicles are not simply there for the taking. We have procedures."

"I see. And the license plate?"

"J47058."

"And this would be one of your blue vans, with 'Bonnard and Sons' on the side, and the bouquet, and so forth?"

"Indeed not," said Bonnard, sounding aggrieved. "Those are our funeral vans. This was our coffin van. Plain black. One wouldn't *advertise* on a coffin van."

"No, of course not."

"That would be vulgar in the extreme. Offensive to people's sensibilities."

"Yes, I can see that."

"Also the coffin that was in the van."

"Sorry?"

"The coffin that was in the van at the time. That's gone too. Well, I mean, it *would* be, wouldn't it?" He uttered a one-note laugh. Policemen were so dumb.

"I see. Yes, certainly it would, sir." *Screw you too, sir.*

"Also the body that was inside the coffin."

"The body that . . . So your van would have been on its way to the cemetery?"

"No, it was coming *from* the cemetery."

"Ah . . . *from* the cemetery."

"Yes, *from* the cemetery. With the remains of a corpse that had been buried fifty years ago. Constable, I've been in business twenty years, and nothing like this has ever happened to me before."

Or to anybody else, odds were. Gray laid down his pen. "Perhaps it would be better if you just carried on in your own words, sir."

Ten minutes later, after promising that someone would very shortly be out to the funeral home, he replaced the telephone in its cradle, shaking his head.

"Teddy," he said to the gray-haired fellow officer whose desk abutted his so that they faced one another. "I believe I just got one that even you have never run into before."

"Gideon, this is Rafe."

"Yes, Rafe. Are we still on for tonight? I know how upsetting Abbott's death—"

"Certainly we're still on. I'm looking forward to it, but that isn't what I'm ringing you about. We've had a bit of a problem with the exhumation."

"Problem?" Gideon was surprised. After lunch at Sully's, he'd swung by the cemetery to see if they'd started yet and found the two-man crew well along and obviously proficient in their task. The excavation had already been dug, with the backhoe that had done the heavy work of getting the dirt out standing nearby, ready to turn around and put it back in with its other end. The coffin had been hauled up and now lay on a tarpaulin spread on the grass. The casket's wood had held up well, he was glad to see. It would make things easier. After a few minutes, he had left it to the workmen and gone back to the hotel. "They were doing fine when I left, Rafe. They were about to winch it up and load it in the van."

"And they did winch it up. And they did load it into the van. And then they drove the van to Bonnard and Sons."

"I sense a punch line coming," Gideon said.

"Gideon, someone *stole* the bloody thing. Right out of Bonnard's private car park."

"Are you serious? With the coffin inside?"

"With the coffin inside. Mike just rang me to tell me about it, and he asked me to let you know."

"But that's . . . Why would anyone steal a coffin?"

"Oh, I doubt that the coffin had anything to do with it. I suspect the wrong sort of person simply happened by at the wrong moment. The key was in the ignition, opportunity presented itself, and he made off with it, probably to England, where he'll have it modified—repainted, and so on—and then sold illegally. He certainly has a rude surprise coming when he opens it up."

"A van parked in a funeral home parking lot with its key still in the ignition, and some random thief just *happens* by and steals it with no idea of what it is or what's inside? Does that strike you as likely?"

"No, not at all, but what other explanation could there be?"

"How about this?" Gideon said after a moment's consideration. "Maybe it was taken because somebody didn't want me to see George's body."

"You mean, to keep you from finding out . . . well, whatever it was that you would have found out?"

"Yes."

"Well, it's a thought," Rafe agreed. "After all, look at what you came up with from a few scant fragments from the tar pit. Who knows what you'd find on a whole body? On the other hand, who would be out there now who'd be worried about what might come from investigating a 1964 murder?"

"Well—"

"And how would they know what's in your report?"

"Well—"

"And how would they know that the reason it was being exhumed was so that you could examine it? I haven't told anyone. The only people who knew about it were you and Mike and me."

"No, there's Abbott too."

"Why would Abbott want to take it? He'd just approved the exhumation. Besides, he was killed last night, long before the van was stolen."

"But we don't know who he might have told," Gideon said, "and then there's the funeral director, and the guys that did the digging—"

"Oh, I doubt very much that they knew what the purpose was," said Rafe. "In any case, none of them could have been more than children in 1964, so they . . . Oh, my God. There *is* someone else."

"Miranda the Dreadful," Gideon breathed into the highly pregnant silence. "Bertrand Peltier's wife. You said she was dead set against doing the exhumation, but you didn't know why. Well, maybe she was protecting her husband, maybe she knew he was the killer, and maybe she thought there was something there that might . . ." He stopped, sensing something coming from Rafe.

"Not Miranda," Rafe said dreamily. "*Peltier* himself. Bertrand Peltier."

"How would Peltier know about it?" Gideon asked. "We have no idea where he is, or even if he's still alive."

"Oh, but I believe he is, and I believe I do know where he is. He's Miranda's boyfriend—Randy Campion!" Rafe's voice had spiked up with elation. "Ha-ha! How could I have failed to see it?"

"Randy who? Miranda the Dreadful has a *boyfriend*?"

Rafe briefly filled him in on Campion. For most of the two years Randy had been around, he told him, Rafe had thought of him as no more than the latest in Miranda's parade of live-in male scroungers, although by far the longest lasting. But since running into him in the street after his visit with Abbott, a number of things had begun to jump out, and they had just now fallen into place.

Item: Randy referred to Miranda as "Mandy," a privilege no one else had been granted for fifty years. And what had been Peltier's pet name for her in the old days? Yes, "Mandy." As far as Rafe knew, only her mother and Peltier had ever gotten away with that. Rafe himself had gotten a tongue-lashing he still remembered for calling her Aunty Mandy when he was little more than a toddler.

Item: She called him "Randy." Wasn't that a nickname for Bertrand as well as Randall? Wasn't it possible that they'd chosen the fake name "Randall" for him instead of some other name, for fear that she might slip up and call him by the old nickname, thus arousing suspicion that he might, after all, be Peltier? This way, being overheard calling him "Randy" was no problem.

Item: Miranda had never accepted the bone fragments that were supposed to be Peltier's, saying she refused to believe he was dead. Wasn't it possible that it was because she *knew* he wasn't dead?

It was a thought Gideon had had too, but he still had reservations. "I don't know, Rafe. Didn't you tell us she got hysterical when she saw the bones? Ran screaming from the police station? That doesn't sound like someone who knew he was still alive."

"Well, that's the way the file describes it, but you have to consider that she might have been putting on a show—she's certainly good enough at it now."

Without giving Gideon a chance to respond, he went on. "Item—and this is the one least subject to proof, because it's a personal feeling, but for me it's the most convincing thing of all. The man exhibits a level of comfort, almost of entitlement, about his living off Miranda that's miles—*miles*—above anything the others have shown. And, for all I can tell, she lets him get away with it. Believe me, *no one* gets along that well with Miranda. No, I'm *sure* I'm right! Well, what do you think?"

"I think you might—"

"And consider this: Mike was looking for some sort of connection between Abbott's murder and what happened in 1964. Well, here it is!

Bertrand Peltier, deeply involved in what happened then, and now, shortly before Abbott, George Skinner's son, is killed, here he is—what do you know about that—back on the scene. Gideon, it's obvious!"

"Yes, Rafe, I hear you, and there might very well be something to it—"

But Rafe was too excited to listen. "Gideon, I'd better ring off. I need to tell Mike about this—"

"Wait, before you hang up—back to the van for a minute? Does Mike have any kind of lead on it?"

"Van? Oh, the van, yes. All I know is that he does have his people on the alert for it, but frankly, if it's found its way into a covered garage or some other hideaway, I don't see much chance of—"

"—my getting a look at it in these next couple of days," Gideon said.

"I'm afraid not," Rafe said.

Gideon sighed. "Damn," he said to Rafe.

Whew, he said to himself.

CHAPTER 24

Not even three hours since Clapper had decided on reopening the old Skinner-Carlisle case, and already he was ruing his decision. The flipping thing was turning into a full-time job . . . but, he had to admit, one that had caught his interest. For the first time, he found himself truly believing that those ancient crimes might not only be solvable but might actually result in a prosecution. He'd been involved in cold cases before, but *fifty years*? If they succeeded, it might be a world record.

Such were his thoughts on hanging up after Rafe's phone call. Wouldn't it be something if Rafe was right? If the prime suspect in the murders of Roderick Carlisle and George Skinner was right here under their noses? And the *only* suspect in the embezzlement of nearly a million pounds from Carlisle Paving and Road Construction? And certainly a "person of interest" in the death of Abbott Skinner as well, although neither Clapper nor Rafe could think of a motive. Abbott had still been in his mother's womb in 1964 when his father and Roddy Carlisle had been killed and Peltier had vanished. Where was the thread that tied him to Abbott?

And would Peltier really have the nerve to come back, even after all that time, protected only by a new mustache, a false name, and fifty years of aging, and to move about as openly as Rafe claimed he did? Well, yes, he just might, if, perchance, he didn't see much downside to being found out; if for example, he was unaware that in 1999, some thirty-five years after he left, Jersey criminal law was amended to eliminate statutes of limitation—not only for capital crimes but for all crimes. If he thought he was home scot-free, he was seriously wrong. He was still on the hook for both murder and embezzlement.

For the first time since transferring to Jersey, Clapper could feel the old, familiar excitement of the hunt building in him. "Vickery," he said in a voice only slightly louder than his normal speech, and in three seconds Constable Vickery was standing at attention just inside the doorway, having shot from his cubicle a few yards down the hall. Clapper couldn't help laughing. Any faster and he would have skidded to a stop with smoke coming from his heels, like a character in a movie cartoon.

"Sir?"

"Two things, Tom. First, I'll need you to see what record we might have of a gent named Randall Campion. He's been here two years, I believe, having come from England. Not only any interactions he may have had with the police, but any record at all—work permit, driving license, car registration, passport record, and so on. All right?"

"Er, sir, you do know . . . travelers from England don't need passports to—"

"Exactly right, my mistake. Well, then, get whatever you can."

"Yes, sir, I'll get right to it and let you know at once." He stopped in midturn. "You said two things?"

"Yes, I want you to check my calendar and find time for us to meet next Monday or Tuesday. A half hour. If my schedule doesn't allow it, then arrange it for before working hours."

"Er . . . just us two, Chief Inspector?"

"Just us. And no need for that look of concern, son. There's nothing wrong, I promise."

Quite the contrary, in fact, Clapper thought as Vickery left. The reason he wanted to talk to the young man was to make sure he intended to sit for the sergeant's exam coming up in a couple of months. Vickery's sterling performance at the morgue had convinced him that he'd been underestimating the boy's potential for police work—probably because Vickery's natural diffidence and shyness were so at odds with Clapper's own blunt personality. But there was more than one way to do good police work, and Clapper was now of the opinion that Vickery not only had what it took to be a good cop but could make a first-rate supervisor too. The boy did need coaching in a few minor matters—self-confidence, deportment—and Clapper was ready to provide it.

He jotted a note to himself about it and returned to the report he'd been thinking about when Rafe had called. This too pertained to the old Carlisle-Skinner affair. It was in the case file begun when the bone fragments had been found in the tar pit in 1969, but this particular item was dated June 1964, which meant that it had been taken or photocopied from the earlier case file. It was signed by Sergeant Mark Lavoisier (he who had taken out the 1964 postmortem on Skinner, had failed to return it, and had then most inconsiderately died ten years ago).

13 June 1964. At 13:35, a man who identified himself as Mr. Edmond Jouvet came to the office to offer "assistance" in the matter and was referred to PC Miller, who requested my attendance as well. Mr. Jouvet, a solicitor at Withins, Wessing, & Overton, was in a state of considerable agitation. His breath smelled strongly of whiskey (noted by PC Miller as well as myself). He insisted he knew why George Skinner had been killed and proceeded to impart a bizarre and disconnected story of exchanged children during the Occupation years and resentments arising therefrom.

After interviewing Mr. Jouvet, it was PC Miller's and my joint opinion that the story was most likely the distorted creation of his alcoholic state and had little or no foundation in fact. Mr.

Jouvet was thanked and provided with transportation to his home, at the termination of which he had to be awakened.

14 June 1964. Today PC Miller was despatched to call on Mr. Jouvet at Withins, Wessing, & Overton to elicit anything further from him concerning his allegations of yesterday. Mr. Jouvet, who appeared to be quite sober, told PC Miller that he had been drinking heavily yesterday as a result of a family problem, that he was not used to drinking, that he had next to no memory of his visit to the police station, and no memory at all of how he had gotten home. He asserted surprise and consternation on hearing a brief summary of what he had said, asserted several times that he had never heard of any matter involving exchanged children, and apologized profusely for taking up the police's time.

Under this, scrawled in pencil, was an unsigned note dated five and a half years later, December 12, 1969.

Called on the above-mentioned Mr. Jouvet this morning just in case he might have something of interest to say. He did not. He was unreceptive, expressing resentment at being "hounded" by the police and asserting that he would file a complaint if there was another instance of it. In this officer's opinion, his hostile and uncooperative manner suggested fear or evasiveness. This officer believes he is worth further questioning.

Clapper's search through the rest of the file had turned up no indication of additional questioning, so apparently it had been dropped, which left Clapper wondering. As it happened, he knew about the exchange of young George and Roddy during the Occupation—Rafe had told him—and Jouvet's actions intrigued him. Jouvet's visit to the police in 1964 clearly meant that he knew about it too. But why did he think it was important in the murder investigations? And why deny any knowledge of it the following day and then again five years later? Like the anonymous author of the note, Clapper believed the man was worth further questioning. He had looked up Withins, Wessing, & Overton in the telephone book, had found that the firm was still in existence in Saint Brélade, and had learned from a telephone call that one Edmond Jouvet had been with the firm for many years, had left twenty years ago, and had been living in retirement in Saint Helier.

At the sound of a gentle throat clearing that he was beginning to know well, Clapper looked up. "Yes, Tom?"

"There's nothing on any Randall Campion, sir."

"Nothing at all? The man's been here two years."

"I know, sir, but he doesn't show up in any governmental records or newspaper indices. I'm sorry."

"For God's sake, Constable, there's nothing to be sorry about. Will you stop this endless apologizing!"

Vickery blanched. "I'm s—" He caught himself before he said it, and after a second they laughed together, a first, and it gentled them both.

"Actually, it's what I hoped you'd find. Tom, do you know if Sergeant Kendry's about?"

"Yes, sir, he is. I saw him just minutes ago. Shall I get him for you?"

"No, that's all right. I'll get him myself. I could stand a change of scene."

Detective Sergeant Warren Kendry's windowless cubicle at the far end of the hallway was a change, but not for the better. At seven by eight feet, it was no larger than the four ordinary detective cubicles, and just as messy, with notices and reminders and lists tacked up on the fabric sections of the walls and taped to the glass parts. Clapper, for whom neatness was generally a priority, was sympathetic; with no room for a file cabinet and only two drawers in the department's standard-issue desk, where were they supposed to put this stuff? Kendry also somehow managed to find space to stick up his "motivational" slogans, which he printed up at home and changed several times a week. There were three new ones today: *Eagles soar, but weasels don't get sucked into jet engines. The problem with the rat race is that even if you win, you're still a rat. If at first you don't succeed, try, try again. Then quit. There's no point in being a damn fool about it.*

Clapper was in a good mood, and they made him smile. He gestured at the third one with his chin. "They got that right."

There was a narrow, not terribly robust visitor's chair jammed in between the desk and the fabric wall, but Kendry knew better than to invite Clapper to sit. That had been tried before, with unfortunate results.

"What's up, Chief?"

"Have you gotten started on the tar pits case yet, Warren?"

Kendry patted the closed folder in front of him. "Just finished going through the background. I'd heard about it before, but I never knew that Roddy Carlisle was Senator Carlisle's father."

"That he was, and, in fact, I've just had an interesting call from the senator." Leaning on the doorless doorjamb and pretty much entirely plugging up the entryway, Clapper briefed Kendry on what Rafe had told him about Campion and on what Tom had been able to find on him in the records, which was nothing.

"Do you want us to bring him in, Chief?"

"No, not yet. I want your people to size him up, that's all—*could* he be Peltier? But make it simple, a routine call, something procedural, nothing threatening. If he is Bertrand Peltier, we don't want him scarpering again."

Kendry, who had been taking notes all along, jotted down a few final ones and pocketed the pad he was writing on. "I assume we'd be most likely to find him out at the writer's place, the old Dechambeaux Manor?"

"That's certainly the first place I'd look. Who do you intend to put on the case?"

"I've already put them: Buncombe and Bayley."

When Clapper responded with a chuckling snort, Kendry said, "You don't think they're right for the job, Chief?"

"No, they're fine. It's the names that get to me. They sound like an old music hall act. Buncombe and Bayley. Can't you just see 'em shuffling out in tandem from stage right, with their striped jackets and their straw boaters, twirling their walking sticks and doing a soft-shoe entrance?"

"Bayley, maybe, but not Harvey Buncombe. Not at eighteen stone. Beg pardon, Chief. No offense."

"Not to worry, Warren. I have no plans to take up soft-shoe dancing."

Kendry smiled. Then he mused for a minute. "Now Laurel and Hardy . . . that I could see."

Back in his office, Clapper caught sight of the notes about Edmond Jouvet on his desk and rang Kendry even before sitting down. "And while they're about it, have them make one more call while they're out. There's an old codger I want them to talk to named Edmond Jouvet, who's also of interest in the matter. Probably best to ring him up first. He lives in Saint Helier . . ."

CHAPTER 25

Kendry's allusion to Laurel and Hardy was apt. Harvey Buncombe was large, wide, and slow moving, while Lyle Bayley was wiry, tight featured, and birdlike in his movements. As with Laurel and Hardy themselves, the conventional fat/thin stereotypes did not apply. Buncombe was not avuncular and jocose but cynical and grumpy. Bayley was the easygoing, amiable one. If they ever practiced the good-cop, bad-cop routine, (which they didn't; to anyone who had access to a television set that particular ploy was familiar to the point of boredom), it was Buncombe who would have been the nasty cop, Bayley the nice guy.

And, in fact, that was the way they worked together, but it wasn't a ploy; it came naturally. It wasn't that Harvey was quick to anger—there was nothing brutal about him—but he was impatient with what he saw as evasion or prevarication, and he was neither good at hiding it nor interested in doing so. He also had developed, somewhere along the line, that heavy-lidded, slightly sidewise detective's look that makes a suspect feel the game was up; he might as well save everybody the trouble and hold his wrists out for the cuffs right now. Bayley, the more literate and educated of the two, had plenty of patience and, without trying to, quickly became the nervous interrogee's friend and comfort, an understanding recipient for whatever the looming, grumbling Buncombe had frightened the poor sod into saying. Because it worked so well, they were often assigned as a team, which pleased them both. Still, Bayley did envy that sidewise look. He'd tried it, but it just didn't work for him.

"It's like a fairy tale, when you think about it," said Buncombe, who despite his prickly nature was a romantic. "The teenage bride and her young lover separated for half a century, and then, in the sunset of their lives, finding each other again and living out their remaining years together."

"*If* it's Peltier," said Bayley. "But then, if it is, it's not going to have a fairy-tale ending. There's still about a million pounds to be accounted for, to say nothing of two dead bodies."

"I suppose that's a point, yes," said Buncombe, who was at the wheel of their unmarked gray BMW. "And there it is, the old Dechambeaux place. She's certainly done a good job fixing it up. It was falling down when she bought it."

"She certainly has," agreed Bayley. "You've seen the lady on the telly, have you?"

"Hard to avoid. A real piece of work, Lyle. If she's with him, she'll make trouble."

"Oh, she's not so bad as all that," said Bayley predictably, and then laughed. "Besides, if need be, you'll give her what for pretty quick."

Buncombe clapped an indignant hand to his chest. "Not I!"

"Yes, right, can't imagine what I was thinking. Ah, that's her there, isn't it? Tennessee Rivers in the flesh. With the gray-haired chap."

"So it is. And I'll wager that's Campion."

"Or should we say 'Peltier'?"

"That's what we're here to render our opinions on, partner."

It was not the manor house they were looking toward but an open-sided stone shed, an L-shaped, moldering, old structure with slate shingles missing from its roof and straw stuffing poking out of the crevices between the stone blocks of its walls. Unlike the impressive and immaculate manor house, this building had obviously been bypassed when it came time for refurbishing, and it still served its ancient functions as stable and tack room. Gear and equipment could be seen in one wing, and four stalls in the other, three of which had horses gazing vacantly out, as horses do, through the open tops of their Dutch doors.

The building served as one corner of a stable yard or corral, otherwise enclosed by a relatively new white rail fence. Campion, if that's who he was, was just inside the fence, using two curry brushes to groom a chestnut horse, and Miranda was on the outside, affectionately stroking the horse's sweaty neck and apparently giving Campion instructions. Campion, wearing jeans and muddy Wellingtons, looked tired. Miranda, in a tailored western shirt, jodhpurs, and riding boots, her short silvery hair windblown, looked sensational.

"Better-looking woman than I realized," Buncombe said appreciatively as Bayley brought the car to a halt on the graveled driveway. "Taller too."

"Fine figger of a woman," Bayley agreed.

"Amazing. Isn't she something like seventy?"

"Wouldn't surprise me. Looks formidable enough, though. I'd watch out for that left hook, Harvey, once you succeed in irritating her."

Miranda and Campion had turned at the sound of tires on gravel and had remained standing on either side of the fence, waiting for them.

"You see? There you are," Buncombe said as the two men walked toward them. "She's already irritating me. She's showing us who's in charge. She's saying, 'You're on my turf now, coppers, you have to come to me.' Clear as can be."

Bayley shook his head. "You are the most hypersensitive man I know, Harvey, you really must do something about that." Privately, he thought that Buncombe was right about Miranda and that Buncombe knew he knew he was right. But this kind of easy raillery was a long-established part of the relationship, and neither of them saw any need for change.

"Pretty quick off the mark to see that we're policemen, though," Buncombe said. "No uniforms, no markings on the car."

"Are you joking? Harvey, anybody can see you're a detective. All they need do is look at you."

Buncombe was wearing a baggy, old tweed sport coat. His tie was loosened, and the top button of his shirt was undone. The points of his collar were curling. Add to that his heavy, world-weary face and his five-o'clock shadow (which was there in the morning an hour after he'd finished shaving), and he did, indeed, look like a cynical, seen-it-all cop. Bayley, on the other hand, had to shave only every other day and was dressed in a light, trim-fitting linen suit and pale-blue shirt that was buttoned up to the top to accommodate his neatly knotted, perfectly dimpled midnight-blue tie.

Buncombe's eyes ran scathingly up and down his partner. "At least nobody's ever called me a pretty boy," he groused.

Bayley barely threw him a glance. "Surely you jest."

They had reached the yard now. Campion had gone back to working on the horse, but Miranda was looking squarely at them, arms crossed and face closed. Bayley, who was younger than Buncombe but first in seniority and nominally in charge, opened and held up his wallet, showing his shield on one side and his ID card on the other. "Good morning, Ms. Rivers. I'm Detective Bayley, and this is Detective Buncombe."

"My name is Mrs. *Atterbury*," Miranda said by way of returning his greeting.

"I beg your pardon, Mrs. Atterbury. Sorry to interrupt what you're doing, but, assuming that this gentleman is Mr. Randall Champion, we have a few questions we'd like to ask him."

Looking up with a relaxed and friendly smile, still holding the brushes and leaning his forearms on the horse's withers, Campion said,

"Good morning, Detectives. How can I help? Not that it matters, but my name's Campion, by the way, not Champion. Like the detective chappie on the telly? Albert Campion?"

"Or the seventeenth-century Jesuit author," said Bayley. "William Campion."

Campion cocked his head at him. "Oh, that's *very* good, Detective," he said smoothly. "I'm impressed. Ninety-nine of a hundred people would have a hard time naming even a single seventeenth-century author, let alone William Campion."

And you'd be one of them, Bayley thought, having made one of his lightning-quick assessments of the man. *You're about as familiar with seventeenth-century Jesuit authors as I am with seventeenth-century Mongolian watchmakers*. To be fair, though, Bayley himself had already expressed just about everything he'd retained about William Campion from his college days, but while they were driving here, he'd done a quick Internet search to see if there was anything about the writer that might be of use in fulfilling their assignment.

And he'd found something. "Interesting thing about Campion," he said offhandedly. "There's also a writer named William Wigmore, born the same year, died the same year. Turns out they were the same man. Campion had an alias, in other words. I don't believe anybody knows why. Must make for an exhausting life, being two people, having to constantly be on guard lest you slip up."

"I suppose that's right," said Campion. "Never thought about it before." He went back to currying, working on the horse's flank now.

Well, that had produced exactly nothing.

Miranda's response was less amiable. "Could we get to the purpose of your visit, please, Detective Bayley? I don't imagine that you've come to chat about William Campion, and we have quite a bit yet to do this afternoon."

She hadn't wasted any time getting under Buncombe's skin. "It's Mr. Campion our business is with, madam. Perhaps you could give us a few minutes alone with him."

She was no less blunt. "I think not."

"Oh, I don't mind, Mandy," Campion said reasonably, straightening up. "Always glad to assist our police officers."

Miranda was unmoved. "But *I* mind. My few experiences with the minions of the law have not endeared them to me, and I am not happy with the idea of a pair of strangely inquisitive detectives coming here, onto my property, unannounced, to interrogate a friend of mine, a newcomer to Jersey who has little knowledge of his rights or of our laws and rules of police procedure."

"Now, now, no one's talking about an interrogation—" Bayley got in before Buncombe could fire a retort of his own.

"Is there some formal objection to my remaining?" Miranda demanded. "Am I not entitled to be here if Mr. Campion wishes it?" She looked at Campion to prompt a reaction of some kind, and he shrugged and smiled. *Whatever.*

"No, madam, you are not *entitled—*" Buncombe said.

"However, you're welcome to remain," Bayley cut in again, "as long as you permit Mr. Campion to answer our questions for himself. You may advise him, if you wish. Is there somewhere we might all sit down for a few minutes?"

"I'm sorry, but there are no chairs out here."

Even Bayley's patience was beginning to thin. It was hot standing in the sun, and not to offer to take them into the manor was calculatedly offensive. He had never understood why so many people chose, right from the start, to alienate police officers. If they had hostile feelings toward them because of negative experiences, that he could comprehend, but to go out of their way to openly antagonize them—that was a mystery. There were plenty of possible downsides to it, but where was the benefit? Whatever the answer, Miranda was obviously one of those people.

"Very well," he said, "then we'll remain where we are. Mr. Campion, what brings you to Jersey?"

"You still haven't explained what this is about," Miranda said.

"Kindly hold your horses," said Buncombe with an unconvincing smile. "We're talking to the gentleman, not to you."

Miranda, not used to this kind of treatment, could do no better than a huffy "I *beg* your pardon!"

"Mr. Campion?" Bayley said.

"What brought me to Jersey," Campion repeated, continuing to brush the horse in slow, steady circles. "Well, first—"

"And if you could stop working on the animal, please?"

"Of course, of course," Campion said contritely. "Sorry about that." He slipped out of the straps that held his hands to the brushes and put them on a rickety table alongside some other horse-grooming implements. "I am here, Detective," he said with an open, earnest smile, "because of the many obvious advantages of Jersey over Merrie Olde England: your beautiful countryside, the marvelous beaches, the low crime rate, low taxes, friendly, welcoming people—"

"Ah, you see, right there, that's one of the things we've come about," said Bayley.

"I don't understand. Welcoming people?"

"Taxes. We have no record of your paying any taxes in the two years—I believe it's two years?—that you've been here."

"That's perfectly true," Campion said easily, "but to the best of my knowledge, I don't owe any."

"How do you support yourself, Mr. Campion?"

"Oh, well, you know, I—"

Buncombe gestured at his muddy boots, the brushes, the horse. "You work for Mrs. Atterbury, do you?"

"You could say that, yes," Miranda answered for him.

"I did say that," Buncombe said sharply. "Is it the case?"

"If you mean by 'work for me,' is he a paid employee, the answer is no. For his assistance, he lives rent-free on the property and is entitled to meals, that's all. Well, and an occasional something for clothing and entertainment and such, but those are more in the nature of gifts than—"

"Unfortunately," said Buncombe, "all of that is considered as income to Mr. Campion, for which he is required to pay taxes."

"I had no idea!" exclaimed Campion. "Naturally, I'll pay anything I owe."

"And back taxes as well, I'm afraid," Bayley said with an apologetic smile.

"Oh, for God's sake," Miranda said disgustedly. "We're talking about *gifts*. Am I supposed to tell my workers how much they cost so they can pay the taxes on them? I don't know myself. I don't keep records of such—" She caught herself, but not soon enough.

"Well, I think you'd better start," Buncombe said with a reptilian smile. "There'll be some retroactive penalties for you too, I suspect."

"How am I expected even to remember—"

"You'll need to take that up with Treasury and Records, Mrs. Atterbury," Bayley said, "not with us."

She shook her head with a weary sigh, then made a hurry-up motion with her hand. "Well, get on with it. Let's hear the rest of it. Obviously, there's more."

"Well, there are a few more little things, yes," Bayley said placatingly. He pretended to check a notepad. "Ah. I gather you're not married, sir?"

"Not me," Campion said with a laugh. "Free as a bird."

"Lucky man," said Buncombe, summoning up a chuckle of his own. "Never been married, then?"

They had planned ahead to ask this question, once again wanting Campion's reaction, but he was only able to blink twice before Miranda again took over, this time more forcefully.

"That's it!" Angrily, she put herself in front of Campion as if blocking the detectives from getting at him, which he seemed more than willing to let her do. With her hands on her hips, at her most handsome and statuesque, she glared at the two detectives. "Where the bloody hell do you two get off asking a question like that? Where do you get off coming here in the first place, bumbling around in his business, my business? I don't know exactly what sort of fishing expedition this is, but I do know that two CID detectives are not sent out on routine matters like these. Please leave."

"I assure you—" Bayley began.

"And I assure you that the instant you venture onto this property again without a warrant, or badger Mr. Campion or myself, I'll be on the telephone to my old friend Chief Bowron at once."

"Mrs. Atterbury—"

"I've asked you to leave once, and I'm not going to do it again. Now get the hell off my property and stay off."

In the meantime, Campion had found his tongue. "Nope, never been married," he said as the detectives turned to leave. "Still searching for the right girl. Think I just might have found her, though." He threw a smiling, manifestly proprietary glance at Miranda and then a smirking, cocksure one at the two cops.

Miranda, glaring at him, looked mad enough to spit.

CHAPTER 26

"It's him, all right," Buncombe said with satisfaction as they pulled out of the driveway and onto Marais Road. "Isn't it?"

"I'm not sure, Harvey. We weren't any too subtle, though. If it is him, I hope we haven't frightened him into bolting."

"You think he's that keen, Lyle? I don't."

"I think *she's* that keen. But we can tell Sarge all about it. He can decide where it goes from here."

"When in doubt, delegate upward," said Buncombe. "That's my motto too. I'll ring him now." He got out his cell but looked up when Bayley turned left. "Why are we pulling in here?"

"Because we are tasked with calling on the old lawyer . . . what's his name, Jouvet?"

"Oh, right. I forgot all about it." He put the phone away. "Don't know what Kendry expects us to get out of him, though. The old boy threw the police out the last time he was approached, and he's on record as stating that whatever it was he'd told them about the Occupation was the result of confusion of some kind. Well, if the old boy was confused fifty years ago, I suspect he's totally gaga by now. He's ninety-five or thereabouts, isn't he? Probably doesn't even remember that there *was* an Occupation."

Bayley laughed. "It'll be a short interview, then. He lives near the Market; we can stop at Rosie's for a cuppa before we head back."

"Or even a couple of sausage rolls," Buncombe suggested, lighting up.

Edmond Jouvet lived in one of a long row of modest, semidetached houses that differed from each other only in their colors, which ranged all the way from white to pale beige. The curtained front bay windows were square and shingle topped to match the roofs, and the front gardens, if they'd ever been present, had been paved over to serve as sidewalk parking spaces, so that to get to the front door of most of them, you had to step around an automobile. Jouvet's was a six- or seven-year-old blue Mercedes.

"For a retired lawyer, it doesn't look as if he's made out all that well," Buncombe observed, running his hand through the layer of dust on the hood.

"Well, we don't know what his expenses might be, do we?"

"Very true. One never knows."

They were let in by a woman in her sixties who didn't seem all that pleased to see them. "My father's in the office back there," she said. "He's anxious to talk to you, but please don't let him get excited."

Jouvet's office was clearly a converted bedroom, but he must have furnished it by moving his old law office there, whole hog. Walking into it was like entering the chambers of a Gray's Inn barrister in the 1930s (assuming the movies could be trusted), or even in the 1880s; neither of the two detectives could tell the difference. The Turkish carpet was threadbare; an old glass-fronted bookcase filled with faded brown books stood against one wall; and framed certificates and portraits of self-important-looking old men hung on the others. The air was a mix of furniture polish and cigar smoke.

Jouvet himself sat at a walnut rolltop desk, his banker's chair turned so that he faced them as they entered. A frail, crabbed old man, who looked every bit of ninety-five and a shaky ninety-five at that, he wore a blue fleece bathrobe over striped pajamas, with tatty leather slippers on his feet. But a single, direct look from his hooded, intelligent blue eyes told them that he was anything but gaga.

"Sit down," he instructed, pointing at a couple of fabric-seated captain's chairs. "Wilma will make us tea." His voice, as expected, was reedy and cracked, but it sizzled with authority.

"That's all right, sir," Bayley said. "We don't need to take too much of your time. We simply want—"

"Sit or stand as you prefer, but I'm going to have some tea, and I advise you to sit down and do the same. This is going to take a while."

Buncombe and Bayley glanced at each other as they sat down, eyebrows slightly lifted, thinking that, as usual, they were sharing the same thought.

They weren't.

Well, well, this is going to turn out to be interesting after all, Bayley was thinking, his curiosity piqued.

Well, there go my sausage rolls, Buncombe thought.

CHAPTER 27

Gideon, Julie, and John were collected in the same dusty Range Rover in which Rafe had picked them up at the airport, driven this time by a husky, outgoing young woman who looked as if she might be a first-stringer on her school's lacrosse team. Indeed, Elissa Prentice was a student athlete—rugby, not lacrosse—at the University of Plymouth, where she was pursuing an MA in Jacobean drama, but in the summers, as she told them, she worked for her "uncle" Rafe as a "shofergopher" (which turned out, on translation, to be a chauffeur/gofer).

Once again, John and Gideon took the backseats and left the front to Julie, who took no time in starting up a lively tête-à-tête with Elissa. Gideon, meanwhile, told John about the theft of the coffin van, but they soon found the women's conversation more interesting than theirs and shortly tuned into it.

"No, he's not married," Elissa was saying to Julie. "Never has been."

"Never? Does he have any women friends?"

Elissa laughed. "He's not gay, if that's what you're getting at. Or maybe he is. I really wouldn't know. But I think he's just a guy that isn't that much into sex one way or another. It just isn't that high priority for him, you know? He's very busy, very involved with the dairy, and his DNA work takes time, and he's really devoted to his work in the Senate, although you wouldn't think it to hear him talk about it. When he gets an evening off from government work, he likes to spend it at home, all alone with his books and his music and a couple of glasses of cognac. Even on warm nights, he'll light a fire in the big fireplace, just for the feel of it, you know?"

"I'm a little surprised by all that," Julie said. "I know he struck us as being pretty sociable."

"Sure did," John contributed from the back.

"Well, I don't mean to say he's not sociable," Elissa said, "it's only . . . he's like one of those wealthy nineteenth-century gentleman bachelors, you know? I mean, who else do you know who talks like someone out of P. G. Wodehouse? Who else do you know who changes into a smoking jacket in the evening when he gets home? Where do you even *get* a smoking jacket? And he puts on one of those, those . . . what do you call them?" She made motions at her throat.

"Ascots," Julie supplied with a smile. "I bet Rafe looks great in an ascot."

"He does, yes. And then, once a week or so, he likes to have friends for dinner. You're this week's contingent. Whatever you have tonight, it'll be good, I can guarantee that much. He's got a live-out housekeeper who's a fabulous cook. You'll see." She turned off the undulating, two-lane "main" road, the Rue de Bas, into a narrow, unmarked dirt track boxed in with hedgerows on either side. "The thing is, he lives exactly the life he wants to live, he knows he's lucky to be able to do it, and he's about the happiest, most contented, sweetest man I know."

"Sounds like you kind of like him," Julie said, smiling.

Elissa glanced over at her. "I *love* Uncle Rafe. We're here, folks," she said as they turned through an open livestock gate and onto a graveled parking area. *"Le Manoir des Fontants."*

As Rafe had told them, the stone structure didn't quite match up to one's idea of a manor, let alone a *manoir*. "An old farmhouse" was what he'd called it, and that was what it was. It did, however, exude a rustic charm. Easy to imagine it on a snowy day, with plumes of peat-scented smoke rising out of a chimney (there were two of them) from the fire in the big stone fireplace. Two stories tall, with a mossy roof and two wood-shuttered dormer windows on the upper floor, it was about the size of a modern middle-class family home, a small one. Caught in the slanting rays of early twilight, the stones were honey-colored, their ridges limned with gold. The stone was unpainted now, but here and there were faint patches of yellow or white left from when it had been painted over in the past. To complete the picture of rural domesticity, a trailing green vine crept prettily up the front wall.

"What a beautiful place!" Julie said. "Is that honeysuckle?"

"Clematis," answered Elissa. "I do the pruning. And behold, cometh the lord of the manor."

"Hello, hello, everyone," was Rafe's smiling, pleased greeting as he trotted down the two steps from the modest front door. To Julie's disappointment, he was not attired in silken ascot and velvet smoking jacket. He had changed from the blue suit he'd had on earlier, though, and was now wearing a newly pressed tan one with a brown vest. His diagonally striped tie was as perfectly knotted as the one he'd worn this morning had been.

"Thank you so much for coming," he said as they climbed out of the Rover. "Isn't it a beautiful sunset? I thought we'd have our drinks in the gazebo while dinner's being prepared." He took their orders—Scotch and water for Gideon, white wine for Julie, beer for John—then said, "I say, Elissa, what would you like? And why don't you join us for dinner?"

"Thanks, Uncle Rafe, but I have other things I need to do," she said, as she was surely expected to say.

"Oh, I'm so sorry. But would you mind stopping in and asking Gussie to bring out the drinks and things?"

"Not me, Unc. I know better than to intrude on Gussie when she's cooking. But what I *will* do is get them for you myself. You lot just go on out to the gazebo."

"Ah, Elissa, what did I do to deserve you for a niece? Yes, that would be wonderful. And there should be a platter of hors d'oeuvres in the cooler. Could you possibly bring those as well? I promise not to notice if one or two are missing. And a glass of sherry for me, please? The amontillado, I think. No, make it the oloroso. No, the amontillado. Thank you, my dear."

He led them around to the back of the house, where a well-cared-for, mildly sloping lawn led down to the gazebo, a simple wooden affair with a shingle roof and four rattan armchairs arranged around a small table in the center. From the raised floor they overlooked what had been the Carlisle Tar Pits until Rafe's mother had had them transformed into these two linked, pretty ponds. In the channel that ran between them—an artificially made one, they now knew—a few mallards, emerald-headed males and their dowdy mates, were babbling softly among themselves and dipping for underwater nourishment. Not far beyond the larger pond was a jumble of rocky outcroppings, presumably the ones from the base of which the pitch had flowed for more than a century and then stopped. A little farther off, cows could be seen in rolling pastureland, tranquilly nuzzling the grass. Refined, pastoral serenity at its best.

Rafe encompassed it all with a wave of his hand. "Isn't the view lovely from here? Mother couldn't have done a better job situating it. I never tire of coming here."

"Oh, it couldn't be prettier," Julie said, after which came an uneasy silence. They were standing yards from the spot where Rafe's father had been murdered and where his body, and then his bones, had lain undetected for five years, but nobody had mentioned it yet. It was practically all Gideon, John, and Julie had been thinking about for the last few days, and now here they were. Were they supposed to ignore it and talk about how pretty the scene was? Everybody was a little tongue-tied.

Everybody but Rafe, who couldn't wait to talk about it. "Now, the bones came up from that area over there," he said, pointing to the opposite side of the smaller pond, directly across from them. If anything, he was even more chipper and upbeat than usual. "I thought seeing the site for yourselves would be of interest. Does anyone have any questions?"

"Yeah," John said. "Didn't you say they found the gun in a nearby hedge? I'm not seeing any hedges. Is it gone now, or were you talking about the one behind the house?"

"No, it's gone all right. Mother had it taken down when she redid the ponds. A gnarly, tangled old thing, must have been planted years and years ago, a screen to hide the pits, I suppose. I don't really remember it all that well, but I know it ran along there for a few meters." He pointed to the border of the smaller pond.

"Which would have been right near where your father was found," Julie said. "I wonder why it took so long for them to find the gun in the first place. You said weeks, I think."

"Yes, that's right. I really don't know the answer to that."

"Well, why would they look there at the time?" John asked. "George was shot over at his place, and your father had taken off, or so they thought. No reason to search here."

Elissa now wheeled up a serving cart with their drinks and several plates of simple but elegantly prepared hors d'oeuvres. She put them on the table one plate at a time: Spanish olives arranged on a wreath of wonderfully aromatic fresh rosemary, dates stuffed with creamy white cheese and studded with crushed walnuts, prosciutto-wrapped melon balls, each with a single flawless mint leaf on top, and an elaborate pewter dish with what must have been two dozen oysters on the half shell, carrying their own briny smell and set artistically among lemon halves and tufts of parsley on a bed of ice.

"Enjoy," she said, setting out the glasses. "I can't recommend the oysters strongly enough, and I speak from recent experience. Unc, ring me up when you want me to take your friends back. Oh, Gussie wants you in there in thirty minutes, no more, no less."

"We shall synchronize our watches. Thank you again, my dear."

Elissa having left, the chairs were pulled up to the table, at which all helped themselves to the hors d'oeuvres.

"Those crags out there," said Gideon, who had been looking at them for a while, "would they be—"

"Indeed they would, the very crags from which the fatal shot was *not* fired by my father."

"So the farmhouse just beyond them—that was George's house?"

"It was. Abbott's too, but he sold it some years ago to move into the city."

Gideon nodded. "I assumed it was much farther away from your house. It's practically right on your property."

"It *was* on my property, or I should say the Carlisle property. My grandfather made a present of it to George's father, Willie, as thanks for Willie's taking care of *my* father when he was a child during the war. And the considerable acreage behind it went with it."

"Some nice present," John said.

Julie nodded. "I'll say. Must be a story there."

"A long one," said Rafe, and proceeded to tell it: How with the German invasion imminent, Howard Carlisle had feared for the health of his sickly son, Roddy. He'd prevailed on Willie Skinner to secretly exchange their young children—Roddy and George—so that the frail Roddy would be relatively safe in England, with the Skinners, for as long as the Occupation lasted, while George, robust and resilient, remained in Jersey with the Carlisles to endure the deprivations that were to come. The boys adapted to their situations as only two-year-olds can and quickly came to believe in their new identities and that they were living with their own families. It was only when the Skinners returned to Jersey at the end of the war, five long years later, and the boys were reexchanged that they learned who their real parents were. They were told to keep it to themselves, of course, and after a while, apparently, they forgot it ever happened. The house and property were Howard's gift to Willie for agreeing to go along with the idea and following through on it.

"Amazing," Gideon said. "Any repercussions when the story did get out? I assume the government wouldn't be interested in taking any action, but I wonder how other people—their friends, their neighbors—felt about being lied to all those years."

"Well, it didn't get out, not then. Georgie did slip up at school early on—he asked his teacher whether he was to be called George or Roddy, and when she prodded him, it all came out. But she was good enough to keep it to herself too."

"Best for everyone," said Julie, nodding.

"Until," Rafe continued, "1999 or thereabouts, when she was well into her eighties and took it into her head to include it in a collection of wartime memoirs that the Occupation Society put out. And somehow"—he paused for a sip of sherry and a roll of his eyes—"Granada TV got wind of it and decided it would make a terrific story for one of those appalling docudramas of theirs."

Gideon smiled. "You have to admit, it is pretty good fodder for one. Did it ever get made?"

"No, thank goodness, but the newspapers got hold of the story. 'Granada is coming to Jersey!' and so on. That was when everyone found out about the exchange—including me."

John swallowed the oyster that he had just slurped up. "Wait a minute—you mean you didn't know anything about it until then? Until 1999?"

"I'm telling you, nobody did. That was when Abbott learned about it too. Well, you can imagine that I wasn't about to permit our family's being made a television spectacle of, and fortunately I was able to do something about it, although I had to threaten a suit to get them to stand down." His mouth curled downward. "*Switcheroo.* How's that for a title? Gives you an idea of how seriously they took it."

For a while the hors d'oeuvres and drinks were consumed in silence. That had been a lot of new information to absorb.

"And how did everything work out for the two boys?" Julie asked at last. "Over the long run."

"About as expected, one would have to say. Unfortunately, George was as feckless as his father before him, not a man to let pass an opportunity for a wrong turn or a misadventure or—"

"A screwup?" John suggested.

"Exactly. And so, more out of compassion than anything else, I believe, my father took it on himself to find positions for him at the various Carlisle enterprises. He felt a sort of familial responsibility for him, just as Grandfather Howard had for George's father, Willie."

"Pretty important jobs for a screwup," Gideon said, "sales manager . . ."

Rafe nodded. "Yes, *too* important. Mother never trusted him, you know, and in the end Father had to agree." He seemed on the verge of enlarging on this, but instead he glanced at his watch, then drained his glass and rather indelicately smacked his lips, signaling the end of a conversation that was obviously depressing him. "And now we'd better report for dinner as instructed. Annoying Gussie is to be avoided at all costs. I've asked her to prepare what I hope will be a treat for you, the most British of all dinners, the very emblem of Old Blighty."

"Roast beef and Yorkshire pudding?" John asked hopefully.

CHAPTER 28

John got his wish: roast beef; carrots, parsnips, cabbage, and broccoli, all roasted with the meat; mashed potatoes; and, of course, Yorkshire pudding—in this case in the form of popovers crisped on the outside, with their centers hollowed out to hold generous lardings of drippings. Gussie, a petite but sinewy Asian woman wearing a white smock over blue jeans and sandals, set the earthenware platter on the table and told Rafe: "Leftover beef goes in the refrigerator. You can leave everything else as is. I'll take care of it in the morning." She waited a couple of beats and dourly added: "Like I always do."

"*Thank* you, Gussie," Rafe said, "what a splendid feast you've made for us."

"Enjoy," Gussie ordered, and was gone.

The two bottles of wine on the table, Rafe informed them, were a 1991 Saint-Emilion from Château Cheval Blanc—"a claret, naturally, and in my opinion, finer even than the Pétrus or Pomerol of that year. But you can try it for yourselves and make your own decisions."

Gideon, John, and Julie tried it for themselves and, unsurprisingly, pronounced it very fine indeed. The roast had already been carved into impressively uniform slices, which Rafe deftly lifted to individual plates, along with portions of vegetables, and handed around. Somehow, he had found the private time to change to a velvet burgundy smoking jacket and pale-salmon ascot, and he looked very much the lord of the manor.

Because Le Fontant had only three rooms on the ground floor—kitchen, sitting room, and a bedroom—there was no separate dining room, so they were eating in the kitchen, the largest of the rooms, the working area of which looked like an exhibit from a twenty-first-century cooking exposition—stainless steel appliances, including a refrigerator the size of a UPS truck; two skylights; dozens of modern, polished copper and aluminum pots hanging from the ceiling; and three work islands, one a vintage butcher block and the other two with pale quartzite work surfaces. The smaller eating area was in marked contrast and could have passed for one of the seventeenth-century rooms at Mont Orgueil Castle, with its rough, thick-legged, old wooden table and chairs to match; bare rock walls; and worm-eaten, adze-carved beams above.

In general, the inside of the manor suited the four-hundred-year-old exterior: small rooms, low, lumpy ceilings with half-buried roof beams in them, and unplastered stone walls. But aside from the eating area, there was nothing humble about it. What had been earthen floors were now covered either with wood or smooth, amber terrazzo tiles. Electrified sconces, placed every three or four feet along the walls, provided the lighting, throwing warm, evocative shadows over the rough granite stones. And the requisite fireplace, carved blackened stone mantel and all, took up almost an entire wall of what was now the living room.

The furnishings had a look often to be seen in the homes of the truly patrician. Everything was cared for and of high quality, but most of it was so old it was just this side of falling to pieces: cracked leather on the chairs and threadbare tapestries, some with holes in them, on the floor and on the walls. Mismatched furniture was thrown together, ostensibly at random. In a poor man's home, it would have been squalid and unkempt; in Rafe's, it was a kind of laid-back, country house chic.

Rafe had just filled his own dinner plate and set it down in front of him when the pleasant flow of casual patter he'd had going abruptly stopped. His mouth dropped open, and rather than sitting down, he more or less fell into his chair—from which he immediately sprang up. "I have proof!" he exulted. With a lighthearted laugh, he smacked his forehead. "I can prove he's Peltier!" With that, he ran for the corner stairway to the upper floor.

John and Julie were understandably puzzled. "Does anybody know what he's talking about?" John asked.

Gideon barely had time to give them a forty-second précis of Rafe's Randy-Campion-is-Bertrand-Peltier hypothesis before Rafe came barreling back down the stairs, brandishing a suit jacket and gloating. "I gave him my lighter to light a cigar yesterday. His fingerprints must be all over it. I didn't want to take it out of the pocket myself because I thought I might do it the wrong way. John, will you do the honors?"

"Sure." John took the jacket. "Have you handled the lighter yourself since then?"

"Ah . . . no, I didn't have a cigar last night, so it would only have been when I took it back from him."

"Good. Got a pair of tweezers I can use? And a plastic bag?"

Rafe got the bag from a kitchen drawer and the tweezers from the bathroom, and John delicately extracted the lighter from the suit coat's inside pocket.

"Ouch," Gideon said. "Crinkled leather. Can you actually lift a print off that?"

John was holding it up to his face, turning it to see both sides. "Yeah, as a matter of fact, they can, nowadays. I've seen them get them off these vinyl money bags they have now, and those are crinklier than this. They use silver nitrate, I think it is."

Rafe had reseated himself at the table. He was starting to look concerned. “Then why are you looking so dubious?”

“It’s not about the prints themselves, Rafe, it’s about what are they going to do with them? I mean, okay, say they now have this Randy guy’s prints. How are they supposed to use them to show he’s really Peltier?”

Rafe looked delighted by the question. “Well, would comparing them with Peltier’s old fingerprints suffice?”

“Sure, it would suffice,” John said, “but how are they supposed to do that? He’s been gone for fifty years. Don’t tell me his old prints are still on file somewhere.”

“But they *are* still on file,” Rafe said, beginning to laugh again. “The Nazis, God bless them.”

In their famously zealous regard for record keeping, he said, they had fingerprinted every single person on the island, even including newborns born during the Occupation years. Since Peltier had been twenty in 1964, he would have been born in 1944 and would be included in the data bank.

“And they’ve been kept all this time?” Gideon asked.

“Oh, yes, mostly for historical records, but I do occasional DNA work for the police, and once or twice in dealing with an unidentified oldster, I’ve made use of them myself.”

John slipped the lighter into the plastic lunch bag Rafe had given him. “Okay, then, you’ve got something to go on. You’ll give this to Mike?”

“Yes, first thing in the morning.” He reached for the bag.

John held back. “No, you want to put this in a bigger paper bag or a small carton, so you don’t accidentally smudge it.”

“Paper bag, paper bag,” recited Rafe, but he had no idea where they might be kept. Instead, from a wall cabinet he removed a bottle of Hennessy cognac from its slender black carton and slipped the plastic envelope inside. “There.”

Julie laughed. "Mike will think he's getting a present."

Rafe patted the box. "He is, and it's better than what was in it before. Speaking of which, shall we defy convention and open the bottle before dinner? We can sip a bit of it while these plates go into the warming oven to be brought back up to temperature." There were already brandy glasses on the table, and into each of them Rafe poured a couple of inches of the cognac, then looked up.

"I trust it goes without saying," he said darkly, "that Gussie must never know that her marvelous dinner was eaten rewarmed."

At eight thirty the next morning, Detective Chief Inspector Clapper was sitting in his office and thinking.

The big window behind his desk was opened to its widest, and he had swiveled his chair to face the gently shifting wall of leaves just outside, so close he could have leaned out and snapped off a branch if he'd wanted to. He had tilted the chair back, clasped his hands behind his head, and put his sizable feet up on the low sill, ankles comfortably crossed. His eyes closed, he was listening to the steady, thin drip of water on the leaves and inhaling the newly washed fragrance of fresh rain on clean pavement. It was a favorite place to sort things out, and the brownish-black smudges on the wood around his heels showed it.

"Chief?"

Clapper turned his chair around. "Yes, Warren?"

Sergeant Kendry grinned. "Just got a call from the lab. We've got him! Pence says it's him, all right, the prints match."

"Brilliant!" Then after a moment, a more hesitant: "He's sure?"

"Well—"

Mumble-grumble.

"No, he's sure, Chief, but he just wants you to know this is a quick eyeball judgment, which is what you asked him for. He hasn't done any formal ridge analysis yet, but in his opinion it's good enough to act on it."

"Then let's act on it. Pence knows his business. Get Buncombe and Bayley out there now. Have 'em bring the tricky sod in."

Another grin from Kendry. "You got it, Chief."

"Oh, Warren?" Clapper called as Kendry turned to leave. "Tell *B* and *B* from me that they did a first-rate job with old man Jouvet. That's quite a story they got out of him. I've been sitting here thinking about just what to make of it."

"Shall do."

Clapper nodded, spun his chair back around, got his feet up on the sill again, and leaned back.

Plenty to think about.

CHAPTER 29

Twenty minutes later, at a little before nine, Miranda opened her Chinese-red front door, looking nothing like the woman they'd met yesterday, looking like hell in fact, like those spiteful Internet photos of movie stars caught without their makeup: wild, spiky gray hair; flimsy, flowered dressing gown; shapeless felt slippers. Her face was as gray as her hair and mottled with red blotches.

"Oh, God, not you two again. Did I fail to make myself clear yesterday? Do you have any idea what *time* it is?"

"*Good* morning, Mrs. Atterbury," Buncombe said with overcooked good cheer. "We're *very* sorry to bother you again, but I'm afraid we really do need to speak with Mr. Campion one more time."

She responded with a barked note that was two-thirds grunt and one-third brusque laugh. "You and me both."

"He's not here?" Bayley said, his heart sinking. Christ, they'd blown it yesterday, as he'd feared. They'd scared him off. He'd bolted. There weren't going to be any commendations from Clapper on this one.

"He's left, has he?" Buncombe asked.

That laugh-grunt again. "Slunk off in the middle of the night like the vile little rodent he is. With thirty thousand pounds' worth of *my* jewelry from *my* safe-deposit box, and two thousand in sterling that I kept in the house."

"History repeats itself," Buncombe said, more gently than Bayley might have expected.

She lifted one unkempt gray eyebrow. "If that's meant to ferret out whether I knew he was Bertrand, the answer is yes, as I'm sure you already know."

"I see," Bayley said. "And did you—"

"Detectives, I don't want to stand here all morning, answering one question after another—"

"We *could* go inside and sit down," Buncombe grumbled, but if she heard him, she didn't let on.

"—so let me give you all the answers you want right now. Yes, I knew from the start about his embezzlement. No, I had no part in it myself; I never saw a pound of it. Yes, I knew from the beginning that he wasn't in that tar pit; I saw him off on the boat myself when he left. Yes, I expected that I would hear from him once he was settled in England."

She paused for a cold smile. "I did too, just as he promised, didn't I? It just took him fifty years to get around to it. It was after a book signing in Derby, no warning at all, and I was bowled over enough to accept his invitation to tea. All 'Sweetkins-this' and 'Buttercup-that,' he was, and what a terrible fool he'd been to leave me behind and begging for forgiveness, the scheming sod. And I took him in, gormless cabbage that I am. So, am I going to be arrested? Accessory to whatever?"

"We don't know, Mrs. Atterbury," Buncombe said truthfully. "He was never formally charged with anything, and it was a long time ago, so, personally, I'd be surprised."

I wouldn't, Bayley thought. *Maybe regarding a 1964 embezzlement, yes, but murder is another matter.* "There's something else, Mrs. Atterbury," he said. "I'm sure you know that Bertrand remains a suspect in the murders of George Skinner and Roddy—"

She flapped a hand at him. “No, no, no, I can disabuse you of that. A suspect he may be, but he didn’t do it. When I saw him off on that boat, they were both very much alive. I remember because that very evening Roddy rang me up to ask if I had any idea where Bertrand was. Naturally, I said I didn’t . . . well, I didn’t, did I, other than that he was in England? It was another two days before he and George disappeared. And then the next day, they found George’s body.”

“Nevertheless, we’d like very much to have a conversation with him.”

“That makes three of us,” Miranda said with another laugh, a heartier one this time.

“Well, do you think you can tell us anything that might help us find him?”

“He didn’t bother to tell me where he was going, I can tell you that, but I might have some useful ideas. If I do, however, you have to promise me five minutes alone in a room with the son of a bitch before you take him into custody.”

Buncombe, who had obviously and improbably taken a liking to her, laughed. “Only if you promise that there won’t be any visible bruises on him when you give him back to us.”

“Certainly, if you’ll lend me your rubber hose.” She too had softened. “Oh, what the hell, boys, come in. Give me a minute to make myself decent, and I’ll get us some coffee, and we can talk about it.”

Buncombe courteously inclined his head. “It would be a pleasure, madam.”

Meanwhile, Julie, John, and Gideon were revamping the day’s plans. Gideon had gotten out of bed at five in the morning, unable to get back to sleep. (In retrospect, he thought, that second helping of trifle might have been a mistake.) He had written and e-mailed the expanded report for Clapper and boxed up the carton of bones. That left the morning free, after all, except for dropping off the carton with Clapper. They decided that Julie and John would take the bus to the wildlife park to get the lay of the land, and Gideon would join them a little later.

As things turned out, it would be a lot later.

CHAPTER 30

"One box of bones, as ordered," Gideon said, placing the Gentleman's Relish carton on the corner of Clapper's desk. With him was Rafe, whom he had run into downstairs. Rafe was there to identify Abbott, and he had come upstairs with Gideon to Clapper's office.

"Ah, thank you, Gideon," Clapper said, sounding very upbeat this morning. "Vickery! Vickery, dammit, where—" And then, when the constable materialized: "The transfer of custody form—I can't find it anywhere. What have you done with the bloody thing?"

"But, sir, you explicitly told me to—" But he didn't finish the sentence, seemingly having learned that excuses to Clapper that began with "But you explicitly told me" were unlikely to end in a happy result. "I'll have it for you in a moment."

As he turned to go, Clapper waved him back and held out a couple of sheets of paper. "And if you would, kindly give us three copies of this. I believe our friends will be interested."

"Sir."

Clapper remained behind his desk, so the two of them took up visitors' chairs across from him. He started to speak, but Vickery was already back with the requested form. Clapper signed it and then pushed it across to Gideon for his signature. "Chain of evidence, don't you know."

Gideon laughed as he put his name to it. "Great, now we've established an irrefutable chain of custody all the way from yesterday to today. It's only that half century in Rafe's garage that might be a little iffy."

Clapper chuckled too. "Well, I don't expect they'll be admissible as evidence, but it's good to have them to go along with your report . . . for which I thank you, by the way. Very thorough."

"Mike, have you had a chance to run those fingerprints of Campion's yet?" asked Rafe.

"We have, in record time, and—get yourself ready for this—you were right: they match. Bertrand Peltier is back among us."

"I knew it!" Rafe said, lifting a victorious fist.

"Two of my men are out there collecting him now."

"What very welcome news." Rafe fell back into his chair, triumphant and smiling. "I expect Miranda may be displeased, though."

"Oh, I think I can deal with Miranda. Gentlemen, have either of you ever heard of an old man, a onetime solicitor named Edmond Jouvet?"

Head shakes from Rafe and Gideon.

"I ask because we have a statement from him that adds another little twist to the case."

"Which case are we talking about?" Gideon asked. "Abbott's or the old one?"

"The old one . . . well, possibly the new one too; I'm not sure yet. I'd like your opinions on it, which is why I've asked Tom to make copies for you."

"If it'll take a while for him to do it," Rafe said, "do you suppose someone could take me out to the mortuary to take care of Abbott's identification? It's got me rather . . . apprehensive."

"They'll call as soon as they're ready for you, Rafe," Clapper said. "I'm sorry it's taking so long. I know what a wretched experience it can be. Ah, here are those copies. Thank you, Tom."

While Vickery handed them around, Clapper said, "I assume we're all familiar with the exchange of children that your family and the Skinners made during the Occupation, Rafe."

"Yes, I gave Gideon the whole story last night."

"Good. Well, it seems Mr. Jouvet was directly involved in it—"

"The lawyer who drew up the agreement?" Rafe asked.

"The very man, and his recollection . . . well, go ahead and read it for yourselves. Tea for myself and Senator Carlisle, please, Vickery. I think coffee for Dr. Oliver."

"Nothing for me, thank you, Constable," Rafe said. "Maybe afterward. My stomach's a little . . ." He made fluttery motions in front of his abdomen.

Vickery left on his mission, and they began reading.

22 April 2015

I, Edmond Lester Jouvet, solicitor (ret.), of 975 Buckingham Court Road, Saint Helier, JE 2, say as follows: (Unless otherwise indicated, what I say in this statement I say from my own knowledge.)

(1) On 27 June 1945 I was present at the Royal Crescent home of Howard and Grace Carlisle. Also present was their son, Roderick, seven, (hereafter referred to as Roddy) and William and Bess Skinner and their son, George, also seven. I was in attendance to assist in concluding the contract originally prepared by myself on 20 June 1940, and in resolving any remaining issues resulting therefrom.

(2) Inasmuch as the 1940 contract referred to in (1) above has now been provided to Detectives Bayley and Buncombe of the States of Jersey Police, I will assume that it is not necessary for me to describe it in detail. In brief, it was an arrangement between the

families in which the identities of the two children were transposed a day before the Skinners were to evacuate to England with their two-year-old son, George. The exchange was instigated by Howard Carlisle to ensure that his son, Roddy, also two, who was unwell, would not have to endure the deprivations of the Occupation but would live in what was hoped would be the relative safety of England.

In return, George would remain in Jersey in Roddy's stead, where the Carlisles promised to treat him in every way as their own son. Certain remunerations from the Carlisles to the Skinners were proposed and accepted. Upon termination of the Occupation and the return of the Skinners to Jersey, the children were to be reunited with their natural parents and remunerations were to be settled to the satisfaction of the signatories.

"Mike," Rafe said, waggling the papers, "why are we reading this? We already know all this. You said it yourself."

"I gather you haven't arrived at paragraph five yet. I don't think anything will be lost if we all leap ahead to it."

But Gideon thought he'd be better off reading it as it was written and continued from where he was.

(3) The meeting on 27 June 1945 proceeded as planned. To all intents and purposes, the two families had lived up to their commitments. The children, showing a natural confusion as to their identities and the identities of their parents, were then reexchanged, the remunerations were transferred by the Carlisles and accepted by the Skinners, and signatures to that effect were appended to the contract, which was placed on the following day in the Jouvet vault at Lloyds Bank, Saint Helier, where it has remained from that day to this.

"My God," Gideon heard Rafe whisper, having apparently gotten to paragraph five. "Can this be true?"

He resisted the impulse to jump ahead himself and plowed steadily on.

(4) It is my understanding that all of the above is generally known to the Carlisle and Skinner families, and to whomever else they have chosen to inform. What follows, I believe to be known by nobody now alive other than myself.

(5) At about eleven, when the Skinners made ready to leave with their son, George, the boy became hysterical and clung desperately to Mrs. Carlisle, who held him close in a most affecting scene. Efforts were made to calm him, to little avail, and at one point Mrs. Carlisle physically prevented Mrs. Skinner from wresting him from her. When Roddy, who was sitting on the floor in a corner, playing with a toy construction set, began to taunt George, Howard Carlisle suddenly stood up and said, and I quote him exactly: "This isn't going to work, is it?"

To my astonishment, within fifteen minutes all four parents agreed that they did not want to give up the children that had lived with them for the past five years and all concerned would be better off if the 1940 exchange were not reversed (i.e., if George were not returned to the Skinners but remained with the Carlisles as their son, Roddy, and Roddy remained with the Skinners as their son, George).

"Wow," Gideon heard himself whispering.

It was agreed that all financial and other responsibilities for the children would be assumed by the couple raising them. The adults were certain that the two seven-year-olds would soon forget that for a single day they had been "someone else," and it is my conviction that this proved to be the case.

Although I had numerous reservations about the implications of so extraordinary an arrangement, I agreed to keep it secret. I believe I can say with truth that it was against my better judgment, and I have regretted it from that day on.

I will also say, however, that when the meeting ended at about midnight and the Skinners went off with Roddy (henceforth, "George"), both sets of parents and children seemed much relieved.

Note: Hereinafter, when the names Roddy and George are used with quotation marks ("Roddy" or "George"), they refer to the names by which they were then and henceforth known and which they themselves came to believe to be their birth names. When quotation marks are not employed (e.g., Roddy, George) they refer to their actual, biological birth names.

(6) In the years that followed I became the Skinners' family lawyer and a continuing mentor of sorts to young "George," doing my best to guide him when the elder Skinner didn't seem to be up to the role of father, which was regrettably often. This relationship, much like that of a fond uncle to a needful (but not always heedful) nephew, continued and somewhat intensified after his (supposed) parents' deaths in 1959 and 1963.

Note: The material that follows may seem improbably exact, considering the length of time that has passed since the events took place. It is, however, accurate, having been faithfully taken from my diary of the time. (I would prefer not to release the diary itself at this time, but will do so should it become useful in any civil or criminal legal proceeding.)

Nineteen years afterward, on 11 June 1964, "George" appeared at my office and told me that he and "Roddy" had had a falling-out and that he had been dismissed from "Roddy's" employ. In addition, as I was already aware, several suits against the two men were in preparation, alleging improper business practices, and prosecution by the Crown on the same grounds was impending. "George," agitated to the point of tears, told me he had lost all hope of ever returning to a normal life; he was virtually penniless, with no means of settling the debts he had already incurred, let alone the burden likely to result from the suits. I assured him that I would serve as his solicitor without payment in any ensuing proceedings. I could also advance him what money he needed to live on for the present, but I was unable to offer him substantial financial aid beyond that.

Thereupon, "George" stated that his only hope lay in flight and he intended to flee to New Zealand or South Africa as soon as it could be arranged. Naturally, I advised against this, but I could see that he was determined to go.

It was at this point that I broke my pledge of almost twenty years: I informed him that he was in reality the son of the late Howard Carlisle and that the man he and everyone else knew as "Roddy" was actually Willie Skinner's son, George, and that a compelling suit could be presented to the effect that he, and not the so-called "Roddy," was therefore the rightful heir to the Carlisle estate and that the outcome was likely to be a very considerable financial settlement in "George's" favor.

"George's" reactions were as explosive and volatile as might have been expected: astonishment, then disbelief, then exhilaration, then anger, particularly at me, whom he had so unquestioningly trusted, for permitting the truth to be hidden in the first place and then allowing it to remain so for so many years.

I accepted his criticism as well deserved, told him I had regretted my part in the deception from the beginning, and said I would willingly testify in his behalf to the facts. His passions having cooled, he refused to allow me to do that, inasmuch as knowledge of my prevarications would surely discredit me as a lawyer and mean the ruin of my career. Greatly moved by his concern, I then offered to arrange and conduct a meeting between him and "Roddy" at which I would inform "Roddy" of the situation and see if things could be resolved privately, perhaps by dividing the Carlisle assets in some fair-minded way.

"George" expressed reluctance, not liking even the implied threat of legal action that would inevitably be suggested by my presence. Their recent falling-out aside, he and "Roddy" had had a near-lifelong friendship, and "Roddy" had done him many good turns, for which "George" remained grateful. He thought it would be better if he spoke with "Roddy" on his own and tried to work out an amicable resolution between the two of them. If that failed, he promised to ask for my help. He apologized for his earlier anger, thanked me most generously for my support, and left.

I did not see him again.

(7) Two days later, on 13 June, I learned to my horror that "George's" body had been found and that his death had been the result of a gunshot wound. My reaction was a mixture of grief and guilt. I had no doubt that what I had told him had led to a confrontation between the two men and to this tragic result. I knew it was my duty to go to the police, but I also knew that "George" had been right: it would be the end of my career as a solicitor, and probably of my life in Jersey. And so, in a state of helpless despair, I made the mistake of fortifying myself with copious helpings of gin, so much so that apparently I was less than coherent when I spoke with the police and made a bumbling fool of myself. I have only the haziest and most unreliable memories of that occasion.

(8) The following day, 14 June 1964, a policeman called to pursue the matter. By then, anxiety and doubt about where my course of action might lead had gained the upper hand, and I had marshaled a good many reasons why no good purpose could be served for revealing what I knew or thought I knew. I will not list them here, except to admit that they were, to a one, self-serving rationalizations, and that I most sincerely regret them now. In any event, I provided no answers to his questions.

(9) Some years later (I have no record of the date), upon the discovery of human remains in the Carlisle Tar Pits, I was called

on by another policeman with similar questions. The results were similar as well.

I make these admissions at this time for three reasons: first, because I know that as a member of the legal profession, I have betrayed its standards and I wish to make what amends I can; second, in the hope that my testimony may be of help in solving some very old crimes; third, in the hope that some of the old injustices that I was instrumental in perpetuating may yet be made right.

I know that others will say there is a fourth reason, viz.: as a ninety-five-year-old man, long retired, I need not worry overmuch about what the effects on my professional career are likely to be.

There is some truth in that too.

Signed this day in the presence of . . .

"So," Gideon said, after rereading parts of it, "'Roddy'"—he raised air quotes with the first two fingers of each hand to extend the clarifying business established in the lawyer's letter—"killed 'George' to keep it from coming out? Is that what it adds up to?"

"It would seem so," Clapper said, "but then why did he let Jouvet live? How did he know Jouvet would keep the secret? And more important, who killed 'Roddy'?" Clapper looked a little embarrassed to be using the air quotes, but there was nothing for it.

There was no reply to that from anyone in the room, and when Gideon put the statement on the desk, he saw that Clapper had his eyes fixed expectantly on Rafe. Gideon joined him. Rafe, unaware of being stared at, continued to peer first at one sheet, then the other, and then back again, delicately tapping his lower lip with a forefinger. When he looked up, it was with a quizzical smile.

"It's rather a sobering feeling," he said mildly, "to learn that one is not the person one thought one was. And not in the figurative sense either, but quite literally. I admit, I did enjoy being 'Rafe Carlisle.'" Rafe's own air quotes were wilted, despondent affairs.

"And you still are," Clapper said supportively. "If you're not, who is? And who are *you*?"

"Who am I . . . yes, that's the question, isn't it?" He was still faintly, dreamily smiling. "But whoever I am, can you seriously believe that I would be a senator if my name were 'Skinner,' which it rightfully should be? Senator Rafe Skinner? Ludicrous. Everything I am, everything I have, derives from being the great Howard Carlisle's grandson. What would I be, what would I have, if I were the 'great' Willie Skinner's grandson? Not the largest dairy enterprise in the Channel Islands, not the—"

"Come off it, Rafe," Clapper said more sharply. He had lit and smoked out a Gold Bond in the last few minutes, and now, impatiently, he ground it out in the meat-pie tin he used as an ashtray when he was at his desk. "If what's eating you is whether or not you still legally own Carlisle Dairies and all the rest—"

"What? Why, no." Rafe looked genuinely surprised. "That's not what I was thinking about at all. I was on a somewhat higher plane, musing on the metaphysics of change and the continuity of identity, considering especially Heracleitus's theory of . . ."

But he couldn't keep it up. "Although, now that you mention it . . ."

"Well, you can stop worrying. I rang Mrs. Morrison in the Law Officers' Department and put the question to her—hypothetically, of course—and she says that there's nothing in the circumstances that would rouse the Crown's interest. If you did run into trouble, it would be in the form of civil litigation from actual—that is to say, biological—descendants of Howard Carlisle who might be lurking about, but whether any such parties exist is—"

Rafe was nodding along, his head lowered, mumbling "Right . . . right . . ." when suddenly he jerked upright. "Wait, wait—Abbott! Abbott is 'George's' son—*he's* Howard's grandson. Wouldn't—" His face sagged. "Oh, my God, I forgot for a moment. Abbott is . . . he's . . ."

"Yes, he is," Clapper said. "Very."

Rafe sighed. "How the gods love their little jokes. For fifty years, everyone in the world—well, except for old Jouvet—accepted me as the sole grandson of Howard Carlisle. I did myself, without question. And then two days, two bloody days, before it turns out that it's not I but he—he dies. It's so . . . so very . . ."

Convenient. The word popped up in Gideon's mind as if someone had slipped it in when he wasn't looking, and immediately he was ashamed. Of all the unbidden, unsupported, totally foundationless conclusions to jump to. This was beyond reprehensible. Aside from the simple ungraciousness of it, the idea that Rafe had murdered Abbott didn't add up. Skinner had been killed two days ago, a day *before* Jouvet had revealed that the boys had been switched and then reswitched in 1945, so how would Rafe have known about it? And if you assumed that Rafe *was* somehow aware of it, then why in the world would he have engaged Gideon Oliver—the bone-picking, nit-picking Skeleton Detective himself—to come and poke around among these safely forgotten bones?

Gideon was starting to think that maybe his problem was too much police work, rather than not enough; he was turning into a cop, finding reason to suspect evil and deceit and culpability wherever he looked. That wasn't the kind of person he wanted to be, and it was a trend he needed to watch out for.

All the same, Abbott's getting shoved off that cliff *was* pretty convenient.

". . . poignant," Rafe finished.

Vickery came in with the coffee and tea—no biscuits this time—and set the platter down on Clapper's desk. "I don't know if you'll want this right now, sir. Dr. MacGowan just rang. Anytime, he says."

"Well, Rafe," Clapper said, standing up, "it seems the moment of truth has arrived. They're ready for us at the mortuary."

"The mortuary, of course, yes," Rafe said, "by all means." He pushed himself up from his chair with all the joie de vivre of a death row inmate looking up and seeing the warden and the prison chaplain awaiting him at his cell door.

CHAPTER 31

If you are either a cop or a character on a TV show and you have to view a body, you will probably do it in the working part of the mortuary, in front of the cooling unit with its ranks of refrigerated, corpse-sized compartments. The body is slid out on its shelf, covered by a green sheet, or perhaps a white one, with the bare feet being the only parts showing, the big toe of one displaying the ever-present toe tag. Even the face is covered, so that the sheet has to be lifted to get a look at it.

That was the way it used to be in the real world too, but mortuaries nowadays have a separate room set aside for the identification of corpses, in which, with the aim of making a disturbing experience a little less disturbing for those there to identify a friend or a family member, it's done differently. The rooms are not so coldly scientific, the bodies are not pulled out of refrigerators like sides of beef, and the dead are arranged to look less . . . well, dead.

Nowadays, the ones that get more business put a little distance, spatial and emotional, between the corpse and the viewer, not even allowing them in the same room. Instead, there is a viewing window between them, much like the one through which a father used to view his new baby in a hospital nursery in the old days. The Jersey mortuary did not have this arrangement (which Gideon had in the past found a little unsettling—the first view of a newly born person and the final view of a newly dead person being so much alike). Here, in the ground-floor mortuary at the back of Jersey General, the viewer is permitted to stand beside the gurney on which the deceased lies, covered by his sheet, except for the face. The big-toe tag is still there, but it's no longer in sight.

"Yes, that's Abbott," Rafe mumbled.

Gideon expected him to turn around and run for the door, but he stood there looking mutely down at Abbott's face while Clapper and Gideon waited. "Why, he just looks as if he's asleep," he said. "He looks . . . relaxed."

Not to Gideon, he didn't. Not with that waxy, blue-gray pallor. He looked dead; that was all. But he'd been cleaned up, and his hair was neatly combed.

"I'm glad I've seen him. I was expecting worse," Rafe said. "But I'm ready to leave now. May we?"

Clapper replied by gesturing toward the door, and they both turned from Abbott and went toward it, Clapper behind. Gideon hung back, drawing a curious glance from Clapper, but nothing was said.

Quickly, Gideon lifted the edge of the sheet along Abbott's right side, just for a second and only for a few inches.

It was enough.

On the walk back to police headquarters, he was unusually uncommunicative, mulling things over, fitting pieces together.

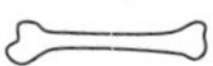

"I'm awfully relieved that that's over," Rafe said as they settled back in around Clapper's desk. "It wasn't as bad as I'd feared, but still . . . I hope never to have to do that again."

Clapper looked over their shoulders toward the door. "Yes, Sergeant? Can it wait?"

"I think not. It's about Peltier, sir. There have been some new developments." At this point the policeman at the door, in his forties but boyish, realized Clapper had visitors and stopped.

"Peltier?" Clapper said. "Well, then, come in, these two are as interested in Peltier as we are. You already know Senator Carlisle, and the distinguished-looking gent beside him is Professor Oliver, the anthropologist who's been assisting us. This is Sergeant Kendry."

Once the appropriate nods and greetings had been made, Kendry advanced to Clapper's desk and remained standing. "He's scarpered, sir. Probably in England by now, or beyond."

"Oh, no," Rafe said quietly, with a discouraged flap of his hand.

Clapper looked grimly at the ceiling. "Bloody hell, Warren. Was the lady involved? Miranda?"

"Buncombe and Bayley don't believe so. They had a nice chin-wag with her this morning."

A brittle laugh came from Rafe. "A nice chin-wag with Miranda? Now there's an oxymoron for you."

"Apparently, he bolted in the middle of the night, taking various valuable possessions of hers with him. She was not in a forgiving mood."

"Well, that's that, then," Clapper said. "We'll do all the usual, but our chances of finding him are nil."

"From what Bayley had to say," Kendry said with the slightest of smiles, "he'll be lucky if we do find him. If Miranda catches up with him first, he's a goner."

"He killed Abbott, all right," Rafe said. "This just about proves it."

"Dammit, Rafe," Gideon muttered, scowling at the floor. The pieces had fallen into place, and the completed picture didn't make him happy.

The others stared at him.

"Sorry?" Rafe said, a friendly, puzzled smile on his face.

"I don't think it was Peltier. I think it was you, Rafe. I think you killed Abbott. You pushed him off that cliff."

Rafe's hand flew to his chest. "*I* killed—?" He started to laugh but cut it short. "If this is some kind of . . . some kind of sick—"

"You're also the one who stole George's corpse before I could see it." His eyes came up to stare directly into Rafe's. "Aren't you?"

"Mike . . ." Rafe appealed to Clapper, but Clapper calmly, neutrally looked back at him.

"This is absurd!" Rafe declared. It hadn't taken him long to work himself up to a righteous anger. His cheeks were flushed, and Gideon could see the pulsing of the arteries in his neck. His hands were shaking as he glared back at Gideon. "If I didn't want you to see the body, I wouldn't have been the one to come up with the idea of an exhumation in the first place, now would I? There never would have *been* an exhumation but for me. I'm the one who talked Abbott into it. I *paid* for it. After all that, why would I want to steal the bloody—"

"Because after you found out—"

"Mike, are you going to sit there and let this continue?" And then, with a bitterly sarcastic tinge: "Should I be calling my solicitor?"

"For the moment, why don't we simply let him finish?" Clapper suggested.

"No, thank you!" Rafe jumped, seething, to his feet. "I don't have to sit here and take this."

And at that instant the last of Gideon's doubts vanished. There is a certain look that can do that for you. He had seen it described in an early nineteenth-century British journal of criminology as "the classic look of the felon caught out," which was true enough, but Gideon thought of it more as the classic look of the kid caught with his hand in the cookie jar: obstinate, belligerent, defensive, humiliated, and guilty as hell. It was exactly the look Rafe Carlisle had on his face.

"Sit down, Rafe," Clapper said.

"I will *not* sit down. I—"

Clapper said it again but with a steelier edge: "Sit . . . down . . . Senator."

"This is scandalous, libelous," Rafe said, practically shouting. "Oh, you want me to stay, do you? Then you'll have to arrest me!" He started for the door.

"I'd suggest you do that, Mike," Gideon said quickly.

Kendry moved to the doorway so that he was now partially blocking it.

"Arrest Senator Carlisle," Clapper told him.

Kendry hesitated, unsure of whether this was some kind of playacting he'd been watching or if Clapper was serious, but Clapper's granite-like face cleared up what doubts he had. He stepped directly in front of Rafe.

"Sir, you are not obliged to say anything—"

"You have no idea what kind of trouble you're getting yourself into," Rafe said between clenched teeth, looking directly at Clapper.

"—unless you wish to do so—"

"Start packing now, Mike. You're through here."

"—but what you say may be put into writing and given in evidence—"

"And as for *you*," Rafe fumed at Gideon, "'despicable' doesn't even begin to . . . ah, the hell with you all." He turned and started his march down the corridor without waiting for Kendry, who had to hurry to catch up.

Clapper sat looking at Gideon for a long, long minute. When he finally spoke, it was more of a deep, slow rumble than speech, but extremely distinct all the same. "I have just now arrested a sitting senator—for murder—on your say-so." His heavy brow lowered. "You want to tell me why? And for your sake as well as mine, it better be good."

CHAPTER 32

Gideon found John and Julie at the wildlife park, finishing their lunch on the terrace of the Café Dodo. Their plates had been shoved to one side, and John had a cup of coffee in front of him. Julie had coffee too and was working at a gooey slice of what looked like banana cream pie with a layer of toffee or chocolate at the bottom.

"About time, Doc," John said. "Afraid we gave up on you. Have something to eat, though. Hey, have you ever seen a Montserrat whistling frog?"

"Nope, never seen one," Gideon said. "That's the one with the distensible internal subgular vocal sac, isn't it?"

John fell back in his chair. "Jesus Christ," he said. Julie just laughed.

Gideon pulled up a chair of his own. "Sorry to be late, folks. There was some . . . stuff that happened."

"Uh-oh," Julie said, laying her fork down. "I don't like the sound of that. What 'stuff,' Gideon?"

"Rafe's in custody. He killed Abbott."

Not surprisingly, they were speechless, or nearly so. "How . . . ?"

"What . . . ?"

They didn't yet know about Jouvet's revelation, so he started with that. It took longer to explain than he thought it would, and by the time he finished, he was tired and depressed. What a mess the whole thing was.

"So . . . Rafe was really a Skinner, not a Carlisle," John said, trying to summarize, "and he didn't know about it until this morning?"

"No, he knew about it the day before yesterday. I'm the one who told him."

"*You* told him?" Julie exclaimed. "But you didn't know about it yourself until—"

"Look, it's been a rugged day so far. I really need some sustenance. Let me get something to eat first."

"Get the quiche Lorraine," said Julie.

"Get the hot roast beef panini," said John.

He went instead for a double slice of the banana cream pie, the name of which turned out to be banoffee pie (from the words *banana* and *toffee*, the server was quick to inform him). And milk rather than coffee.

Julie was concerned. "Cream pie for lunch? This thing has got you really feeling down, hasn't it?"

"I don't feel good about it," Gideon said, after which they gave him enough time to consume most of the first slice before they took up where they'd left off.

"You told him he wasn't really Howard Carlisle's grandson?" Julie said more explicitly.

"Yep. Well, he learned it from me, yes." The rest of that first slice of pie and all of the second had lost their allure. He moved them aside.

"Aw, no, wait a minute," John said. "You didn't know about it the day before yesterday yourself. You just found out this morning too, or am I missing something here?"

There was a round of delighted children's laughter from some of the other tables. The Dodo's terrace directly overlooked the park's

"Discovery Desert," home to its meerkat colony, and several of the little creatures had popped out of their burrow to stand at rigid attention, three of them, all in a row like little toy soldiers, on the lookout for whatever dangerous predators might be lurking nearby. That there hadn't been a single predator in all the years they'd lived here counted not a whit. As always the behavior charmed onlookers. Even Julie and John turned to look and smile.

Gideon took advantage of the break to marshal his thoughts and decide where to begin.

"You ever hear of syndactyly?"

Julie hadn't. John thought it meant too many fingers.

"No, fused fingers, webbed fingers, a hereditary condition. And when I saw Rafe at the States Building the other day, we were looking at a portrait of Howard Carlisle, his grandfather, and it came out, thanks to brilliant me, that Carlisle had a case of it, which was news to Rafe, who doesn't have the condition. But Abbott Skinner did, which is pretty good evidence that it was Abbott who was Carlisle's descendant, and not Rafe. Rafe clicked to it immediately, even if I didn't. That put Rafe's inheritance—which was most of his wealth—in jeopardy, and so . . . Abbott had to go."

"Back up a little, Gideon," said Julie. "How do *you* know Abbott had it? You never met him."

"Right, and Rafe wanted to keep it that way. That's why Abbott had to be gotten rid of that same night—before I had a chance to meet with him in the morning. And he was."

Julie repeated her question. "So how do you know Abbott *did* have it?"

"I didn't until a couple of hours ago. We were at the mortuary. I peeked under the sheet. The second and third fingers on his left hand are fused."

"But Rafe must have known that all along," John said. "Why would he set up a meeting with him where *you* could see . . . oh, yeah, he didn't know that it was hereditary, that it ran in the Carlisle line. He didn't realize that until—"

"Until I pointed it out to him," Gideon said dejectedly. "That twenty minutes or so at the States Building—that changed everything. That got Abbott killed. Damn."

"Well, what are you looking so depressed about?" John said. "You didn't kill him, Rafe did. Jesus, you look like your dog died."

"I'm just tired of the whole thing, that's all. It's been a lousy morning. First the scene with Rafe, and then I had to go through it all with Mike, and here I am doing it again."

He knew that was only part of it, and Julie, so sensitive to his every expression, his very posture, the set of his head, the slope of his shoulders, knew it too. "You feel guilty about it, don't you?" she said softly, placing her hand on the back of his. "You shouldn't. John's right: if you knew Rafe was a murderer, of course you had to tell Mike."

Gideon nodded. "I know that. That's not really what's bothering me." He moved his hand so that it covered Julie's, rather than the other way around. "I feel . . . well, sure, guilty, but I also feel responsible."

"Responsible!" John blurted. "Gimme a break, will you? There's only one person responsible and—"

"Let me put it this way. Do you really think that if I'd never shown up in Jersey, Abbott would be dead and Rafe would be a killer?"

"Well, nobody can know—"

"Come on, you know it wouldn't have happened, not ever. I feel as if I was part of some entrapment scheme. I provided the motivation, I created the opportunity, the *reason* for him to be killed. If I hadn't come here, if I hadn't seen that picture of Carlisle, if I hadn't opened my big mouth about syndactyly and how it ran in families, if—"

"If Rafe hadn't *asked* you to come," Julie said sharply. "That's what brought you here. You didn't offer to look at those bones and pry into his affairs, he practically begged you to do it."

"She's right, Doc," said John. "It's not entrapment if you never intended to trap anybody. And you didn't."

"I know, but . . . aw, hell."

"And do you remember what Rafe said the first day we were here?" Julie asked. "In the bar at the hotel?"

No, he didn't, and neither did John.

"His toast: 'Let the chips fall where they may.' Rafe set all this in motion all by himself. And the chips fell where they did. And here's another quote, this one from a famous anthropologist I know: 'I just say what I find.' Well, you did."

"Yes, that's all true, but . . . well, there we were last night at his house, a convivial dinner—"

"Doc," John said flatly. "Tell me. How'd he look to you last night? Like he felt guilty?"

"Rafe? Not at all. He was happy, he was obviously enjoying the evening, he—"

"Well, if he was 'obviously' happy one lousy day after shoving Abbott off a cliff, if he didn't feel guilty about anything, then why the hell should you?"

That stopped him. Gideon smiled. "You're actually making me feel better, you two." The banoffee pie had begun to look good again. He loaded the last of the first slice onto his fork and moved the second into position.

"While we're on the subject," Julie said, "why do you suppose Rafe asked you to get into it in the first place if he . . . oh, that's right, he didn't know there was anything fishy going on, family-wise. He just wanted to know what happened in 1964."

"Right. It was that few minutes at the States Building, that picture of Carlisle, that changed everything."

"So you think he stole the coffin van too?" Julie asked. "He was afraid George had syndactyly and you'd find it?"

"Yes, I'm pretty sure that's what happened."

"I wonder where he put it. Hiding a van and a coffin and a corpse for very long on an island this size would take some doing. Even in his garage, it'd be bound to be seen sometime."

"I suppose," said Gideon, who was still focused on the bigger picture. "It's ironic, isn't it? At one he's talking to Abbott, convincing him to allow me to see George's body and arranging a time for me to meet Abbott. Two hours later he's realizing that he can't let any of that happen, and so . . ." He said aloud what he'd said to himself a few minutes earlier. "What a mess."

He was down to the crust of the second slice now, and he was already regretting it. Should have stopped after one. He reached for his glass and drank down a cool, creamy, welcome slug of milk. *I wonder if this came from Rafe's cows,* he thought.

"So what now?" John said.

Gideon thought for a moment. "How about showing me that Montserrat whistling frog?"

They saw the Montserrat whistling frog (which had no interest in whistling for them), they saw the Andean bears, they sat in on a behind-the-scenes "Animal Encounter" with the Sulawesi crested macaques, and they watched a baby orangutan climb all over its slow, patient father, who only occasionally swatted it off with a huge hand. The baby obviously thought it was part of the game (perhaps it was) and came running eagerly back for more.

After that, they did what a lot of other people were doing: they flaked out on one of the neatly mowed lawn areas for a midday siesta of sorts, not quite sleeping, but lying back, propped on an elbow or against a tree trunk, and chatting or eating ice cream or, most likely, just enjoying watching bulbous wads of dense cumulonimbus clouds shaping themselves into towering white stacks against a cobalt-blue sky. More rain was on the way, but no hurry, not for a while yet.

Gideon found his mind drifting back to murder, not the one that had happened two days ago but the two that had happened fifty years ago. He was more at a loss than ever in trying even to approximate just what it was that had happened that day in 1964. Not the motives that drove it or the background that led to it or the results that resulted from it, but simply, literally, what had *happened.*

He knew, with reasonable certainty, that the two men had been killed on the same day (because they'd disappeared on the same day, and by the following morning "George's" body had been found, and "Roddy" was not to be seen again until they hauled those pitiful few remnants out of the nearby tar pit five years later). And he knew, with reasonable certainty, that "George" had been killed first because it was "Roddy"—with reasonable certainty (it was "Roddy's" gun, after all)—who had killed him. With the recent appearance of Jouvet's statement, "Roddy's" motive for doing so had become one of the few undeniably distinct threads in this whole bloody intergenerational birthright tangle.

Beyond that (and the nearly identical thread of Rafe's own nearly identical motive, all these years later) everything was foggy. Who killed "Roddy"? Had it been Peltier? Someone else nobody knew about? Had the two murders been part of a single violent falling-out between the two or maybe the three of them, or had "Roddy" been murdered later, perhaps hours later? He'd been killed by being struck with a rock or something like it (even this was, again, only a reasonable certainty, because how could Gideon know for sure that the cracked and repaired cranial fragment represented his only injury?). But assuming that it *was* the cause of death, why had "Roddy" not used, in his own defense, the revolver later discovered in the hedge? Only one bullet had been fired, and that was resting in "George's" hip at the time. Had "Roddy" been caught by surprise, attacked from behind? No, because it was the forwardmost part of the parietal, and thus the forward, upper part of the head, that had been struck—a pretty unlikely place for someone standing behind you to brain you with a rock or with anything else.

He was troubled too, and had been obscurely troubled from the start, with the notion that two different murderers were involved: "Roddy" (as he was then called), who had killed "George," and then Peltier (or someone else) who had killed "Roddy." And yet, what other possibility was there? *Somebody* had killed "Roddy," and it certainly hadn't been "George."

There was no end to it. The questions sprouted questions that sprouted questions. Too many unknowns, too many possibilities. *That's it, I give up,* he thought, and lay all the way back on the cool grass, fingers linked behind his neck, emptying his mind, watching the clouds, inhaling and trying to separate the aromas in the air: the musky, gamey smells from the nearby gorilla enclosure, the odors of sunscreen and insect repellent, cologne, mowed grass, congealing vanilla ice cream. After a while he gave that up too and just watched the building cloud pillars. He was two-thirds asleep, comfortable and drifting, when the breakthrough came. He sat up.

"Pluralitas non est ponenda sine neccesitate," he said.

John and Julie, who had been lazily chatting, stopped and looked wordlessly at him, until Julie said, "Occam's razor?"

He nodded. "'Entities should not be multiplied unnecessarily.'"

"The law of parsimony," said John. "And you are telling us this, why?"

Gideon pulled himself closer to them. This was not something for the ears of the many kids scrambling about. "I've been knocking myself out—well, everybody has—trying to figure out who killed whom back in 1964."

"I thought that there was general agreement that it was Peltier," Julie said.

"Peltier or possibly someone else, but—well, two murders by two different people—but that just didn't sound convincing to me. Too many entities."

"So what's your theory?" John asked. "You don't think it *was* Peltier?"

"It's not quite a theory, just a hypothesis. But I realized that we don't absolutely need Peltier. We can account for what happened without him."

"Who, then? One of the people they screwed?"

"No, nobody. We don't need anyone at all beyond—" Two fingers came up alongside each ear, but with a head-jerk of exasperation, he brought them down again. "Do I really have to go through that routine every time I say their names? How about this: Whenever I say just *Roddy* or *George*—no air quotes—I'm not talking about the names they were born with, I'm talking about the names they lived by from the time they were two years old, the names they *thought* were their real names, right up until the day Jouvet let the cat out of the bag, all right? That'll make things simpler."

This was fine with John and Julie. "You were saying?" Julie said. "'We don't need anyone beyond . . .'?"

"Anyone beyond Roddy and George themselves to account for their deaths."

John thought about that. "I don't see how, Doc. Roddy killed George, we're pretty sure of that, right?"

"Yes."

"So then it couldn't have been George who killed Roddy. Or are you saying that he *did* kill Roddy, whacking him in the head with a rock, or maybe the gun itself, but Roddy didn't lose consciousness right away and shot him before he died himself?"

"That's a possibility, yes."

"No, no, no, wait," Julie put in. "If they killed each other, then what was George's body doing back on his own property and Roddy's doing in the pond? Shouldn't they have been found together?"

"Yeah, that's right," John said, "and also . . . okay, all right, we'll shut up, and you tell us your theory—pardon me, your hypothesis."

"All right, remember what Jouvet said? He finally told George that he—not Roddy—was Howard Carlisle's son, and that he had an excellent basis for challenging Roddy's inheritance—the dairy and whatever else had come down to him."

Nods from Julie and John.

"Okay, now imagine this: George walks over to see Roddy—they lived practically next door, right?—to tell him he wants his fair share, some kind of settlement. They argue, maybe they fight. Roddy goes into his house to get the gun, which, if you remember, is right next to the door. Maybe he means to frighten George, or maybe to kill him—"

"For the very same reason Rafe killed Abbott fifty years later," Julie said. "All right, so far so good."

"They wrestle," Gideon continued, "as in the diagram I drew. George on top, Roddy on the bottom. Roddy shoots George, but George still has enough oomph to brain him, maybe with the gun, maybe with a rock. Roddy falls into the pond and dies, and George tries to get home, but he only makes it seventy or eighty feet, to the foot of the crags, before he collapses and dies. And that's it. Roddy kills George, George kills Roddy. No other entities need apply."

The two of them were looking at him with virtually the same doubtful expression.

"What?" he said. "Problem?"

"Just a teeny, little one, Gideon, dear," Julie said. "I think you haven't been getting enough sleep. You've forgotten. George was shot *through the heart*. His heart was 'shredded.'"

"Yes, and so?"

"So how could he run seventy or eighty feet?" John put in. "You can't run two feet if your heart's shredded. You're dead."

"No, you're not."

"Getting shot in the heart doesn't kill you?"

"That's right, you can live without a heart—"

"You can live without a heart—?"

He wasn't sure which one of them the high-pitched cry of disbelief came from, maybe both.

"Right, you can," he told them. "Not too long, I admit, and your quality of life isn't going to be that great."

The thing is, he explained, it isn't the destruction of your heart, per se, that kills you; it's the death of your brain, due to the loss of the oxygenated blood that gets pumped up *from* your heart. Without a functioning heart, you're still alive . . . for a while. Without a functioning brain, you're dead right now. But even when the heart was "shredded," the brain could continue to function for ten or fifteen seconds, and probably more, on the blood that was in it already and what had already been on its way in the carotid arteries.

"But wouldn't you lose consciousness?" Julie asked.

"Yeah, you would, wouldn't you?" John said.

"Usually, you do," Gideon said, "but that's not strictly because of the lack of blood to the brain. It has more to do with overall systemic shock and everything that follows from it. And some people are simply more resistant to that than other people are. They stay conscious, right up until the millisecond they die. People have run a lot more than seventy or eighty feet after taking a fatal gunshot to the heart."

Julie leaned back, thinking it over. "And you think that's what actually happened."

"That or something close to it. It makes more sense to me than a second killer, Peltier or anyone else."

"Okay, Doc," said John, "since it's coming from you, I'll buy it, but I don't see how you're gonna prove it."

Gideon grinned. "Happily, I don't have to. All I have to do is tell Mike. It's up to him what to do with it."

"He'll buy it too," John said. "It'll let him clear the case, which every policeman loves more than anything else."

"To tell you the truth," Julie said, "I never did have much faith it was going to get solved, not definitively, even with you working on it, Gideon. Too many uncertainties, too much water under the bridge. Did you honestly think you were going to get anywhere with it?"

Gideon considered but not for long. "Not really," he said.

CHAPTER 33

Gideon told Clapper about it that afternoon. The chief inspector was noncommittal, but a week later, when Julie and Gideon were home in Washington State and taking a breakfast hike along nearby Dungeness Spit, a wild, curling, six-mile-long finger of sand and driftwood, Clapper called from Jersey. Gideon took it on his iPhone and was gratified to hear that his hypothesis, while far from incontrovertible, was as good a solution as Clapper was likely to get (which was exactly the way Gideon saw it), and he was closing the file. Again.

"But what I've really rung you about is to tell you that we've gotten some evidence against Rafe that *is* incontrovertible—"

"Nothing's incontrovertible when you've got a jury involved," Gideon said.

"You're right enough about that, mate, but this comes close. We got a warrant and sent a couple of men out to his house, and they came back with a pair of boots, one of which had some very interesting material on the sole."

"Ah, limestone."

"Better. A clump of gray fibers at the toe that have now been identified as four-ply, medium-weight Aran yarn . . . identical to the ones in the cardigan that Abbott was wearing."

"He *kicked* him over?"

Clapper shrugged. "So it would seem."

"Well, that's it, then."

"That's our opinion too, but of course there'll be a trial, probably in July sometime, and we'll need you to come and testify."

"Sure, that won't be a problem."

"Good. Would you be able to bring Julie? I know Millie would love to see her, and July is a very fine month here. Of course, we wouldn't be able to pay her passage—"

"Just a minute, Mike, let me ask her."

Julie had stepped down to the shoreline while he was speaking and was up to her bare ankles in the gentle surf.

"I'm going to have to go back to Jersey in July for a few days, Julie. Care to come along?"

"Love to."

"Great. Mike, she says—"

"Gideon," said Julie, "why don't you put it on speakerphone? Then I can talk to him myself."

"An iPhone has a speakerphone?"

She laughed. "Gimme." He handed it to her, and she tapped in a few mysterious commands and gave it back to him. "Mike?" she said from three feet away. "Hi, I would *love* to come back to Jersey in July."

Mike's voice floated tinnily from the speaker that Gideon hadn't known was there. "Well, that's wonderful, luv. The missus will be delighted. Did you two enjoy your stay at the Revere? If you like, the department can have you put up there again—now, it won't be in the lavish suite that the senator provided, but—"

"That's fine," she said, checking with Gideon, who nodded. "I'm dying to go back to the Revere. It's been preying on my mind."

"Good. Oh, I wanted to tell you two . . . we've found the coffin van and its contents, thanks to my excellent associate PC Vickery. On a hunch, the young man looked through local French papers from the three regions to which car ferries run back and forth from Jersey. And in one of them he found an item—yes, he reads French—about an unmarked black van, license plates removed, with a coffin inside—an inhabited coffin—that was found at the Saint-Malo ferry car park, paid for ten days."

"He took it to France?" Gideon said. "But he was back in Jersey, having dinner with us, that same day. Is that possible?"

"The ferry journey takes an hour and twenty minutes. Assuming he drove the van on, drove it off, left it in the car park, and came back on the turnaround ferry, we're talking about less than three hours in total. So yes, it could have been done. It *was* done, I have no doubt."

"Sonofagun," Gideon said. "He's really smooth. He couldn't have been more relaxed that night."

There was a little more chitchat between the three of them, and Clapper rang off. They continued on their walk, heading for a giant driftwood tree trunk that they liked to have their breakfast on (today, bacon and egg sandwiches from home) because there always seemed to be seals or otters playing just offshore.

"Julie?" Gideon said as they walked. "Why are you 'dying' to go back to the Revere? Why's it been 'preying' on your mind?"

She looked up at him, smiling. "Because I never did get to sit in that chair that Ringo sat in. Obviously."

AFTERWORD

The first few chapters of *Switcheroo* are set in the Channel Islands during the five years that they were occupied by German military forces. While the main characters in the book and the story it tells are fictional, the background details are not. The evacuations, the Churchill speeches, the return of evacuees at the end of the war—all are from the historical record.

For those who would like to know more about this unusual chapter in English history (these islands were the only British territory that suffered occupation in World War II), an Internet search will provide plenty of factual material and excellent references. But for those who prefer a more intimate perspective, let me recommend a couple of fictional treatments: *The Guernsey Literary and Potato Peel Pie Society*, a novel/memoir by Annie Barrows and Mary Ann Shaffer that is every bit as charming as its title, and *Island at War*, a *Masterpiece Theatre* TV miniseries.

In writing this book I was greatly helped by PC Chris Ingham of the States of Jersey Police, who was most cordial when I showed up, unannounced, at police headquarters with a notebook full of questions on local police procedure and who then patiently and amicably continued to answer additional ones by e-mail over the months that followed. Thank you, Chris!

ABOUT THE AUTHOR

Photo © 2015 Bob Lampert

Former forensic anthropology professor and Edgar Award–winner Aaron Elkins can't seem to let go of the past—he has written his eighteenth book featuring the globetrotting Skeleton Detective, Gideon Oliver. Often credited with launching the forensic mystery genre in the early 1980s with *Fellowship of Fear*, Elkins has written nonfiction articles for the *New York Times* travel magazine, *Smithsonian* magazine, and *Writer's Digest*. His books have been made into a major ABC television series and have been published in over a dozen languages. In addition to the Edgar, which he won for *Old Bones*, his fourth Gideon Oliver book, he has also won a Nero Award and shared an Agatha Award with his wife and coauthor, Charlotte Elkins. Elkins lives in a small town on the Washington coast, where (when he's not writing) he serves as the forensic anthropologist for the Olympic Peninsula Cold Case Task Force.